THIS PLACE

A HOLMES CROSSING BOOK

CAROLYNE AARSEN

Misty Ridge
PUBLISHING

CHAPTER 1

 y life had come full circle.

Abandoned child. Check.

Uncertain guardianship of said child. Check.

Only this time I wasn't the one crying upstairs, cast off yet again by my biological mother, rejecting hugs offered by a loving foster parent.

This time it was my niece who lay prostrate, staring sightlessly at her bedroom wall, so quiet it seemed she was afraid to draw even the smallest bit of attention to herself.

Earlier in the evening, I had sat beside her until she fell into a troubled sleep, my hand curled around hers, my heart breaking for so many reasons. I wanted to stay at her side all night. To drink in features I had imagined so many times. To be there for her if she woke up, crying.

But I had other issues I couldn't put off. So I reluctantly drew myself from her side, and returned downstairs to find a small blaze crackling in the corner fireplace of the living room. The heat warmed the house but did little to melt the chill in my bones. It had settled there, deep and aching, as I watched her parents' coffins being lowered into the icy ground.

Duncan Tiemstra, Celia's uncle, hovered by the fire as if attempting to absorb all of its warmth, one arm resting on the mantle, looking at a picture he held in his other hand. He had aged since that first time I met him at Jer and Francine's wedding. Then he looked young. Fresh. Ready to face life. And very interested in me.

Now he looked like a grieving Visigoth, with his blond hair brushing the collar of his shirt and framing a square-jawed face. The hint of stubble shadowing his jaw made him look harder and unapproachable. When we met at the funeral all I received was a taciturn hello. No memory of the feelings we had shared six years ago.

My heart folded at the contrast from then to now.

Then we were dancing on the edges of attraction, flirting with possibilities. I was twenty-two, my life ahead of me. He was twenty-seven, looking to settle down. We laughed together. Even went on a couple of dates.

Now, we were separated by years and events that had pushed us apart, yet connected by the little girl that lay upstairs.

"Is she sleeping?" Duncan asked setting the picture he had been holding on the mantle.

"Yes. Finally." I plumped a throw pillow and set it on the large recliner I guessed had belonged to my brother. I folded an afghan that had fallen onto the floor and laid it on the matching leather couch.

"Poor kid. She must be exhausted." He dragged his hand over his face and heaved out a sigh. "I know I am." Then he glanced my way, his eyes holding mine. "How about you, Miriam? How are you holding up?"

His concern touched me, but I sensed he was merely being polite.

"I'm tired. There were a lot of people here," I said, pushing a love seat to face the fire, resisting the urge to gather the few coffee cups remaining on the low table, traces of the mourners that had filled the house only moments before. "I didn't think Jer and Fran got to know that many people in the few months they lived here."

"That's Holmes Crossing," Duncan said, stifling a yawn as he shoved his hands in the pockets of his crisp blue jeans. "Everyone knows everyone, and we all show up at the funerals." He moved closer to a second love seat flanking the fireplace. "You going to keep fussing, or are you going to sit down? We need to talk."

His words were ominous. I knew exactly what he wanted to discuss and it wasn't our previous relationship. This conversation had been lingering on the edges of my grief ever since the lawyer had called to let me know that while my brother had named Duncan as Celia's guardian in his will, in a strange and unexpected complication, Duncan's sister had named me.

I lowered myself to the couch across from him, folding my ice-cold hands together, trying to still my wavering emotions.

"It was a nice service," I ventured, not ready to delve into the convoluted guardianship issue. And for sure not ready to make a trip down memory lane.

"Nice." He almost snorted the word as he leaned back on the couch. "I don't know how a double funeral could possibly be considered nice."

I understood his anger. When I got the news of my brother's death, I was in the cramped little apartment I shared with my friend, Christine. Alone.

I remember clutching the phone in both hands as my world spun out of control, sinking to the floor, trying to make sense of what Duncan was telling me. All I heard were the words accident, snowmobiling and mountains.

My first thoughts were of their daughter Celia, and what would happen to her. Behind that came an unreasonable fury that Jer and Fran would be so stupid and reckless.

Then came the waves of grief, and everything after that was a haze.

"You're right," I murmured. "Nice is a lame word. But I did appreciate the message."

"How the dark threads of our lives give contrast to the others?" He released a harsh laugh.

I let the rhetorical question slip past me. The dark weavings of my own life kept me tossing and turning with regret in the lonely hours of the night. Losing my foster mother—Jer's mother— six years ago, had added yet another dark thread. She had been the only solid anchor in my life.

And now Jer was gone as well.

"So, how do you see this happening? This

5

guardianship thing?" Duncan stretched out his long legs, crossing his muscled arms over his chest.

My feet and head both ached, pounding with the beat of my grieving heart. I wanted nothing more than to drag myself upstairs and slip into bed beside Celia. Pull the covers over our heads, and give in to the grief that held me in a relentless grip.

Not to be reminded of the one thing I wanted more than anything else but couldn't allow myself to.

Take care of Celia.

"I don't know," I said.

"The estate isn't settled yet, either," Duncan said. "I'm worried what will be left for her."

I was too. This house was huge. I wasn't sure how my brother had afforded it on his electrician's income. Phil, the lawyer for the estate, had hinted that there were a few insurance and estate issues to be dealt with and not to make any hasty decisions.

"For now, until all the legalities are done, I feel I should stay here at the house with Celia," I said. "I want to make sure everything is settled in her life before…"

I stopped, realizing I was jumping ahead of the scattered plans I had made on the flight here.

"Before what?" Duncan asked, his voice curt.

I tried to hold his narrowed gaze, reminding myself that his anger wasn't directed at me. At least, I hoped it wasn't.

"Actually, to be honest I haven't thought beyond getting to bed tonight and trying to figure out what to do tomorrow morning."

My throat thickened at the thought of Celia living the rest of her life without her parents. However, years of suppressing my own emotions for the sake of peace, for the sake of the greater good, kicked in. Lessons learned the hard way through the dark and rocky paths my life had taken. I tried a different tack.

"Do you know why they each made separate wills? Why they named different guardians?" I asked. Or why Francine thought that I, with my itinerant lifestyle and too many scars from the past, would be a suitable guardian?

The slow shaking of his head was his only answer.

"I thought maybe, because you lived close to them, you might know their reasons..." my voice trailed away, and I pulled in a deep breath.

"They'd only been here a couple of months, and I hadn't spent a lot of time with them." He sighed again, tunneling his fingers through his thick and unruly hair. He looked over at me and for a moment his gaze softened, and I caught the faintest glimpse of the old attraction. But this wasn't the time or place and we both had other priorities.

"Jer had always said they'd agreed to make your parents Celia's guardians," I said. Though part of me had struggled with his reasoning, I knew I wasn't guardian material.

"My father's accident in the bush last year changed all that," Duncan said. "There's no way Mom and Dad can take care of a young girl right now." Duncan sat straighter, scratching his temple with a forefinger. "Now all we need to know is how long you're sticking around?"

"I won't leave until things are settled in Celia's life."

"So not right away?"

"No. Of course not. It's her birthday next week—" my voice tangled on the words, and I stopped, memories of the day of her birth ingrained in my memory.

"Of course. I can see that you want to keep her here till then," he said.

The direction of the conversation puzzled me.

His impersonal tone warned me to simply take his question at face value. I doubted he was looking to fan the old, barely glowing spark between us. I certainly wasn't, though I would be fooling myself to deny the attraction he still held.

"My parents will be glad to hear that," he continued, leaning forward, clasping his hands between his knees. "I'm sure they are also hoping you'll stay until Christmas."

"I'm hoping the guardianship issue will be resolved before then. As well as the estate." Besides requiring taking a month off work, I wasn't sure I wanted to be around for Christmas. That family-centered season had become more difficult each passing year. Each dark twist and turn of my life had removed more people from it. My own mother and her crazy life, my foster mother.

Now my foster brother.

Christmas was a season when all those losses created a darkness that no amount of candles or carols could brighten.

"What's to resolve?" he asked. "You're the guardian. At least, according to the lawyer."

I frowned, trying to piece together what he was saying. "I was under the impression that we would do this jointly."

"You won't need my help. I can't do much."

"What do you mean? You're as much her guardian as I am."

I had presumed the joint guardianship was the reason for his smoldering-by-the-fireplace act. I thought he resented my presence in Celia's life.

"I don't have the foggiest clue why Jerrod named me," he snapped. "After my father's accident, I thought they would name my sister, Esther, as guardian. Not me. I'm not capable."

"I'm sure you're more than capable. Plus, you have a lot of support." As I sat in the church, filled to capacity with friends and community members, a peculiar poignancy had filtered through my grief. I realized that Jer, through Fran, had found something here in Holmes Crossing that I hadn't in my peripatetic wanderings.

A place where they belonged. A place where Celia would have grandparents, an aunt and an uncle who lived normal lives, in a community of people who cared.

"That doesn't change anything." Duncan heaved out a sigh as he rubbed his forefinger over his temple. "You may as well know that I can't... can't help you out with Celia. I've got too much going on in my life. I'm not in any position to care for her."

His words were a jolt.

"But how...? Why would you want to...? Jer wanted you as guardian...you can't just walk out on her."

He looked up at me, his eyes flat, as if all emotion had been drained out of them. "I'm not walking out on her. I just won't be involved in the day-to-day stuff. She's all yours. I won't fight you for her. I can't be her guardian. I just can't."

She's all yours.

His words plucked at a deeper, harder pain. And yet, for a moment a tendril of hope, of yearning, slipped upward.

She's all yours. You don't have to share.

Then a chilling thought occurred to me. "Is this because she's adopted?" I asked, the words spilling out before I could stop them. "Because she's not a blood relative? Is that why you won't take responsibility?"

"That has nothing to do with it. She's as much my niece as any natural child of Francine's would be." He shot one more glance over his shoulder at the pictures behind him, as if something there had triggered his outburst.

For the tiniest moment, I thought his resistance was due to the few days we'd been together all those years ago, then dismissed that thought as crazy. The key words were, *all those years ago.* I stopped replying to his texts after those few blissful days we spent together. After I returned to the States to my job and my own messy life and realized I was only fooling myself. I assumed he'd given up on me. In fact, I knew he had given up, because he had gotten married six months after we parted ways.

"Seriously. I can't take care of that little girl," he said.

"I realize that you're busy, but you're saying you won't help me out at all?"

He shook his head again, rising from his seat. "Sorry. It won't work for me. I just… I can't. I've got the logging operation to deal with, and a farm to run. And there's no way I can." He stopped there then swung away from me.

He grabbed the heavy coat draped over the back of one of the chairs, slipped it on and glanced my way again. I don't know if it was my fragile emotional state, or my own reaction to him, but I seemed to catch a glimpse of warmth in his eyes, a softening of his features. Then there was a shift, and it was gone.

"Goodbye. I'm sure we'll be in touch," was all he said, and then strode out of the room. The closing of the door echoed harshly in the silence he left behind.

I sat a moment trying to absorb what had just happened. Did he seriously think I could do this by myself?

I thought of Celia upstairs, alone and my throat thickened.

This wasn't right, I thought, leaning back on the couch, confusion mingling with sorrow. Celia was supposed to have been settled in a stable, loving family. When I heard that Jerrod had died, though it cut me to the core, one sliver of my soul was thankful that Celia at least had an uncle, an aunt and grandparents. She would be taken care of, and surrounded by people who loved and supported her.

What was Francine thinking, naming me Celia's guardian? She knew where I had come from, and what my life was like. I pressed my hand to my mouth, my emotions doing battle.

I didn't deserve Celia then, and much as my lonely, aching heart yearned to take her in, to take her home, I knew I couldn't be the mother she needed any more than my mother could be the mother I needed. Celia deserved a better legacy.

And even as my mind tried to process this latest complication, another thought sifted through the fog and settled with startling clarity.

Was Francine trying to undo what had happened almost five years ago, when they had adopted my baby? My daughter Celia?

#

Duncan twisted the key in the ignition of his truck and threw it into reverse, making sure to avoid the huge SUV that used to belong to his sister. He slammed the truck into drive and hit the accelerator, tires spinning snow as he barreled down the driveway.

He clenched the steering wheel, staring at the twin cones of light his headlights cast on the snowy road ahead, thinking only of escape. Every moment he spent in that house, listening to the never-ending words of condolence, was like a twisting of the knife that had been embedded in his soul three years ago.

He banged one hand on the steering wheel in a mixture of impotent rage, laced with grief.

He had argued with Francine about their trip to the mountains. About the cost, the stupidity of leaving Celia behind while they ran off to indulge in their newfound snowmobiling hobby.

What had been more troubling was Francine pulling him aside before they left, telling him she and Jerrod needed this holiday. She had pleaded with him to just leave it be.

And now that 'break' had cost them their lives,

and put another pair of graves in the Holmes Crossing graveyard.

Duncan swallowed down a knot of pain, fighting the flood of emotions, pushing them back where they belonged. He hit the dashboard fan controls, blasting warm air over the iced up windshield. He rubbed it with the sleeve of his coat as old questions and an old anger with God threatened to take over.

But dwelling on those things meant letting feelings take over. He figured God didn't care about the grief of working slobs like him.

He turned on his radio and country music blasted out of the speakers, bouncy, happy, and trite.

Didn't matter. It was a distraction.

Think about your horses. That new one you want to buy, he reminded himself. He hoped to hitch his other horses, Bonnie and Clyde, to the sleigh again. They were a good team, and he enjoyed working with them. Maybe this spring, after he was done seeding, he'd be able to take them out to the wagon rally that the Wildmans held every year down in Silver Valley.

If the logging season didn't last too long.

And on the heels of that thought came plans

that weighed more heavily and required imme-diate attention.

Skyline was talking about reducing their log-ging contract. He had to get the air brakes fixed on that new Kenworth. Les said they could move into that new block tomorrow.

He sucked in a breath, then another, as he mentally blocked off that portion of his life, shifting in his seat.

When his wife Kimberly was alive, she had often accused him of compartmentalizing—throwing the word out like some kind of accusa-tion—but it was the only way he'd been able to juggle all the different aspects of his life and stay sane.

It served him well now.

He drove down the road that followed the river, past the other acreages along the river. Francine and Jerrod had bought the acreage from a friend of their father. They could barely afford it but Francine was never one to count the cost before starting a project. And now the lawyer, Phil, was saying there might be problems paying out the insurance.

Duncan sucked in a long breath, pain lancing his chest at the thought of his sister. Another person swept out of his life.

And Celia...it had been difficult enough seeing the little girl around Holmes Crossing the past few months. The thought of being responsible for her was more than he could comprehend, and Jerrod should have known that. Why had he thought he could be his niece's guardian?

He thought of the look on Miriam Bristol's face when he said he couldn't do this. Her disappointment bothered him more than he cared to admit.

When he saw her coming into the church, it had been the first time since their date after Jerrod and Francine's wedding that he'd seen her. The years had narrowed her features, given her a haunted look that made him wonder what she'd been through. With her presence came the might-have-beens that slipped through his mind whenever he thought of her. He had been surprised at the faint quiver of attraction he'd felt.

Did she think the same of him?

He arrived at the fork in the road and slowed down. Left sent him to town. Right brought him to his house.

His empty house that felt even emptier the past few days. Actually, the past couple months. Since Francine had moved back to Holmes Crossing with her perfect life and her perfect family, his house, which had been hard enough to live in before, now seemed even more inhospitable and unwelcoming.

And empty.

He turned left.

The neon 'Closed' sign shone in the window of the café but at the funeral Terra told him to stop by if he had time.

As he stepped inside the cafe, the warmth came over him and he shivered, shucking his heavy jacket.

Jack De Windt, still wearing the Mountie uniform he had worn at the funeral, sat at his usual table halfway down the café, nursing a cup of coffee, smiling that half-smile he had perfected at something Lester Greidanus was telling him. Probably some questionable joke. Then Terra came by to refill Jack's mug. Her hand rested on his shoulder and he looked up at her, his expression shifting. It wasn't much, but in that look Duncan caught a hint of what he had been hoping for in his own marriage.

As though there'd been some unspoken signal, they all turned at once, and he could tell, to the split second, when they saw him.

Their smiles froze, then shifted into a sorrow that made him second-guess the wisdom of coming here. Though they had attended the funeral, seeing them now, isolated from the crowd of people, made their sympathy suddenly more personal.

Then Jack was up on his feet, striding toward him.

"Hey, man. Glad you stopped by."

Jack's words were made all the more poignant by his gruff voice. His hand on Duncan's shoulder, squeezing once, settled Duncan's uncertainty in coming here. He needed his good friends.

He joined Lester at the table and without a word, Terra appeared with a cup of coffee for him. "Still got some Saskatoon pie," she said.

"That'd be nice." He hadn't eaten anything since he choked down a piece of bread at home, and sipped half-heartedly at mugs of cold coffee at Francine and Jerrod's house.

But in the quiet familiarity of the café, ordinary was finally given some space in his life.

Lester fidgeted across from him, his hands turning the fork around in his hands. "So, today kind of sucked."

"Les. Seriously," Terra scolded, as she set Duncan's pie in front of him.

"Well, it did," Lester protested.

In spite of the emotions still surrounding him

like remnants of fog, Duncan smiled at Lester's succinct and honest précis of the day and everything surrounding it.

"You're right, Les. It did suck." Duncan shot Terra a grateful glance and then sat down between him and Jack. "Thanks for the pie. And thanks for bringing all that food to the house."

"There's probably mountains of it left over," Terra said, resting her elbow on the table and spinning a curly strand of auburn hair around her finger. "Judy and Gloria told me they would bring food as well, but I didn't think they would recreate the feeding of the five thousand."

Duncan smiled as he dug into the flaky crust of the pie. "Miriam won't have to cook for months with all the leftover food in the house."

"I don't remember seeing her around before," Jack asked. "Where does she live?"

"You gonna run a background check on her?" Les joked.

"See, Les, this is where things get complicated for you," Jack said, leaning back, crossing his arms over his chest. "What I'm doing is called conversation. Showing interest and asking questions."

"If you weren't still in uniform, with all that hardware strapped around your waist, I'd think it was just chatter instead of the third degree," Les said with a lift of his eyebrow.

"Trust me, you would know when I'm giving you the third degree," Jack returned, his grin belying the gruff tone of his voice.

Les turned to Terra. "Let me know when he's on shift, okay? So's I don't speed when he's patrolling."

"Nuh-uh," Terra said adding a shake of her head. "You're on your own, there."

Les released a nervous laugh.

This was why he came here, Duncan thought, easing out a sigh of contentment. Chit-chat. Easy give-and-take.

"So how do you know Miriam?" Jack asked.

"I met her at Jerrod and Francine's wedding." Actually it was at the rehearsal. Miriam sat beside Jerrod's mother, laughing, her long, tawny hair framing a face with large, expressive eyes and a gentle mouth. And he had been smitten.

Les snapped his fingers. "Right. Now I remember why she looked familiar." He turned to Duncan. "You two danced every dance at the wedding. Looked really cute together."

Duncan kept his head down, concentrating on getting the exact ratio of filling to crust on his fork, ignoring Les' comment.

Les didn't know they had done more than that. The day after the wedding, they had gone on a date. Laughed. Had fun and left with promises to stay in touch.

"Wasn't that after you and Kimberly broke up?" Les asked.

Duncan just shrugged his response. He didn't want to talk about Kimberly. At all.

"Kim dumped him a couple of months before the wedding," Les put in helpfully for the benefit of Terra who hadn't lived in Holmes Crossing at the time.

"Something like that," was all Duncan would say.

"So why didn't you go after Miriam, then?" Les pressed.

Duncan wished his chatty friend would just put a sock in it. "I texted her a couple of times after the wedding, but didn't hear anything. So that was the end of that story. " Duncan gave his friend a meaningful glance that he hoped conveyed the message, 'Hush your yap'.

When he got the brush-off from Miriam after the wedding, Kimberly had gotten into contact with him again. She tearfully promised things would be different this time and his mom was pushing him to get back together with her. They never liked the fact that he had broken up with her.

And then, when Kimberly got pregnant, the choice was made for both of them.

"So, how are your parents doing?" Jack asked.

Duncan looked over at Jack and gave him a tight smile. "Dad's busted up. Mom's being Mom," Duncan said, thinking how his mother managed to hold in her emotions, even in this darkest of times. "But it's tough."

"Of course. Tough for you, too," Terra said, gently placing her hand on his. "And now this guardian thing with Celia."

Duncan just shrugged and looked down at his pie, poking his fork into the flaky dessert.

"Might be a bit soon for Duncan to talk about this," Jack said.

"Sorry. Like I said. Nosy," Terra apologized.

"That's okay," Duncan said giving Terra a forgiving glance. "I think it's been on everyone's mind, but no one has dared bring it up."

"Except motormouth me," Terra said. "Again. Sorry."

"Does seem kind of weird," Les said. "I mean, Francine is your sister and all, and Jerrod is just the in-law. Seems kind of twisted. Unless they were trying to get you two to hook up again."

Duncan caught Terra's exasperated eye roll directed at Les, and grinned at her reaction.

"The last time Jerrod and Fran talked about Celia, my parents were supposed to be her guardians," Duncan said.

"What do your mom and dad make of it?" Terra asked. "They must be wondering why the sudden switch?"

"Mom and Dad don't like it at all," he said, breaking off another piece of pie. "But Dad's still in a wheelchair, and Mom can't take on more."

He knew they would like the situation even less once they found out what he had told Miriam. He wasn't emotionally ready for that conversation yet. Bad enough he had spilled his intentions to Miriam. He had hoped to wait a couple of weeks, at least, before letting her know she would be on her own where Celia was concerned.

He blamed the picture of Kimberly and Tasha that he'd found on the mantle for evaporating any last bits of self-control he had clung to through the entire afternoon. He had thrown away all his own pictures of his wife and daughter right after their funerals, but as soon as he saw this one, it was as if everything came back.

The photo was taken on Celia's second birthday. He and Kimberly had flown down to visit Jerrod and Francine, who were living in Toronto at the time. They had taken Tasha with them.

It was the last photo of Tasha that he had. Three days later, she was dead. She and her mother.

"What's Miriam like?" Terra asked, her question jerking his dark thoughts back to the present. "Do you think you'll be able to work with her?"

"She's hot," Lester said. "Maybe you should get together with her again."

Terra shot him an 'are you kidding' look.

"What?" Lester protested, lifting his hands up in a gesture of puzzlement. "She is."

Duncan had to admit his outspoken friend was right. Miriam had been pretty then; she was gorgeous now.

"I understand that she was Jerrod's foster sister?" Jack asked.

"Yeah. They grew up in Halifax. Miriam had a lot of crap in her life dealing with her natural mom. I'm thinking she got tossed back and forth between her mom's home and foster homes for a few years before she finally settled in with Jerrod's family for good."

"And don't I know what that feels like," Terra

said with a wry note. "Leslie and I were moved enough when we were growing up. At least Miriam had some stability by being returned to the same foster home every time."

Duncan shot her a sympathetic look, understanding Terra's reference to her and her sister's erratic upbringing with a mostly absent mother. "Well, she'll have someone to relate to while she's here."

"Miriam might not want to talk about her past with a complete stranger," Terra said with a shrug. "Or an incomplete one, for that matter."

Jack groaned at the old joke as Duncan finished off the last of the pie, the headache that lingered all day slowly returning. "Can I bug you for some Tylenol?" he asked Terra.

"Of course," she said.

"Should let you know, I got things under control in the bush." Les folded and refolded the paper napkin in front of him. "Got five hundred cubic meters logged and skidded today."

"That is a good day," Duncan said.

"I don't think Duncan wants to talk about logging," Jack muttered.

"Actually, I don't mind." Work was territory he could negotiate without all the emotional landmines. "I'll be back tomorrow," he said to Les.

"I need routine and work. It's been a crappy week."

Dealing with the legalities of bringing Francine's and Jerrod's bodies back from Blue River, the funeral, and the other stuff that came with it, had dragged everything out of him. He longed for the simple. The straightforward. Even with breakdowns and problems and stress, working in the bush was less emotional than dealing with his sister's death.

"Here you go," Terra said, setting a cup of water with ice cubes in it and a couple of pills on the table. Duncan tossed the tablets back and chased them with the water.

"So I imagine you'll be busy the next while, helping with Celia," Terra said. "Getting her settled in. That's quite a responsibility for you as well."

Duncan finished the glass of water and set it on his plate, knowing that he had to tell them. He didn't want unrealistic expectations, or to have to deal with constant questions about his niece.

"I don't think I'll be helping much with Celia."

"Does Miriam not want you involved?" Terra asked.

Duncan dragged his hand over his face, his stubble rasping against his fingers as he eased out a sigh, not sure how to say what he had to. "First off, from a legal standpoint, I'm not Celia's principle guardian."

"Why not?" Jack asked.

"Apparently, the lawyer said there's this whole insurance thing about how, statistically, a wife lives longer than her husband, so when they die at the same time, the wife is deemed to be last to die. Which means everything that would have gone to Jerrod goes to Francine, and is then handled by Francine's will."

"So what has that to do with Celia?"

He thought the legal explanation would have been enough for his friends. Black and white. Nothing he could do.

But he felt a need to get this out of the way before anyone got too many wrong ideas. He knew his parents would be angry. Hurt. But he couldn't do anything about that. He couldn't live their life for them. Now, after the horrible emotions of the past week and all they brought back to him, he needed to get his life settled.

"I told Miriam that because Francine named her as guardian, I was willing to leave it at that. To let her do with Celia what she thought best."

"But she's your niece, too," Terra protested. "You have some rights."

She still didn't get it.

"I'm a single guy with too much on my plate. Between the farm and the logging, I'm too busy. Besides, I can't be involved in that little girl's life. I can't do this."

"But Duncan—"

"Leave him be." Jack spoke softly, laying a hand on his wife's arm. "Duncan has his reasons."

Duncan shot Jack a grateful glance. Jack had been on duty when Kimberly and Tasha died. In fact, he had been the one to bring Duncan the news. Jack knew exactly what Duncan lost that horrible day, and why he was balking at taking on the responsibility his brother-in-law handed him.

Celia was too visible a reminder of that loss.

#

"So what is he like?" Christine's voice over the phone line sounded eager, greedy to ferret out whatever details I'd toss her way. "Francine's brother."

I groaned, realizing what a tactical error I had made when I told her about Duncan and his position as co-guardian.

Trust my dear friend to concentrate on the peripherals, edging past the hard places. I was glad I had never told her Duncan and I had met before. She would be relentless.

"Good-looking, in a brooding, Norse god kind of way." I switched my phone to my other ear as I sat back on the narrow, single bed in the spare room. I couldn't stay in Francine and Jerrod's large room and king-size bed. Besides being slightly creepy, it was like an explosion had gone off in there. Clothes and personal items were strewn across the bed and spilling onto the floor. It looked like they had packed in a hurry before they left.

And all that stuff seemed too personal to deal with until I was ready.

"Ooh. Sounds yummy already."

"I'm not interested," I told her, cutting her off mid-gush.

"But why not?" she half groaned, half whined. "You haven't had a date in ages. He's right there. Available. Like you."

"Sorry, but this is hardly the time to be talking about guys and dates." Too late, I realized how snappy I sounded but figured I had to stop her before I started crying again. My emotions had been teetering all day, and I didn't want to start now while I was alone.

Christine was immediately contrite. "Sorry.

Being insensitive again. So, now you've got this little girl to take care of. How's that's supposed to work?"

Little girl. Such cool, unfeeling words to describe my daughter.

My heart hitched again at the thought. I had checked on her before I left and I wanted to pull her into my arms. Hold her close.

But I didn't dare confuse her like that. She barely knew me as an aunt let alone as a mother.

"I have no idea how that will work." I leaned back against the wall, looking out the window, still unable to comprehend how utterly dark it got out here in the country. I could see a band of stars spread across the sky and, once again, felt amazed at the vastness of creation. And, even worse, how completely isolated I was out here. "You know as well as I do that I can't bring her back to Vancouver with me."

"True that. There's barely enough room in the apartment for the two of us, let alone a little girl." Wasn't too hard to hear the relief in Christine's voice, which underlined my determination to keep Celia here in Holmes Crossing. "But what else will you do? Would you think of staying there and taking care of her?"

"I don't think I'm the right person to do it."

"What do you mean? You love kids. All of your sketches and paintings are of kids." Wasn't hard to miss Christine's surprise.

She never knew that my painting children, creating those pouty-lipped, adorable faces was a way of living out a dream that wouldn't become reality. I had never told Christine all the down-and-dirty details of my life. I had met Christine A.D. Anno Domini. After Christ. After Celia. They had both arrived about the same time.

"No. I just like other people's kids," I said, folding an arm over my midsection.

"I'm sure it's tricky for you, if Duncan doesn't want to be involved," Christine continued.

"I think he's just grieving. I'm sure he'll come around." It was what I prayed for. My life was too unsorted to take in Celia. Exactly the kind of life my biological mother lived. The apple doesn't fall far from the tree.

At least my mother dropped her dead-beat boyfriends before they pulled her too deeply into their horrible lives.

As opposed to Gregg and me.

"Anyhow, I'm beat," I continued. "I should check on Celia again and get to bed."

"Do you know when you'll be back here?"

I hesitated, thinking of the complication that

had entered my plans. "I think I should stay around for Celia's birthday..." I let the sentence hang, not daring to think what would happen past that. I simply had to convince Duncan that he needed to be involved. That he was the better person to take care of Celia.

"Do you think Gillian will keep your job for you, if you stay longer?"

The concern in Christine's voice only made me more nervous. Gillian Dempter was a great boss, but she couldn't be expected to put my job on hold while I sorted out my life. She had already extended her own comfort zone in hiring me. "I can't think about that now. I'll deal with that when the time comes."

"Sure. Of course."

But I knew that Christine had her concerns, as well. If I didn't have a job I wouldn't be able to pay rent. I hadn't gotten an illustrating job in eons. Since Celia was born, actually. So my only gig was my job at the hotel. And given the current economic climate and my sketchy résumé, anything else was either minimum wage work or hard to come by.

I heard a whimper from Celia's room and my heart jumped as I waited, straining as I listened.

"Miriam?"

"Sorry. I thought I heard Celia crying."

She had been restless since everyone had left. Waking up and complaining that it was too noisy, that it was too loud, even though I was the only person in the house. Exhaustion finally pulled her into a twitchy sleep.

I listened, but then nothing, so I turned off the light and walked to the window, trying to still my spinning head.

The first night I was here, I stood outside, in the snow and the cold, looking up at the stars tossed across the sky like crushed glass on black velvet. I was still trying to absorb losing my brother and Francine. Wrapping my head around Celia's orphaned state.

And then I saw it, a band of light spread across the sky in the north. I couldn't figure out what was going on at first and then it shimmered and moved, waving like a curtain and I realized what I was seeing.

The Northern Lights. Aurora Borealis.

I'd heard of them, but never seen them before. And as I watched them dancing across the sky, bands of blue and green with flashes of pink, I felt as if I were in the very presence of God.

And for a moment, I realized that my grief was a small part of a larger cosmos. I felt as if

God had given me this small sign of His vastness. His greatness. And I felt a flicker of comfort that in spite of what happened, Celia would be taken care of and given the family she deserved.

But now, after what Duncan had told me, that certainty had been tested.

"I still think it's weird that your brother didn't even name you guardian," Christine continued. "That he named his brother-in-law without consulting him."

I thought it more hurtful than weird, even though Jer, Fran and I had all agreed that his parents were to care for Celia. Not me.

"Francine never talked to me, either," I said, weariness clawing at me. "Duncan told me his parents were supposed to be guardians. Apparently, his father's logging accident changed all that for them. He has a sister, Esther, but she's in college and I don't think she'd be able to take Celia on. But still..." I let my voice trail off, still trying to absorb the implications of the conflicting wills.

"It's a big job," Christine said. "I hope you can manage while you sort it all out. But I should go. Need my beauty sleep. I hope you can sleep, too." She paused a moment, then, "You take care. I bet you'll be praying about this?"

I heard the skepticism in her voice, and in spite of everything, had to smile. "Yes. I will."

"Hope it makes a difference," was all she said.

And as I said goodbye, I had to echo her thoughts. I hoped so too. Somehow I had to find a way to convince Duncan that he was the best person to take care of Celia. It was the only solution that made any sense. The only solution that was the best for Celia.

Then I heard Celia crying out again, and I realized that the long night of trying to comfort an inconsolable child was only beginning.

CHAPTER 2

"What do you want for breakfast?" I gave Celia my brightest smile, determined to try to keep things—air quotes—as light as possible as I wiped down the stove in the kitchen. I couldn't believe it had gotten this grimy in the short time Fran and Jer had lived here.

Celia sat across the island from me, shoving her doll's arms into the sleeves of a cheerful, apricot-hued party dress. She had spent the night complaining about noise and voices only she seemed to hear. As a consequence, I slept less than she did as I stood, or rather, sat guard over her, ready to console her.

I wasn't sure how I was allowed to feel about

her. This whole 'me and her' wasn't something I had imagined or prepared for. Her life was supposed to take place far enough away that I could spin any fantasy I wanted, imagine any life for her I chose.

Jer encouraged the distance, saying that he didn't want to confuse Celia and upset me. At least that had been his line. I saw the sense in it, though my heart always yearned for time with Celia. For a chance to see my little girl in the flesh. To hold her on my lap. Read her a story. Instead I was only allowed to send her birthday cards and gifts from her Aunt Miriam. Call her once in awhile.

And now I was dropped into her life with no preparation. No rulebook on how to deal with a daughter I barely knew. A daughter who pointedly ignored me, as she fussed with minuscule snaps on the doll's dress. Finally, she smoothed it out, apparently satisfied with her work. She tilted her head and I caught a glimpse of myself as a young girl.

And it hit me.

She was the only biological family I had.

I almost staggered under the reality of that, and behind it came an even more tantalizing thought.

I have a chance, another chance, with my daughter.

For a dangerous moment, I let the idea settle as my imagination wove other fantasies. Mother and daughter together. My child restored to me again.

I swallowed a knot of emotion, tried to still my suddenly racing heart.

Then my practical and unselfish side shoved the sentimental feelings aside. Celia came first. Jer had taught me that well.

When, as a single mother, I had found out I was pregnant and had been betrayed by the man who was Celia's father, I had turned to the only person I could count on. My foster brother. The only family I had left after his mother, my foster mother, died.

Jer was the one who encouraged me to think of adoption when I had no other choices left. So when Jer and Fran asked if they could be the ones to adopt her, I saw this as a chance to give Celia the best possible life and the stability I never knew with my own mother.

Even after she was whisked out of my arms, a part of me had hoped to stay involved with her. To hold the connection. But my brother firmly closed the door on any type of open adoption, and I knew he was right. By naming Duncan Celia's guardian he sent me a clear post-mortem message.

I was not the right person to care for my little girl.

My heart stuttered again over the words. My little girl.

But I caught myself as once more I veered too close to places I had no right going. I gave up my right to Celia all those years ago, and for good reasons.

Now, she had someone else responsible for her. Her Uncle Duncan. His refusal to be involved surprised and disappointed me. This didn't seem like the loving, caring man I had met at my brother's wedding.

Forget the past. Do what is in front of you.

My foster mother's words wove into the moment. Words she whispered to me whenever I felt overwhelmed and couldn't figure out which way to go in my life.

Right now, what was in front of me, was finding a way to get Celia to eat.

"Celia, honey, what can I make you to eat?" I repeated my request, hoping this time I would get a response.

Celia looked up from the vigorous hair

brushing she was giving the American Girl doll sitting in her lap. The doll had almost as extensive a wardrobe as Celia herself. And I should know. I had contributed many of the overpriced clothing items as well, not even balking at breaking my budget to buy fake baked goods and a doll-sized electric mixer that cost more than the secondhand Sunbeam that sat in the drawer of my apartment kitchen.

Guilt. The great motivator.

"Jane wants waffles," Celia finally proclaimed.

Jane being said doll with said extensive wardrobe.

"Okay. Jane can have waffles. What do you want?"

"Jane wants waffles." Celia said in a monotone voice. She bent her head over the doll, her own blonde hair a tangle that she refused to let me touch. I didn't push the issue, but it bothered me that her doll would be more neatly coiffed and dressed than Celia. "So just make Jane some waffles," she continued.

Well, if Jane wanted waffles, I could oblige. Maybe Celia would eat some of them in the process.

"Do you know where your mom—where the

waffle iron is?" I caught myself from referring to her mother just in time, wondering simultaneously at the protocol of dealing with a grieving child. I had always been on the receiving end of the forced good humor and smiles. The overeager desire of others to smooth rough patches away from a life stumbling through unknown territory, unsure of which steps to take.

Somewhere along the line, Celia would need outside help. Until then, however, it was guesswork on my part until the Tiemstra's took over.

"Jane says the waffle iron is in the pantry," Celia informed me, still avoiding eye contact.

Since I met her just before the funeral, Celia had been an obedient little automaton, acknowledging hugs and kisses with a passivity that I recognized all too well. Every time I was moved to a new foster home I held back the same way, unsure of how to behave until I found my footing.

That Celia had to deal with the same sorrow broke my heart. This wasn't the happy ending I had hoped for her when I gave her up.

"Thanks for the help, Celia."

"It was Jane who told you. Not me." Celia looked up at me, her eyes snapping. "You have to thank her."

I veered between confusion and concern at her angry reply. I knew nothing about psychology but I assumed this was Celia's way of keeping me at a distance until she knew who I was and where I belonged in her life.

I wasn't about to thank the doll, so instead I turned to the pantry. My heart sank once again when I was confronted with the mess. Ripped bags and open boxes with contents spilling out fought for space with tin cans, empty grocery bags, cleaning supplies and an excess of appliances.

I recognized a panini maker, four-slice toaster, blender, stand-up mixer, coffee maker, an espresso machine, the waffle maker I had come to fetch and an array of gadgets and contraptions whose function was lost on me. And all were caked and grimy.

I shoved cans and plastic containers aside to get the waffle maker, and set it gingerly on the counter. It was coated with grease and drips of questionable age. As was the mixer. It took a few tries to find the pancake mix. I just hoped it wasn't stale.

The fridge was as difficult to negotiate after yesterday. The plethora of food containers made me feel like I was playing Jenga—pulling some containers out, setting them aside and digging through others—all while trying not to cause an avalanche. The eggs were buried on the second shelf toward the back. The milk was in the door and, out of habit, I checked the date on the container. My own refrigerator was also a haphazard affair and the quality of the contents veered from fresh to landfill-worthy. Checking best-before dates was a survival skill I learned early on.

Then my heart clenched as the date on the carton registered. Francine had been alive when she put this in the fridge. Her hands had been warm. She'd had plans for this milk.

Sadness washed over me, and for that moment, all I could do was cling to the handle of the refrigerator door for support. Would this happen every time I bumped against a memory of Fran and my brother?

I dropped my head against the door of the fridge. *I can't do this, Lord,* I prayed. *I can't do this on my own.*

And as the grief slowly subsided, another thought rose up.

I wasn't supposed to do this alone. I was supposed to have help.

"Jane says you should close the door of the

fridge." Celia's quiet voice slipped into my tortured thoughts. "She says you're wasting energy."

I turned to her as I closed the door, hearing my brother in her comment.

"Your daddy used to say that all the time," I said.

"Don't talk about my daddy," Celia cried out, her eyes wild, her hands slamming on the counter. "My daddy isn't here anymore, and my mommy is dead. And you're not my mommy."

Her words struck like barbed arrows in my heart.

I remembered saying the same thing to Jerrod's mother the first time I came into their home. Trouble was, in this case, Celia was wrong.

Don't even venture into that quagmire. Francine and Jerrod adopted her into their family. She is Celia Carpenter. You can't lay claim to her.

But for now I didn't know what to say. What did Sally Carpenter, my foster mother, do each time I came back from visits with my natural mother with a few more emotional scars? A few more bad memories?

My thoughts scrabbled backward. But all I dredged up was the feeling of arms around me, a gentle hug, and an acknowledgement of my grief.

So I went around the counter separating us

and I tentatively put my arm around her shoulder, but she jerked away.

I knew why she did it, but nevertheless, her rejection cut deep.

I waited a moment, but she held her shoulders stiff under my arm, and I knew this wasn't working. No violins would accompany this tactic.

So I went back to cleaning the waffle iron, mixing batter, and struggling against the sorrow I couldn't indulge in.

Ten minutes and a few taciturn replies later, I set the waffles and a cup of milk in front of Celia, who promptly pushed them over to Jane, sitting on the counter, legs splayed, hair neatly braided, her permanently cheerful face mocking both of us.

"She needs a fork," Celia said, still not looking at me. "And a smaller cup."

I remembered seeing a small baby fork in the cutlery drawer and hoped this would do the trick for the increasingly demanding Jane. I also found a smaller cup and poured some juice into it.

Celia forked a piece of waffle, and held it in front of Jane. I half expected the doll to open her mouth.

"Jane doesn't like it when you watch her eat," Celia grumbled.

Chastened, I turned around, busying myself with cleaning the mixer and washing the bowl. Jane was getting to be a pain but I needed her on my side. So I kept my mouth shut.

When I was done, I snuck a peek over my shoulder, thankful to see both juice and waffle gone.

"Jane wants to go upstairs to her room," Celia announced, stepping off the stool, her doll tucked up against her.

"Do you want to do anything else today?" I needed to keep busy and while the messy house promised me at least a few days' worth of work, Celia was my priority.

Celia conferred with her doll, still not making eye contact. "Jane wants to stay home today." Then she trudged up the stairs, a sad, little ragamuffin with her wrinkled nightgown and tousled hair.

As she left, I sank back against the counter.

Help me, Lord, was all I could pray.

Then, a ringing of the doorbell pulled me away from the counter, and I hurried to the front entrance, grateful for the distraction.

Duncan and Francine's mother stood on the step, her smile tight, her heavily-made-up eyes staring me down, her bobbed hair looking as if she had just stepped out of the beauty salon. A cream-and-orange silk scarf filled the open neck of a brown pea coat worn over beige slacks. Gold hoops swung from her ears. She was an elegant study in neutrals that made me feel like I should have thought twice about putting on the faded blue jeans and old T-shirt that were my go-to wardrobe choices. And I should have spent more time cleaning up the house.

"I hope this isn't a bad time?" she asked, stepping quickly inside. I cut off the blast of winter air as I closed the door behind her. "I just wanted to make a quick stop to see how my granddaughter is doing."

My resistance to her claim on Celia surprised me.

"She's struggling, as I'm sure you are," I said. "Can I take your coat?"

"Thank you," she said finding a spot for her purse on the overflowing bench in the porch. She slipped her coat off, tucked the silk scarf in the sleeve and handed it to me. "I wanted to stop and see Celia though I can't stay long."

I opened the door of the closet in the foyer to hang it up, pushing aside the other coats that still hung there, my heart fluttering at the sight of my brother's and sister-in-law's clothing.

"Oh, my." Mrs. Tiemstra's hand flew to her mouth at the sight. "I'm sorry, I should have arranged for someone to clean up."

"You've had enough on your mind," I said. "I'll deal with it."

"Are you sure?" Mrs. Tiemstra asked, her voice tight as she held back her own grief. "Though Jerrod was only your foster brother, I'm sure this has been difficult for you as well."

I tried to stifle my own hurt feelings at the casual comment I'd heard dozens of times before. 'Only a foster child' seemed to be a steady refrain in my life. As if my birth mother's lack of concern for our relationship gave everyone else permission to devalue it as well.

"It's hard," was all I could manage.

Mrs. Tiemstra patted me on the shoulder, her smile tight, then she walked past me directly into the kitchen. She glanced around the room and I felt a flush of guilt when I saw Celia's syrup-covered plate still sitting on the counter.

"I just gave Celia breakfast," I said, hurrying over to clean it up.

"At least she's eating. I haven't been able to swallow a single bite," Mrs. Tiemstra said, hugging herself.

I nodded in agreement, but then my heart

sank as I came around the eating bar to clear the plates. The floor below Celia's chair was littered with pieces of waffle and, near as I could tell, it was everything I had served up for her.

Guess Jane wasn't hungry, I thought as I bent over to pick them all up. As I stood I caught Mrs. Tiemstra's concerned look. "I thought she had finished them," I mumbled, dumping the sticky pieces on the plate, then scraping the plate into the garbage. "She didn't want me watching her eat."

I wasn't about to relay the disturbing information about how Celia was communicating through her doll as well.

"Did you want something to drink? Some tea or coffee?" I offered, as I rinsed out a dishcloth.

"I only have a few moments. I wanted to see how Celia was doing." She wove her fingers together, glancing around. "I hope you don't mind my being rather forthright," Mrs. Tiemstra said, as I hastily wiped the floor. "But I have a delicate matter to deal with."

My radar tingled as I walked around the island to the sink again. In my history, delicate matters usually involved whispered conversations between my foster parent and the social worker, usually having to do with my mother demanding my return to her home. Which invariably ended in yet another truncated and disastrous stay with my mom.

"Go on," I encouraged, swallowing down my paranoia.

"It has to do with the guardianship of Celia." Mrs. Tiemstra stopped there, as if waiting for me to fill in the blanks.

One of the survival techniques I learned early on in both my biological mother's home and consultations with social workers was to wait before offering an opinion or comment.

"What about it?" I countered, glancing up the stairs to make sure Celia wasn't there.

"I need to express my concerns about the situation," Mrs. Tiemstra continued. "I understand that you have a home in Vancouver. I am sure you'll need to get back to your obligations..." She let the sentence trail off and I knew precisely where she was going.

"But you're wondering why Duncan was named guardian by Jerrod, and me by Francine." May as well toss it out on the table.

"Yes. That's exactly it." She seemed to wilt in relief and as I looked at her drawn features I reminded myself of her own loss.

"All I can say is that currently everything is in flux," was all I could give Mrs. Tiemstra.

"Exactly. In flux." Mrs. Tiemstra latched hungrily onto the word. "I would think until everything is settled you'll be staying here?"

"Like I told Duncan, I don't want to disrupt Celia's life. This is her home." I wanted to tell her about my own decision, but this wasn't the time.

"That's wonderful. And this gives you and Duncan an opportunity to work together. He and Jerrod were close. That's why he named Duncan guardian." She tugged at her lower lip. "I'm thankful he did that. I know my son will want to be intensely involved with any decisions you make."

"That's not what he told me last night," I said, puzzled at her comment.

"What do you mean?"

The sound of footsteps coming down the stairs prevented me from answering and then there was Celia, her hair still a nest of tangles, still in her nightgown, still clinging to Jane.

Which put an end to that conversation.

"Honey, there you are," Mrs. Tiemstra called out, rushing toward Celia and scooping her up in her arms.

"Hi, Nana," Celia said, pulling away from her kiss.

Mrs. Tiemstra set her down, kneeling down in front of her, pushing her hair back, stroking it gently. "How are you feeling, sweetie? Miriam said you didn't eat your waffle this morning. You love waffles."

"Jane said she didn't like the way Aunt Miriam made the waffles." Jane's critique of my cooking didn't bother me. What did bother me was the way Celia avoided eye contact with her grandmother.

I could see the confusion on Mrs. Tiemstra's face at this pronouncement. "Jane can't eat waffles, honey," she said.

"Yes. She can. But she didn't want those waffles." Celia's voice was matter-of-fact.

"Why don't you get me a brush, sweetie, and we can brush your hair," Mrs. Tiemstra said, pushing herself to her feet.

"Jane likes my hair this way."

Mrs. Tiemstra gave me a puzzled look. "Why does she keep talking about her doll?"

"Her name is Jane," Celia said with a touch of anger.

"I know that, honey, but she's not real."

"She is. She is real and she doesn't like the way

you're talking." Then Celia spun around and scooted back upstairs.

Mrs. Tiemstra watched her leave, then turned to me. "What in the world is going on?" she demanded, as if I had abetted this sudden transformation of her granddaughter to this strange person who talked via a doll.

"I'm not sure, but I'm thinking right now it's easier for her to make it seem like Jane is the one making the requests and talking," I said. "It might be her way of distancing herself from her grief."

"That is the oddest thing." She shook her head, frowning at me. "I am not entirely sure I like the way things are going here."

She wasn't the only one, but for now, this was the way 'things' were.

"We need to get this guardianship thing straightened out with the lawyer. The sooner the better." As if that was all it would take. Clearly, Duncan hadn't told his parents what he had told me. And the sooner I got this out of the way, the better.

"We need to talk." I would have liked to consult her in Jerrod's office but that door was locked and I hadn't found a key yet. So I brought Mrs. Tiemstra to the mudroom, just off the front entrance.

"What is this about?" Mrs. Tiemstra demanded. "Why are we talking here?"

"I don't want Celia overhearing this," I said, closing the door as Mrs. Tiemstra entered. I turned to face her, wondering how she would take what I had to say. "After the funeral, Duncan told me he didn't want to be involved with Celia."

"Of course he does," Mrs. Tiemstra objected. "He's her uncle just as much as you are her aunt. Maybe even more. Francine was his blood relative, Jerrod was just your foster brother."

Again I struggled to brush off her comment.

"Then you'll have to talk to Duncan about this," I said. "Because that's what he told me."

"I can't believe Duncan would have said what he did." She sucked in a quick breath. "He would never turn his back on his sister's daughter. His niece."

I didn't want to tell her that I was as surprised at the news as she was.

"This came straight from Duncan," I insisted. "With no prompting from me."

She just stared at me as if trying to figure out what to do with me. "You can't appeal to him? Get him to understand? I know that at one time you two were...well, you had some type of connection."

I was surprised she would mention this. Also surprised that after all these years she thought that 'connection' would give me any pull with her son.

"That was a long time ago," I said.

She frowned then glanced at her watch, her eyes narrowing. "I'm sorry. I really have to go. My husband and I will be speaking with Duncan as soon as we can. We need to get this straightened out. Celia must stay here."

I wanted to say I was on her side. Wanted to tell her exactly what I thought, but I didn't want to run the risk of Celia overhearing two adults discussing her future, tossing her back and forth like a ping pong ball.

I'd had enough of that in my own life.

Besides, this way I could allow myself a few more foolishly hopeful moments pretending I was the only one in Celia's life.

Pretending that, in spite of my past, I could be a true mother to her.

#

"I CAN'T DO IT, Mom. Sorry." Duncan focused on stirring the cream into the coffee his mother had given him, steeling himself for what was coming. "I can't be Celia's guardian."

He knew when his mother called him last night and asked him to stop by their house before going off to work that this 'talk' would be on the table. Not the best start to his working day, but he figured he may as well get it out of the way. Thankfully, it was Saturday, which was often a slower day in the bush. His crew would be okay without him breathing down their neck for a couple of hours.

"But honey, why?" Cora sat down beside his father, both of them facing him, an immoveable wall of disappointment and familial duty.

Duncan carefully set his spoon down and took a slow sip of his coffee, dragging out the moment.

"Jerrod named you guardian for a reason," his father said, his hands clenching the arms of his wheelchair. "You should honor that."

Duncan was sure the logging accident that had broken his father's spine nine months ago was why Jerrod made the changes to his will. He just wished his brother-in-law would have consulted him first.

"And what about Francine?" Duncan returned. "Seems kind of strange that my own sister didn't name me guardian."

His father's lips thinned at his cheap shot and he grimaced as if in pain.

Guilt immediately took a seat at the table, but the comment bought Duncan some time as he cobbled together his arguments. He'd practiced them on Miriam and had all last night to fine-tune them.

"Had you fought with Francine?" his mother asked. "I know you two didn't always get along."

Duncan's thoughts slipped back to the argument he'd had with his sister before she and Jerrod took off on this stupid trip. He'd tried to convince her that it was irresponsible. But Francine had told him, an unusual note of pleading in her voice, that she needed to do this. For her and Jerrod's sake.

"We disagreed about their sledding trip," was all he would say

"Do you think that was the reason she made the change?" his mother asked.

Duncan shook her head. "She wouldn't have had time beforehand to do that." He pulled in a deep breath, marshaling his arguments. "But we need to respect her reasons, whatever they may be."

"It doesn't make any sense," his mother continued. "You should be taking care of Celia. She's no relation to that girl."

Once again his mother's quick dismissal of Miriam was a vivid reminder of that afternoon, a few days after Jerrod and Francine's wedding, when his mother tried to convince him that dating Miriam was a mistake. That he should get back together with Kimberly. When Miriam ignored his texts he ended up doing exactly that.

Once in a while he wondered what would have happened if Miriam had replied.

"Miriam is as much Celia's aunt as I'm her uncle," Duncan said shooting his mother a warning glance. "And she's suffered a loss as well."

"Jerrod was just her foster brother," his father put in. "It's not like they were close."

"Regardless of what didn't or should have happened, Celia is in a good place for now. I can't give that girl the time she needs," Duncan continued. "I'm in the middle of the busiest season. I've got major contracts to fulfill and higher productions standards to work around."

The words that sounded so reasonable last night came out trite and heartless when spoken aloud at the dinner table where his family had made many good memories.

"I can't give her what she needs," he said. "I'm not capable."

"Is it because of Kimberly and Tasha?" his mother asked, her voice measured. Quiet. Devastatingly accurate. He was surprised that she brought up his wife and daughter. His mother had barely spoken their names in the three years they'd been gone, but she was already looking away, as if regretting her outburst.

Duncan clutched his mug as his mother's words opened a crack to the dark place he'd been edging toward since Jerrod and Francine's death.

He tossed down the last of his coffee, the hot liquid almost scalding his throat, then pushed the chair back, its feet screeching out a protest as it slid over the tiled floor. "Sorry, I can't sit and talk more about this. I gotta get to work."

He spun around and dropped his coffee cup into the sink. The spoon toppled out, creating an angry clatter.

"I'm sorry, Duncan," his mother said, her voice quiet. Composed. "That was unacceptable. I just don't want to lose another granddaughter."

Another granddaughter. The words cut him with deadly accuracy.

Duncan heard the heartache in her voice, but he had to set everyone else's expectations and unhappiness aside. It was the only way to get through the next few months.

"Sorry, Mom. I wish I could help." He drew in a ragged breath and looked over at his mother, knowing full well the pain she was dealing with. "And even if I could, I don't think I have a case against Miriam. Phil had told me that according to the insurance policy, Francine was deemed to have been last to die, so everything gets handled according to her will. And in her will she named Miriam the guardian."

"Are you sure about that?" his father put in.

It had taken several visits to the lawyer's office, and a few conversations with Phil before he got it all straight himself. The lawyer had presented it as a scenario—a possibility—not necessarily something they had to abide by. But Duncan saw it as a way to satisfy the letter of the law and protect his own heart.

Cold as that sounded.

"I'm not sure that's entirely correct," his father said. "We'll need to look into it."

"You go ahead," Duncan murmured, taking his coat off the back of the chair and shrugging it on, tamping down his growing emotions. "I'm not pursuing it."

"Aren't you being a bit selfish?" His father's

gruff voice brought guilt back into the conversation. "We have a stake in the situation as well."

It was on the tip of his tongue to tell his father to take on guardianship of Celia then, but he caught himself. His father's disability required his mother's full-time care. There was no way she could take care of a small child as well.

"I'm not only thinking of me," he said. "I'm thinking of what's best for Celia. And I don't think I'm best for her."

If a picture was worth a thousand words, his father's glower spoke volumes. But Duncan knew he couldn't give in.

"You should know why I can't do this. Why I can't take care of her. She's the same age—" He stopped there, looking down at the chair, surprised it held under the strength of his grasp.

Then old habits and coping mechanisms kicked in. He focused on his hands, thinking of the work waiting for him in the bush, and slowly released their pressure on the chair.

Then his cell phone buzzed, and he glanced down at the screen. With relief, he noticed it was a text from Les.

"Sorry. I gotta go," he said. "We have a breakdown."

"That new skidder you bought?" his father asked, looking up.

Duncan shot him a puzzled look, then recognized the question for the peace offering it was. The usual Tiemstra deflection.

"Yeah. Looks like the grapple isn't working." Duncan latched onto the change in topic with relief. He had taken over the logging operation from his father over four years ago. But his dad still liked to stay up with the news, and keep up when he could.

"Might be the hydraulic hoses. That brand of skidder is known for that."

"How can you two do this?" his mother cried out, surprising him once again with her emotional outburst. "How can you talk about these ordinary things with your daughter and your sister barely in the ground?"

Then she left the room, her head down, trailing her misery behind her like a raggedy old blanket.

Hank looked back at his son and blew out his breath. "You were right about Celia. You've got enough to deal with. We'll find a way to work through this."

Duncan heard the suffering in his voice and once again couldn't figure out why God had been so capricious with his family. His own wife and child. His father's accident. And now this.

"Sure. Of course," was all he said.

He yanked his truck keys out of his pocket and, giving his father a quick nod, left. As he drove away, he hoped his parents would leave him out of it. There was no way he could let himself be pulled into that little girl's life.

It would be too painful.

CHAPTER 3

I sat across from Celia on the floor of her bedroom, a hairbrush in one hand, hair ties in the other, dresses splayed out on the bed. It had been more than two days since the funeral, and fifty-six hours since I started taking care of Celia.

And I still hadn't managed to get the girl to brush her hair. Or change into ordinary clothes. She had trudged around in her pajamas since the day after the funeral. But today was Sunday and I wanted, no, needed to go to church.

Mrs. Tiemstra had stopped by again yesterday afternoon, and again Celia had held herself back. Then, Celia had spent most of the night curled up in a ball on the floor, arms wrapped around her knees, whispering complaints about the noise in the house, tears sliding down her cheeks—which was almost harder to take than the loud sobs of the night before.

"I think this will look really pretty on you," I said, holding out a pink-and-gray knit dress. "Your mommy bought it for you."

"My mommy is dead," Celia spat out, avoiding my eyes, still clutching her doll. And from the way she said it and the way she glowered at the dress, I guessed that if Francine was dead to her, so were any of her wishes.

I sent up another half-formed, half-baked prayer for wisdom and strength. Anything to help figure out how to handle Celia and how to sort out my own emotions concerning her. Each hour we spent together created a growing connection and a troubling vulnerability. Small glimpses of a life with my daughter teased the edges of my thoughts like forbidden fruit. I knew I couldn't indulge, and yet...

I went back to the closet, once again sorting through the frighteningly vast array of clothes, each one rejected with a firm shake of Celia's head.

As I pulled out yet another dress, I realized I was falling into the definition of insanity—repeating the same action over and over again, and expecting different results each time.

Then, I saw the answer, lying on the floor underneath a heap of other clothes. A tulle-and-satin confection decorated with sequins and still on a hanger. More a party dress than anything a young girl would wear to church. But it was the smaller, matching dress hooked onto its hanger that caught my attention.

I figured out how I could make this work. I unhooked the smaller dress from the hanger, brought it over to Celia and crouched down in front of her and her doll.

"Isn't this a beautiful dress, Jane?" I asked as I held out the dress for the doll's perusal, letting the light from sun pouring in from the window dance over the sequins on the dress. "Do you think you'd like to wear it to church?"

In my peripheral vision I caught Celia's puzzled expression as she looked from me to the doll, but then, to my surprise, Celia took the dress from me.

"She says she likes it," Celia said.

I almost turned to Celia to ask her about the matching gown, but caught myself in time. "And, Jane, there's a big-girl dress, too," I said in a fake, sing-songy voice that I assumed young girls used when speaking to their dolls. "Do you think Celia might like to wear it? Then she can look the same as you."

This was how far I had fallen. I was talking to a doll.

Celia bent over Jane, as if listening to her, then nodded. "She said that would be fun."

Relief sluiced through me and I smiled at the doll, then realized the absurdity of what I was doing. Too many more days of this and I would be able to hear Jane's elusive voice myself.

"That's great. I'll get the dress out of the closet." And while I was on a roll, I added one more proviso. "And maybe you could help me do Celia's hair the same as yours? Then you'll really be twins."

To my surprise and relief, Celia nodded.

Jane had spoken.

Actually, she hadn't, but I didn't care anymore. She had served her purpose.

Half an hour later, we were dressed and coiffed and headed out of the house.

I felt like I had made a major breakthrough. That it came from the help of a lifeless doll didn't matter to me one bit. There were ways to get through to a grieving little girl, and Jane had just become one of them.

As we drove to church, for the first time in days I felt like this situation could be borne. Endured.

And in spite of the sorrow that still clawed at me, a tiny part of me wondered if Duncan would be in church.

* * *

I PULLED into the parking lot of the church, my eyes slipping to the graveyard beside it. My throat closed at the sight of the two fresh mounds of dirt.

For a moment, I hesitated at the wisdom of returning to the place where, only a few days ago, Celia and I had sat through a service for her parents and my only family.

But I needed to attend church this morning. Needed to hear assurance that God was in control. Needed to be part of the community of believers.

Thankfully, Celia didn't even glance toward the graveyard, but as we stepped out of the SUV, into the cold, I wished that Celia had a coat that matched Jane's.

Because while Jane was all kitted out in a toque with matching scarf, puffy pink coat, and faux leather boots, Celia chose to weather the below-freezing temperatures in the same thin party dress her doll wore underneath her warm clothes. She shivered as she walked through the snow to the church, clutching her doll, but didn't voice one word of complaint. It was as if she had no emotions of her own. As long as Jane was warm she was fine.

I held open the door of the church, trying not to feel guilty at my own down-filled jacket. I had pleaded with her to put on even a simple sweater but she wouldn't budge. I put my jacket on, however, though my boots were borderline suitable. Just because Celia chose not to wear a coat didn't mean I should suffer.

However, as we walked into the crowded foyer, I felt like a neglectful parent as the people gathered there glanced our way.

I could tell the moment they remembered who we were. That first spark of recognition, then the slow slip into sympathy. Some looked away. Some hesitated, as if unsure of the grief protocol. But a surprising number came up to us, expressing their condolences. Lots of hands on shoulders and prolonged eye contact.

Though Fran and Jer had only moved to Holmes Crossing a couple of months ago,

Francine was a returnee and native daughter. I had noticed a number of gravestones in the graveyard with the Tiemstra name carved into the slabs and planted into the earth. Francine had roots here. I heard from Jerrod that her great-great-grandparents had settled here in the early 1900s—Dutchmen farming cheek-to-jowl with Italian, and other immigrants lured from Europe by the promise of cheap farmland.

Her great-grandfather and grandfather both farmed, and her father expanded into the logging business, which, I had found out via my brother, Duncan had taken over, as well as the farm.

And then, as if my thoughts had conjured him up, the doors on the opposite side of the foyer opened up. Cold air swirled across the floor, and there he was, tall, broad-shouldered, taking up an inordinate amount of space. His leather jacket, plaid shirt and blue jeans made him look like a walking cliché—a lumberjack brought to life. His head was bare and, as he looked around, he finger-combed his thick hair away from his face. And when he caught my gaze, foolish girl that I was, I couldn't help the old attraction that flickered through me.

He stopped, his hands dropping to his sides, and time seemed to slow. Then his deep-blue eyes shifted from me to Celia, his expression suddenly grave. Then Celia yanked her hand away from me.

"Dunkle," Celia called out, running toward Duncan, sounding surprisingly chipper. "Look, Dunkle. Jane is wearing your dress."

Dunkle—Celia's way of bringing Uncle and Duncan together in one word—stopped in his tracks, people in the foyer looking sympathetically on as Celia held her doll up for his inspection.

Her enthusiasm was as unexpected as it was surprising. This was the most life she had shown since the funeral.

"'Member you bought this dress for Jane?" Celia pointed to hers. "And one for me. They're samesies."

"Hey there, Celia," Duncan said giving her a vague smile and an awkward pat on her head, looking obligingly down at the doll but I could see that he didn't recall what she was talking about.

"For Christmas," Celia insisted. "You bought my dress and Jane's dress for Christmas. Last year."

From the confusion on his face I ventured a guess that Dunkle had had little to do with said purchase, and suspected that his mother had taken care of the gift.

Which explained why I had trouble getting the zipper up Celia's slender back. If the dress was a gift from last Christmas, it was a year old, and one size too small.

"Yeah. Of course," he said gruffly. I could tell he was uncomfortable even as he was trying to connect with her.

"Celia was excited to wear her dress," I said to him, touching Celia on the shoulder to let her know I was there.

"Jane told me to wear it," she insisted, annoyed with the fact that he didn't seem to know what she was talking about.

"You both look really pretty," he said his smile wavering.

"Miriam. I'm glad to see you here." With a wave of flowery perfume and a flutter of her gloved hands, Mrs. Tiemstra joined us, her eyes as blue as her son's, flicking from me to Celia to Duncan. Her bobbed hair brushed the velvet collar of her black coat, swathing her slimly elegant figure.

In her presence I was suddenly aware of the frayed cuffs of my down-filled jacket that looked okay when I put it on this morning.

"And Celia, you're wearing your dress that Uncle Duncan gave you...last year." Mrs. Tiemstra shot a look from Celia's bare arms to me, one perfectly plucked eyebrow lifting in question.

"It matches the one her doll is wearing," I said, hoping Cora understood the significance. "And Celia doesn't have a matching coat."

"Jane loves this dress," Celia said, her eyes still on 'Dunkle' who now stood with his hands shoved in the pockets of his blue jeans. "She told me to wear it."

"It's minus ten out there," Cora said, her confusion showing me that she still didn't understand Celia's current thought processes.

Music started up in the sanctuary, signaling the beginning of the service. This was my out from an increasingly awkward situation.

"I imagine we should get going," I said, reaching to take Celia's hand, but again she ignored me.

Mrs. Tiemstra shot another look at her son, who had turned away from us and was now heading up the stairs. She pressed her lips together then gave me a pained look. "I'm sorry about Duncan. He's...struggling..."

He wasn't the only one, I wanted to say, but kept my thoughts to myself.

"I know you've much to handle now," Mrs. Tiemstra said, pulling me aside and lowering her voice. "But I was hoping we could get together sometime this week to discuss Duncan and Celia."

"I'm taking Celia to kindergarten on Monday," I told her still fighting my own inclination to lay my claim on her. "I'm hoping to get her back into a normal routine as soon as possible. We could meet after that."

Now, didn't that sound all practical and stoic.

"That would be perfect," Mrs. Tiemstra said, her look of relief reinforcing my own feelings about taking care of Celia. "And I was hoping you could join us for lunch today after church, as well. When Jerrod and Francine moved here..." She paused, an infinitesimal break in her voice, then she put on a bright smile and plowed on. "They always came for lunch after church. A kind of tradition in our family."

The thought gave me a mixture of warmth and regret. Traditions. The glue of any family and community. Something Celia would need.

"Sure. We can come."

"Wonderful. It's just a simple meal. Soup and buns."

"I'm sure it will be great," I said.

She gave a nod of approval then walked away.

I followed Mrs. Tiemstra up the stairs, letting the music draw me on, Celia at my side.

And as I stood at the back of the church, the memory of the funeral and the ensuing heaviness threatened to drag me down into sorrow once more. But I had Celia with me, and I couldn't let that happen.

I just hoped I could keep this up, I thought as the usher brought us to an empty spot in the pews. I just hoped I would get the strength I needed.

CHAPTER 4

uncan stepped into the porch of his parents' house, stamping the snow off his boots, wishing he'd had the guts to turn down his mother's invitation to come for lunch. But his mother had insisted, saying that at this sad and difficult time, they needed to be together.

And from the sight of Jerrod and Francine's SUV parked outside, Miriam and Celia were part of the 'together' time as well. His heart had sunk when he saw the vehicle, knowing full well what his mother was doing. He would have turned around, but he also knew that the family needed to be together, in spite of his personal discomfort around both Celia and Miriam.

"Duncan, there you are," his mother said with

a forced smile, holding open the door leading to the kitchen as he hung his coat up on an empty hook. "Come on in. Celia and Miriam are here already. We're just about ready to eat."

"I can't stay long," he warned her as he followed her through the door and down the wide hallway. "I need to get some bookwork done this afternoon. Got a busy day tomorrow."

"You stay as long as you can," his mother said, tossing the comment over her shoulder as she walked through the kitchen to the dining room beyond. "I'm just thankful you came."

Blessed warmth and the scent of his mother's beef soup greeted him as he followed her toward the murmur of conversation.

Every Sunday, for as long as he could remember, his mother served soup and grilled-cheese buns for lunch after church. The smell brought out other memories of Sundays from his youth, and more recently from the many times he, Kimberly, and Tasha used to come.

He knew that Jerrod, Francine, and Celia had come a few times since they moved here, and though he couldn't avoid every Sunday, he'd managed to keep it to a minimum.

In the dining room, his father was already wheeled up to the table, Miriam sitting beside him. Her white sweater set off her long hair pulled up in a loose bun, errant strands framing her narrow features. She was biting at her lip, her face pale as she fiddled with a spoon in front of her.

Again, he was struck by the differences in her the years had created. And how hard it was to keep his eyes off her. Did she ever think of him after she'd left? Had he even crossed her mind?

He pushed the thoughts back.

"So Duncan tells me you live in Vancouver?" his father was asking Miriam. "Rains a lot there doesn't it? Isn't that kind of depressing?"

"Hank. That's rather rude," his mother said with a nervous laugh, as she lifted the lid off the pot of soup parked in the center of the table.

"Well, it does," his father said, his tone a bit defensive.

"I don't mind all that much," was all Miriam said. "But it can get a person down, if you let it."

"Yeah. I bet," his father said, nodding his head quickly, clearly scrambling for something else to say. As Duncan sat down, his father turned to him with a look of relief. "Glad you could come, son. Miriam and I were just...getting to know each other. Or trying to."

Duncan couldn't help but grin. His father had

always seen small talk as a sign of small minds. He preferred to jump straight into the meat and potatoes of life, so his casual conversation with Miriam was a struggle for him.

"Now that we are all here, we can eat," his mother said. "Celia, do you want to come and sit with us?"

Duncan finally spotted his niece tucked in one corner of the dining room, hunched over at a child's table and chair set his mother had purchased many years ago. Celia had her back to them and didn't respond.

"Celia, honey. We're ready to eat," his mother repeated, but still no response.

"Celia. Come now." His father's voice held a note of exasperation.

Duncan could see from the tightness around his father's mouth, and the way his fists were clenched on the table, that today was not a good day physically or mentally. Which was probably why he hadn't been in church this morning.

"Dad, I think—"

"She's been sitting there since she got here," his father said, cutting him off. "Didn't even come to sit with me."

"Things are all messed up for her, too," Duncan said, keeping his voice low, recognizing that his father's distress was tied in with the sadness that was crushing him.

His father glared at him but then sat back, breathing slowly, as if riding out both pain and grief.

"I'll get her," Miriam said pushing away from the table.

Duncan wanted to tell Miriam to simply leave her be. He recognized Celia's desire to retreat from people and sympathy, but after he'd relegated his responsibility concerning her, he didn't feel he had any right to hand out advice.

Miriam crouched down beside Celia, her head bent over the little girl.

"Aren't you hungry?" she was asking Celia, her husky voice lowered, trying to make eye contact with his niece. "Don't you want to come sit with Dunkle?" Her hand came up to touch the girl's hair, but Celia recoiled. Duncan saw Miriam press her lips together, then, without another word, she returned to the table.

"You couldn't convince her?" his mother asked as she set a plate of buns on the table beside the pot of soup.

Miriam shook her head and sat down.

"Has she eaten at all since the funeral?"

"I don't know. There's a box of animal

crackers in the pantry that's getting depleted. And yogurt tubes keep disappearing from the refrigerator." Miriam's concerned sigh made Duncan feel momentarily guilty again.

What could you do to help? he reminded himself. *Celia misses her mom and dad. No amount of hovering or fussing can change that.*

"Then we'll eat before the food gets cold." His mother sent a questioning glance over at his father, who gently shook his head.

It appeared his dad didn't want to pray a blessing over the food today. Not that Duncan blamed him. He'd had a hard enough time sitting through church this morning himself. He'd only gone to make his mother feel good. If he had his way, he'd have stayed home, working with his horses, instead of trying to figure out what God was thinking, dealing such an ungodly amount of death and tragedy to his family.

"Duncan?" his mother asked, her tone hopeful.

He just shook his head as well. He didn't feel like talking to God either.

"Then, I think it's up to me." His mother paused a moment, as if giving the men in the household a chance to change her mind, then lowered her head and began. "Dear Lord. I know we're all hurting today, and we don't understand why we are being led through this dark valley. But we know that You will provide. And thank You for the food that we have. May it nourish and strengthen our bodies. Amen."

Her simple prayer tugged at his soul. His mother's faith had always been strong. Even after his father's accident. It was something he envied. He wished he trusted God as simply as she did.

"So, Miriam, tell us a bit more about yourself," his mother asked as she handed around bowls of steaming soup. "Jerrod told us a few things but not that much. He said that you draw?"

Miriam nodded as she took the bowl. "I did some illustrating for children's books at one time, but anything I've done since then has been for myself."

Duncan shot her a look of surprise. He didn't recall her saying she was an artist during the time they spent together —the short time they spent together, he reminded himself.

"That's right. Francine said that you used to do that. I suppose you quit because you couldn't make a living at it?" his mother asked.

Duncan shot his mother a warning look. "That's a bit personal, wouldn't you think, Mother?"

His mother blinked her surprise as she sat down. "Well, I'd read that somewhere."

"Actually, the truth is I do other work now," Miriam said, her half-smile showing that she didn't mind the digging into her financial situation. "I haven't illustrated a book in years."

"Have I seen any of your books?" his mother asked.

"I gave some to Jerrod and Francine. For Celia. The first one is about a princess who loses her crown."

"I remember now. Francine did show them to me. I'm surprised she didn't mention that you'd done the artwork on them. Have you seen them, Duncan?" His mother turned to him. "They're adorable. Beautiful illustrations."

Duncan gave Miriam an apologetic smile, feeling bad that he knew nothing about the books or her contribution to them and, apparently, neither did the rest of his family. "Sorry. Not much for princess stories."

"I can't imagine why not," Miriam said, giving him a smile that held a hint of mischief. "You strike me as a man who can embrace pink and glitter."

He laughed and the sound and the feeling surprised him as well as the desire to come up with a clever reply. "Sorry. More of a plaid guy myself."

"So I noticed." Her eyes ticked down to his shirt then back to his eyes.

As he held her gaze, he felt it again. That flicker of attraction he experienced the first time he'd seen her. That same flirtation disguised as teasing they had indulged in then.

He caught himself, surprised and a bit disappointed that he could so easily revert to this in spite of everything that had happened to him in the meantime.

"We'll have to make sure you get a chance to look at the books, Duncan," his mother said. "Maybe you could read them to Celia."

Duncan knew what his mother was doing, and he wasn't biting.

He looked away from Miriam, then, in spite of himself, he glanced over at the table where Celia still sat in isolation. He could hear a low murmur, as if she were talking to herself.

Or her doll.

"You said you do other work now?" his mother continued, turning to Miriam, clearly determined to find out more about her. "What else do you do?"

"I work in a hotel," Miriam said with a light shrug.

He could tell his mother wasn't satisfied with Miriam's vague answer.

"I'm sure she keeps herself busy," his father put in, coming to Miriam's rescue.

"I try to stay out of trouble," Miriam said, giving him a thankful smile.

"Glad to hear that," he said, turning his attention back to his soup.

Miriam gave him a puzzled look but then turned back to his mom. "By the way, Cora, I love your house. It's cozy. Did you decorate it yourself?"

Duncan had to smile again at Miriam's deflection and her perceptiveness. "Mom's house is a work in progress," he said. "If you're not careful, she'll get out her iPad and show you all her Pinterest boards."

"And what do you know about Pinterest?" his mother challenged him.

"Only that you talk about it endlessly," he responded.

"I enjoy it."

"And endlessly share that enjoyment," his father said bringing a lighter note to the discussion.

"I actually found something the other day that

Francine showed me..." His mother's voice trailed away as she realized what she had done. She blinked rapidly as her lips pressed together, and he felt his own heart clench.

Here we go again, he thought, making fists of his hands, struggling to compose himself. He glanced over at Miriam, surprised to catch her looking at him, her own features holding that pressed-in look.

It will pass, he reminded himself, sucking in a quick breath, suppressing the emotions.

"Francine never told me she liked Pinterest," Miriam was saying, her lips curving in a soft smile. "What kind of things did she pin?"

His mother pressed her knuckles to her mouth and gave a light shake of her head, as if dismissing what Miriam had just said. She held the pose a moment, fighting for self-control.

Then she picked up her spoon and gave Duncan a forced smile. "Do you think I put too much salt in the soup?"

He recognized what his mother was doing.

The same thing he always did whenever Kimberly and Tasha's names came up around people other than family members. Deflect, detach and dig down.

And above all, don't create a scene.

He caught Miriam's hurt look, and for a moment wanted to explain how things happen in the Tiemstra household. That emotions were embarrassing, that grief was private and that they didn't talk about hard things around other people.

His father's accident was a problem they would receive grace to deal with. His wife and child's deaths a hardship in which they needed to find meaning. Now, his sister and brother-in-law's deaths would also be tucked neatly under the category of God's will.

He suddenly felt an urge to sweep his arm over the neatly set table and create exactly the scene his mother was avoiding. He wanted to shout that he missed Francine and Jerrod, that he was furious with God for taking Tasha and for dumping sorrow on their family and again.

But he knew he wouldn't. Because if he gave in to that one, other feelings would ride on its coattails.

And those he hadn't found a way to deal with, either.

A movement behind Miriam caught his attention, and he took a deep breath. Celia stood beside Miriam, holding her doll.

"Jane wants to know about my birthday party," Celia demanded. "When are we having it?"

"I'm not sure, yet," Miriam was saying. Duncan could hear the pained note in her voice. "I have to think about it."

"Jane says she wants a horse birthday party."

"I'm sure Miriam can arrange that, Celia," his mother put in. "I can help her plan your party."

"Jane wants the party," Celia insisted.

"Of course, honey." His mother looked over at him. "A horse party. Maybe at Uncle Duncan's place?"

"I don't think I'll have time," he said, sending his mother a warning look. "Things are picking up in the bush. I've got some new equipment I've got to babysit."

He fought down the pull into his mother's needs and wants. He knew life had to go on, but somehow, planning a kid's birthday party so soon after his sister's death seemed too trivial.

Then his eyes unconsciously drifted to Miriam. He knew he didn't imagine the disappointment in her expression. And as he held her soft, brown eyes, for just a moment, he wished he could be that guy. The sensitive, caring person who was only too willing to put his own needs aside to help out this hurting little girl.

It had taken him years to find the tiniest slice of peace after Kimberly and his little girl died. He didn't think he could let himself fall into that space again.

Celia tucked her doll under her arm and walked back to her table.

"She's still doing that?" his mother asked Miriam, lowering her voice.

"Doing what?" Duncan asked.

His mom shot a quick look at Celia then leaned closer to Duncan, almost whispering. "Celia won't talk to any of us directly. She only talks through that doll. Jane wants this, Jane wants that. It's rather strange."

"I think it's her way of coping," Miriam said. "She won't ask me a direct question or make a direct comment. Like your mother said, everything goes through Jane."

Duncan frowned. "She doesn't talk to me that way."

"I noticed. It's like she has a unique relationship with you," Miriam said, giving him a direct look, as if she expected more from him. He held her gaze, fighting a mixture of attraction and annoyance.

"Well, I don't know why. I certainly haven't encouraged it." He bent over and focused on his food.

The rest of the lunch limped along, and as

soon as it was reasonably polite, Duncan said goodbye to his parents and Miriam, wishing he didn't feel like such a heel.

And as he drove away, he wasn't sure what bothered him more—that Celia hadn't been able to count on him, or that he had disappointed Miriam.

* * *

"I'm glad you came to see me." Mrs. Lansing, the principal of Holmes Crossing Elementary, sat down in her chair at the desk between us, and folded her hands on its surface.

I glanced around the room with its schedules and diplomas and air of authority, and had to fight down a familiar anxiety. I'd spent far too many hours in the principal's offices of various schools growing up to feel entirely comfortable in this hub of academia. Too often, my time in that place meant yet another change. Another adjustment. Another dose of grief.

"First off, I want to express my sympathy with the loss of your brother," she continued. "I understand you stayed with him and his mother as a foster child?"

I dragged my attention back to her. "Yes. For

about seven years." I skipped the 'off and on' part that often accompanied my comment. No need to delve into that mess.

"This is a difficult time for you, I'm sure. I know my words are too small to encompass your sorrow, but be assured that we will do everything we can to see that Celia is taken care of."

"Thanks. That means a lot."

Mrs. Lansing gave me a sympathetic smile, then leaned back in her chair, the light from the window behind her casting her features in shadow. "So why don't you tell me what you think should happen with Celia?"

I released a short laugh. "That's why I'm here. I don't know." Another flush of guilt accompanied that confession. Surely, on some level, I should be aware of what she needs? Wasn't that some automatic emotion ingrained in mothers? Didn't it come at the same time the baby was born? "I was hoping you could give me some guidance. I'm sort of making stuff up as I go along. Kind of like building a boat while I'm sitting on it in the water."

Mrs. Lansing chuckled. "That's fair enough. So what would you say is your first priority with her?"

Getting her to eat, I almost said.

Yesterday morning and this morning again, Jane had chosen waffles. And once again, every piece of waffle had ended up on the floor. Just like her lunch and supper had yesterday. Correction, Celia's lunch and supper.

I still wasn't sure whether to call Celia out on it, or simply hope that at some point soon, Jane—correction, Celia—would get hungry.

"I don't know if you noticed, but she took her doll, Jane, with her to school today," I said, instead. "It seems that all her communication goes through the doll. If I ask Celia something, she first asks Jane, and then she tells me what she wants. Kind of disturbing to me, but for now I'm playing along."

"That's wise."

I was surprised how good her words of affirmation made me feel—that I was doing something right, somewhere.

"But how long should I let her keep this up?"

Mrs. Lansing rocked in her chair a moment, frowning. "I'm not sure. But I think a counselor would suggest you continue for a while yet. Celia had to make a number of adjustments even before her parents' death. Moving to a new community where she didn't know anyone, and starting kindergarten. It's been barely a week since her parents died. I'm sure it will take her some time to deal with her own sorrow."

I nodded then, and to my dismay, my face tightened and my eyes welled up. I tried to blink the tears back, but one escaped and slipped down my cheek.

"Oh, my dear, this must be so difficult for you as well." Mrs. Lansing pushed up from her chair and came around the desk. On her way she tugged a couple of tissues out of a box and handed one to me, taking my other hand in hers as she sat down.

She had done this before, I thought, as I swiped at the tears.

"You have a lot to deal with," she said, her voice quiet, assuring. "I think you're doing an amazing job."

I sniffed then gave her a watery smile. "How do you know? You just met me."

"It's what I'm supposed to tell you. To make you feel good about yourself," she said with a wry smile.

I laughed at her blunt honesty.

She patted me on the shoulder. "But I'm partly serious. The fact that you are willing to play along with the doll issue and that you let her take the doll to school shows a quiet wisdom."

"Or a quiet desperation," I said. "I feel like I'm swimming on my own on this."

"You aren't," Mrs. Lansing said. "We're here to help you in any way we can."

"Thank you. I appreciate that." And I did. I needed every scrap of support I could get.

"So, first off, we need to talk about our approach concerning Celia and her doll," Mrs. Lansing continued, her sudden, matter-of-fact tone making me feel more grounded. "My feeling is to let it play out. I'll set up an appointment with a counselor. I'm afraid it might not happen until the new year, but until then, just play along. I suspect her play with Jane might be a way of giving herself a buffer between life and herself."

"The situation is ironic," I said with a shake of my head. "I used to hate playing dolls. I always preferred playing boy games with Jerrod. But now I'm forced to talk to a doll."

Mrs. Lansing gave me another curious smile. As if she was trying to figure me out, as well. "Did you and your brother get along when you were younger?"

Her question surprised me, but at the same time I felt a sense of relief at her interest. Yesterday, at Duncan's parents' place, I got the idea that they didn't want to talk about Francine or Jerrod.

I was thirsting for every bit of connection I could make to my brother. I wanted to know everything I could, even if it made me sad.

"For the most part," I said. "Every time I came back there was an adjustment period which, thankfully, my foster mom understood. My biological mother always—" I stopped there, not sure why I had even said as much as that. Though I wanted to talk about Jerrod, I drew the line at my biological mother. Too close to home, maybe. "Anyhow, I've got this to deal with and I want to do the best I can for Celia."

"She's lucky to have you," Mrs. Lansing said.

I didn't know about that, but I just returned her smile, then glanced down at my watch.

"I've promised Mrs. Tiemstra I would meet her at the café in town," I said, "So I'm sorry, I need to go. I'll come back as soon as I'm done."

"If you wish, but there's no need. We can notify you if there are any problems."

"I'm not sure I like to leave her alone."

"She's not alone. She's got her teacher and her classmates. She's been in this class since September, so at least that part of her life is ordinary," Mrs. Lansing said.

As opposed to me, who erratically popped

into her life the last few years. The thought choked me a moment, but I brushed it aside.

"Okay. I'll be here before dismissal, unless I hear from you," I said, as I slung my purse over my arm and rose from the chair.

"You can stop by her classroom and discreetly look in before you go, if you'd like," Mrs. Lansing said.

"That would be nice."

I followed her out of the office and down the hall. We stopped at the kindergarten room. The door had a window in it and I peeked in. I could make out Celia sitting at a small table with three other girls.

It looked like they were all talking to Jane and not Celia. I touched the glass with my fingers, wishing I could rush in and help her. Take away her pain. Help her know that people loved her.

Baby steps, I reminded myself as I drew back, disturbed at the sight. Baby steps.

The same kind of baby steps I would need to use when it was time for me to move on.

* * *

"So Celia wants a horse-themed birthday party," Mrs. Tiemstra said, taking a sip of the tea she'd ordered at the café. "I was wondering if you've had a chance to think about that."

"Not that much," I said looking around the café. Local art hung on the cream-colored walls. Red burlap curtains held back by brown gingham strips hung at the windows. The mismatched wooden chairs and tables lent an air of country coziness, which was enhanced by the twang of country music.

The café wasn't full. A couple of older men sat at one table. One wore a priest's collar. The other was a larger man, with bright-green suspenders snugged over a faded blue chambray shirt. They looked like they were in deep discussion.

"I know she's developed a passion for horses lately," Mrs. Tiemstra said, pulling my attention back to her. "What do you think of planning around that?"

"Sorry," I said, taking another sip of my coffee. "I don't know much about birthday party planning."

"Would you mind if I helped you out?" Cora gave me a tentative smile that puzzled me.

"I could use all the help I can get."

"As can we all," she said, with a melancholy smile. She pressed her lips together and pulled in a quick breath. "I'm sorry. It's just been—"

"It's been barely a week is what it's been," I said, reaching across the table and touching her arm in a show of sympathy.

"Thank you for your understanding," she said, giving me a careful smile as she brushed a strand of hair back from her face, quickly composing her features again. As before, her hair was perfectly styled, her makeup runway-ready, her brown turtleneck sweater, gold chunky necklace, and cream blazer giving her a look of elegance and grace.

As I looked at her, I couldn't help but compare her to my foster mother, with her gray furze of flyaway hair, sweatshirts, and jogging pants.

"So, how should we do this?" I asked, feeling a moment of disloyalty to Sally. She was a loving woman who had given me a home when my biological mother, a polar opposite of Sally with her tattoos, bright-red lipstick, bedazzled denim jackets, and tight blue jeans, didn't.

"I could order a cake with a horse theme from Alana at the bakery. Have a horse piñata, and napkins, and paper plates with horses." Then she held my eyes, her own growing suddenly bright. "Duncan has horses, and he could give the girls a ride in a sleigh at his place."

"Would he want to do that?" I distinctly remembered how he had said he didn't want to be involved with Celia.

Mrs. Tiemstra waved away my question with one elegantly manicured hand. "I'll tell him he has to help out."

I wasn't comfortable with this. Though I wanted him involved, I wasn't sure we should force Celia so quickly into his life.

Why not? The sooner the better? He has family support. It's what you want for Celia.

I knew this was my ultimate goal, but at the same time I felt a flash of resistance, which I immediately quashed. I couldn't indulge in even the smallest 'maybe'. The longer I stayed here, the harder it would be to leave. Already, each moment I spent with Celia dropped another barb into my heart that would tear when it was time to go.

"You're his mother. I'm thinking that would give you some leverage," I said. "So I'll let you talk to him."

"I have a better idea. We'll go to his place tomorrow night and present him with the idea. That way he can't say no in front of both of us."

The plan seemed like an ambush in my opinion, but at the same time, a small part of me didn't mind the idea of seeing him again.

Mrs. Tiemstra toyed with her fork, her lips pursed, and I sensed she had something else she wanted to discuss with me. "I spoke with Duncan. About what you told me the other day. His reluctance to take care of Celia."

I sat up straighter, a chill raking through me.

"What did he say?"

"You were right. He told his father and me that he didn't think he could do this." Mrs. Tiemstra tapped the fork on the plate, the tempo increasing. "I feel like I should let you know why. It's because of Tasha."

"Tasha being...?"

"His daughter."

My breath caught in my throat. I knew Duncan had lost his wife and child in an accident. I just didn't know the little girl's name.

"I'm sure it hurts him to see Celia. Tasha would have been the same age."

"I sensed there was a deeper reason to his reluctance," I said, feeling sorrow pressing against my chest. He knows, I thought. He knows the same heart-wrenching loss.

Though I didn't know what would be worse. To have Celia swept completely from my life, or living, as I had, with the regret and the steady reminder of what I couldn't have.

"He has to be made to see his responsibility," Cora continued. "It's not just him, it's...it's us as well. I know Celia is adopted, but she's as much our granddaughter as Tasha was. I can't lose... can't lose Celia—" Mrs. Tiemstra stopped there, her voice trailing off.

I buried my own pain, touching her gently to make a connection.

"You need to know that I agree with you," I said, fighting down old longings, feeling as if I were betraying Celia, even as I did what I knew was best for her. "I also don't think I should be taking care of my...of Celia. I agree that Celia should stay with your family." I spoke slowly, laying my words down like leaves on a stream. Deliberate and careful. "Duncan is in a better position to take care of her than I am. Much as I'd love to...to take her back with me to Vancouver, I can't."

I swallowed again, fighting for self-control, blaming my fragile emotions on my grief.

Mrs. Tiemstra frowned at me, as if she didn't comprehend what I was saying.

"I am not exercising my guardianship to Celia," I said, keeping my voice quiet.

Her eyes widened in shock and she raised one hand to her trembling lips. "Oh, my goodness.

This is…this is wonderful news. I was so afraid…"
She blinked away the moisture I saw gathering in
her eyes. Then she nodded decisively, as if underlining my decision. "This is the right thing to do."

Then why does it feel so hard?

"You are a good person," she said, reaching out
and grasping my hand, squeezing it gently.

I wasn't, but I still appreciated her affirmation.

"I'm just trying to do what's best for Celia. She
needs stability and a home. I can't…" My own
voice broke again, and I stopped, wishing I didn't
feel so vulnerable. For a few glorious moments, I
had allowed myself some 'what ifs' when it came
to Celia. But I had to think only of her. Why I
gave her up was still woven into my past and
present, and I couldn't hand that legacy to her.
My mother had clung too long and hard to me -
had turned my life around with her selfish demands. I wasn't going to be that mother. I wanted
to do what was best for my daughter.

I cleared my throat. "Like I said, I can't give
her what you all can here."

"I'm sorry for you," Mrs. Tiemstra said, still
holding my hand. "Losing Jerrod, your foster
mother…so many blows in such a young life. I'll
be praying for you."

I pressed my lips together, fighting, again, a

surge of grief. And as she held my hand, for a moment, I didn't feel so alone.

"Thank you. That means a lot. My mom—foster mom—always prayed for me. I feel like it's been awhile since I was on anyone's list."

"Well, you're on mine now." Mrs. Tiemstra cleared her throat and gave me another squeeze, then drew her hand back. "And now we have to figure out what to do about Duncan."

I had no idea, but I was sure she did.

For now, I was content to follow her lead.

CHAPTER 5

*D*uncan turned down his driveway, exhaustion pulling at him. He'd stayed later than he liked at work, but at least the skidder was fixed and pulling trees again. He'd grabbed a bite to eat at the diner before it closed. Caught up with Terra who was working today, chatted a moment with Cor and Father Sam, and then left.

Now, he was looking forward to a few moments of reading the news, nosing through the Ritchie Brothers' website for equipment, and checking out that saddle he'd seen advertised on the horse-and-riding forum he frequented.

Another barnburner of an evening, he thought

with a vague smile as he turned the last corner. Living the dream.

But his house, which should have been dark, blazed with light, and as he came closer, his heart sank when he recognized his mother's car.

And right beside it was Francine and Jerrod's SUV.

Frustration with his mother and her meddling bubbled up inside of him, followed, surprisingly, by a tiny spark of anticipation at the thought of seeing Miriam again.

Which he immediately stifled. He wasn't looking. Besides, he looked like five miles of bad road after working on equipment all day. He probably had grease stains on his face and he needed a shave.

He grabbed his Thermos, his lunch box, and gloves, and got out of his truck. The same icy wind that had bedeviled him all day while he worked on equipment, swirled snow around him as he trudged through the drifts on the sidewalk to the house.

What was his mother doing here? She usually called ahead, giving him enough time to toss the books under the couch, wash the piled-up dishes, and create some semblance of order in a house that was decorated in Twenty-first Century Bachelor.

Find that on your Pinterest boards, he thought, as he pulled open the door and stepped into bright warmth, trying not to feel embarrassment at the thought that Miriam was seeing his house in its natural state.

His mother's tall leather boots, gleaming and polished, stood at attention just inside the door. A pair of worn, and battered boots stood beside them. Miriam's, of course. And Celia's small Sorel boots lay in a heap beside them.

He dropped down on the worn deacon's bench Kimberly had picked up at a yard sale. She'd paid way too much and had pouted when Duncan had said she got taken. He felt like a heel for stealing her joy, and his penance was to scrape fifty years of bad painting decisions off the surface. Tasha always climbed up on it to reach out to him—

Pain seized him and he closed his eyes, riding out the discomfort resurrected by his sister and brother-in-law's deaths.

Thankfully, that was followed by anger, an easier emotion to face. He jerked his boots off and dropped them beside his mother's, hung up his coat, tossed his gloves and toque into the bin above the coat rack. Before he entered the house he drew in a long, slow breath, preparing himself, and slid open the pocket door separating the porch from the rest of the house.

He set his lunch box and Thermos on the table just inside the door, and quickly scanned the kitchen ahead of him, guilt stabbing in his gut. The last four days' worth of dishes were cleaned up. The counter shone, and his taps gleamed.

A woman's touch he thought, steeling himself to face his mother, his niece, and the girl that had danced in and out of his thoughts the past few days.

And, of course, as he stepped into the living room, Miriam was the first person he saw. She was hunkered down by the wood stove, carefully feeding another log to the fire, her long, tawny hair spilling down her back in a shining wave.

"Be careful," his mother warned as she tidied up the magazines and newspapers that had once covered the couch. "You don't want to burn yourself."

"I've stoked a few stoves in my life," Miriam was saying.

Celia sat on the couch, tying a scarf around her doll's neck, the same heartbreakingly lifeless expression on the girl's face. "Well, you're home later than usual," his mother said when she noticed him.

"Had some trouble with the skidder again," he said vaguely, looking past her to Miriam who stood, running her hands down the sides of her blue jeans in a nervous gesture. "What is going on? Everything okay?" Then he felt ice slither through his stomach. "Is it Dad? Is he okay?"

"Yes. He's okay. Cor is visiting with him right now. They're playing crib and sharing old-time bush stories." His mother gave him a quick smile that only served to shift his nervousness.

"So...why are you here?" he asked, as he walked over to the kitchen sink and made a quick stab at washing his hands, trying in vain to work the grease out from under his fingernails.

His mother glanced over her shoulder at Miriam, who was looking at Celia, who was looking at her doll.

"Mother? What are you doing here?" he prompted, drying his hands on the tea towel that hadn't been there before he left. In spite of the thorough washing, he left a few dark stains on the towel, which he tossed in the sink to deal with later. He scrubbed his hands through his hard-hat hair, wishing he didn't care so much what he looked like.

His mother clasped her hands in front of her and took in a quick breath. "As you know, it's Celia's birthday next week. And we asked her what kind of birthday party she wants." His mother walked over to Celia and knelt down in front of her. "Celia, darling, can you tell Uncle Duncan what you told me and Aunt Miriam?"

Celia didn't look up, but continued tugging on the doll's scarf. "Jane wants a horse party."

Duncan's panicked gaze flicked from Celia, to his mother, then landed on Miriam who was watching him, concern etched on her features.

"I told you I won't have time," he protested, wondering how much more he should have said when his mother first brought it up.

His mother walked toward him, her hands up in a placating gesture. "You won't have to do much," she said. "Miriam and I will take care of the birthday stuff. We just want you to take the girls out on a sleigh ride with the horses. Nothing more than that."

Duncan dragged his hand over his face. He felt shanghaied. He didn't have time. But how could he say no with Celia sitting right there, a sudden ray of hope shining in a face that had looked so blank and unemotional the past week.

Then his mother took a step closer, lowering

her voice, and Duncan knew she was hauling out the big guns.

"Celia is in a hard place," she said softly. "And we need to do whatever we can. I know it's difficult for you, but I am hoping you can put your needs aside for her sake."

And didn't that make him sound like the most selfish uncle in the world?

Trouble was, part of him knew she was right, even as his survival instincts kicked in. When his sister and her family moved back to Holmes Crossing, he found that every time he saw Celia, he had to fight down a bitter ache at the stark reminder of what he had lost. Keeping his distance had been the only way he'd found to keep his own grief at bay.

And now he was dealt a new sadness, when he hadn't yet handled the old.

"Your niece has lost everyone important to her," his mother continued. "And you know yourself how hard that can be. She's just a child."

His mother's words were like a chisel, pick, picking away at his stony resistance.

And she wouldn't quit until she got what she wanted.

"Okay, okay. I'll help," he said, giving in. "But you'll have to get everything ready and set everything up at your house. She and her friends will only come here for a sleigh ride." He gave her a hard look, underlining his comment. "And only that much." He knew his mother was an artist when it came to blurring boundaries.

"I didn't expect that you would do anything else," she said, patting him on the shoulder as if he were only ten, instead of thirty-three. "We'll take care of everything." Then she shot a surreptitious glance at her watch, and grimaced. "I'm sorry, but I have to go. I promised your father I wouldn't be long."

At least the visit had been short. And Miriam had kept her distance, which was also helpful. She was too pretty, and he was too lonely, and he knew she was going back to Vancouver. All in all, a dangerous combination.

"Good. Let me know what you want and when," he said as his mother walked over to Celia and gave her a kiss. Celia didn't even look up.

His mother looked crushed, but then pulled herself together and stood.

"I'll let Miriam tell you what is happening," his mother said, as she picked her coat up off the couch and slipped it on. "She and I discussed how we'll do this."

"Pardon me?"

"What?"

He and Miriam spoke at the same time, both questions directed at his mother, who was already hurrying out of the room, waving at them both.

"I have to run. Sorry. I trust you two can manage."

And then, before Duncan could register a protest, she was gone.

Silence descended and for a moment, Duncan had no clue what to do next.

He turned to Miriam, who now sat on the couch with Celia, watching him, her expression one of puzzlement. "Did I just get roped into something?" she asked.

"Welcome to Manipulationville. Cora Tiemstra, Mayor-in-chief."

Miriam chuckled, easing his resentment over his mother's maneuvering.

"Sorry about that," he said, trudging over to a chair across from her and dropping into it. His hand rasped over his whiskers, and once again he wished he looked more presentable. "If you want to leave, that's fine. Mom can tell me what I need to do."

"I'm here now, I may as well let you know what we arranged," she said.

Which created a small feeling of anticipation.

"So, what did you want me to do?"

Miriam pressed her hands between her knees. "Your mother and I thought we could have three of Celia's good friends come to Francine and Jerrod's..." Her voice trailed off. She cleared her throat and continued, "Have them come to the house. We would do the cake and gifts there, and then come here after that. Your mother said you had some horses you could hitch up to a sleigh?"

"Yeah. Bonnie and Clyde."

"Is the fact that they're named after bandits any indication of their character?" she asked with a light laugh.

"They're reformed. And broke to harness. Very compliant, unlike their namesakes."

"That's reassuring."

"So the sleigh ride is the only thing I'd have to do?"

Miriam nodded, then turned to Celia. "What do you think, sweetie? Would you like a sleigh ride with Uncle Duncan and his horses?"

Celia gave Miriam a disdainful look. "I don't want the sleigh ride, Jane does."

"So, Jane, do you think you'll like it?" Miriam asked, her tone reasonable, but Duncan could see the difficulty in her expression as she talked to the doll.

Celia held the doll's head close to hers, then nodded. "Jane said she will love it." Then Celia slid off the couch, walked across the room, and trudged up the stairs.

"Celia, come back," Miriam said. "This isn't your house." But Celia kept going, and Duncan had to fight down his own resistance to his niece's intrusion.

"I'm sorry. I'll go get her," Miriam said, getting up.

He clenched one fist even as he waved off her comment with his other hand.

"It's okay," Duncan said, even though Miriam had no idea what it cost him to say that.

No one had been upstairs since his mother cleaned out Kimberly…and Tasha's…things.

Miriam sighed, as Celia turned at the top of the stairs into the hallway. "I probably should have asked Jane to come back."

Duncan heard the anxiety in her voice, and saw the weariness on her face, and he felt a flicker of concern.

"Are things going okay for you?" he asked. Abruptly coming to Holmes Crossing, a place where she didn't know anybody, couldn't be easy.

"Yeah. I'm fine." But he could see she was anything but. His practical side told him to leave it at that, but he felt sympathy for her. She'd had her own loss and now she was responsible for this little girl.

She doesn't need to be.

But even as he entertained that thought, Duncan's chest heaved, and he knew he had to keep his distance. Old emotions were already crowding too close to the surface.

He sucked in a breath, but at the same time, he couldn't ignore what Miriam was dealing with.

"I just asked 'cause you look really tired," he said. But as soon as the words left his mouth he felt like doing a face-palm. His sister always accused him of being too blunt, and he knew telling a woman she basically looked haggard was not the way to win points.

"Was your first clue the oversized luggage under my eyes?" Miriam asked, scraping her hair back from her face. "I should probably get charged for that."

"Actually, you look pretty good for looking tired," he said, realizing too late that he had just jumped straight into the fire.

"I'll take that as a compliment."

"I guess that's what I was trying for," he said

releasing a frustrated sigh. "Sorry. I'm not so good with the small talk."

"Probably better at the medium talk?"

"Don't know about that either."

"Well, I'm not so good with the birthday party stuff. I'm glad your mom is making the plans."

"Hope she wasn't too overbearing. She can be kind of pushy."

"She was helpful, though she did try to convince Celia to go with a princess theme. She thought I could draw some pictures for her. Like from the book."

"The ones you illustrated?"

"Yeah."

"I should have a look at these books," Duncan said, dropping his head onto the back of the chair as he watched her. She sat half on the couch, half off, as if she was ready to launch herself out of her seat on a moment's notice. "I've never met an illustrator before."

"Well, we're even. I've never met a cowboy logger before. I didn't even know there was such a thing." She gave him a small smile that brushed lightly over his heart.

"The two don't really belong together," Duncan said, surprised at his reaction to her. "It's not like I rope trees."

"Now there's an interesting concept." She looked past him as if considering the idea. "That would make a cute story."

"You said you don't illustrate anymore. Why not?"

She looked down at her hands, now twisted around each other, a frown creasing her forehead. "I had my chance but then…well…I needed to pay bills."

"Don't we all," he said.

Her eyes rested on his, and for a moment, their gazes held. He felt, once again, a low thrum of awareness, an echo of older emotions. Wondered if she felt it too.

Behind that came a wondering if she ever thought of him after their almost-romance. They had gone on a couple of dates after Francine and Jerrod's wedding. He thought things were moving along. Then he returned to Holmes Crossing, she went back to the States, and didn't reply to any of his texts.

Not that he would ask her why. He blamed his feelings for her on the heightened romance that always accompanied weddings.

But then, as now, she was easy to talk to, and he enjoyed their casual conversation. Something he hadn't indulged in with a beautiful woman for so long he wasn't sure he even remembered how.

Since Kimberly, he had gone on a total of two dates, both of which were set up by his well-meaning sister, and both of which were disasters. Though he wouldn't deny that he was lonely, he wasn't looking.

But Miriam drew out emotions he thought he was done with.

A log in the food stove fell, sending a shower of sparks up the chimney, catching his attention. He was about to get up to push the log back, but Miriam was already there, nudging the charred piece of lumber back onto the flames with a poker.

"Did you light the fire?" he asked.

"I did," she said, shooting a glance at him over her shoulder. "I hope that's okay."

"It's amazing," he said, closing his eyes just for a moment. "The house is usually chilly when I get home."

A rustle of movement caught his ear, and he sensed Miriam wanted to get things moving. And so should he. He was enjoying this time with her too much.

"So, the birthday party," he said, opening his

eyes, straightening, and clasping his hands between his knees. "When is this happening?"

"Friday. At about two-o'clock."

He did a bit of mental juggling. It could work out if Les was willing to supervise that day. They would be finished in the block Thursday and doing an equipment move Friday. He didn't need to be around for that.

"How long do you want the ride to be?" he asked.

"No more than half an hour," Miriam said. "Depending on the weather. I imagine if it's blowing hard we'll have to cancel."

"I've got a good trail cut through the trees on the property," Duncan said, stifling a sudden yawn. "We'd be out of the wind there, so that will help."

"Another thing, your mother said something about doing a marshmallow roast afterwards on the yard."

Duncan frowned. "I thought I was just doing a sleigh ride."

"And you would be," Miriam said, tapping her fingers together. "We just thought it would be fun for the girls to make s'mores while we're here anyway. Your mom said you have a fire pit. If you could bring some wood back from the bush and have it ready I can take care of the fire."

"Which you seem to be capable of making."

"I have a few life skills."

The slightly harsh tone of her voice kindled his curiosity. All he knew of her life before coming to Jerrod's mother's house was that she had been bounced between her biological mother's place and the Carpenter home. After the wedding, when Jerrod heard Miriam hadn't returned any of Duncan's texts, he'd said it was probably just as well. That Miriam's life was complicated.

But he hadn't gotten that impression when they spent time together at the wedding. She seemed fun, spunky, and full of confidence. Quite different than how she came across now.

"As long as you're okay with me just taking care of the sleigh ride, I can help out," was all he said.

"Then it's a start."

Before he could ask her what she meant by that, she walked toward the stairs and called out for Celia.

But there was no reply from upstairs.

"Celia. It's time to go. Jane." Still nothing. "Can I go up and get her?" she asked, turning to him.

Again, that reluctance for her to go up there,

and again he fought it down. It shouldn't matter anymore.

"You didn't have to ask," he said.

"Sorry. Force of habit. Every house has its own boundaries."

As did this one, he thought. Boundaries Celia had already slipped over when she went upstairs.

But even as he fought his resistance to that, he also found himself wondering about Miriam's comment about boundaries.

And he found himself wanting to know more about her.

* * *

IF YOU HURRY, you'll fall, I told myself as I beat a hasty retreat up the stairs, forcing myself not to look back to see if Duncan was watching me.

It had been so easy to talk to him. Just as it had the first time we met. Then, he'd worn a suit, and the next day, blue jeans and a clean shirt.

Now, he looked rough and hardened, worn down by the sad events of his own life. Which made me wonder what I looked like to him? How much I had changed because of what I had been through?

At the top of the stairs, I paused. Ahead of me

was a bathroom, to the left, a closed door, to the right, one that was open just a crack.

"She's probably in the room to the right. The other one's mine."

I jumped at the sound of Duncan's gruff voice behind me. I spun around, my feet catching on the carpet, and would have fallen, but for his hand steadying me. His skin was warm and his touch sent a current of awareness that bothered me on so many levels.

You can't do this, I reminded myself. You weren't right for him then, and even less so now.

My brain knew that on one level, but the loneliness that grew with each passing year, the need for companionship, made me hesitant to pull away.

But my practical self won out.

I drew away from him, turned to the right, carefully pushed open the door and stepped into a darkened room.

My heart melted when I saw Celia curled up, asleep, on the carpeted floor, her doll clenched tightly in one arm, her knees tucked up. She looked so alone.

I bent down to pick her up, but to my surprise, Duncan pushed past me, gently took the doll from her, fitted his arms under her and stood. But it was the subtle softening of his expression as he looked down at her that snagged my attention. He had been a father. Had held a child before. He knew what to do.

The thought pierced me.

"You get her coat ready, and I'll bring her down," he said quietly. Then he glanced at me and for the whisper of a moment that connection that once sang between us rose up again.

I wanted to hold his gaze but made myself look away, turning to leave. Then I stopped. I hadn't noticed it before, in my rush to get to Celia, but a small child's bed took up one corner of the room. Pillows in the shape of hearts lay neatly along the wall. A quilt, also decorated with hearts, was tucked around the mattress.

This was Tasha's room, I realized, glancing around at the prints on the walls, the toy chest in one corner. Frozen in time, like it was waiting for his little girl to come back.

And suddenly, everything that Duncan had lost hit me like a jolt of electricity—shocking and immobilizing.

He knows, I thought, struggling not to look over my shoulder, to acknowledge, in this moment, what had been swept from his life in the accident that also took his wife.

He knows what it's like to lose a child. He has felt the same loss.

A sob crawled up my throat, and I wasn't sure whether it belonged to what I had just seen, the little girl that lay in Duncan's arms like she belonged there, or the relentless compounding of losses in my life.

I took a deep breath, dug down like my foster mother always told me to do, and sent up a prayer for strength. I couldn't break down. Not here. Not in front of Duncan.

Without looking back, I walked out of the room and down the stairs, clutching the wooden railing. The last thing I wanted was to stumble again.

I went directly to the porch, snagged Celia's coat off the hook and turned to Duncan to put it on her. I hesitated again. The sight of that little girl resting so peacefully in his arms looked so right it gave me an ache.

I wanted to grab her, hold her close. Stake my claim. And warring with that urge was the feeling that, in spite of Duncan's reluctance to take care of her, this was exactly where Celia belonged.

"Sit down and take her," he said, still not looking at me. "I'll go start your vehicle."

"It has a remote starter," I mumbled, digging

through the pockets of my coat, needing a few moments to compose myself. "I'll take care of it."

I stepped into my boots and out into the freezing darkness. A click of the fob turned on the vehicle's lights, illuminating the light snow drifting down, deadening the rumble of the SUV starting up.

For a moment, I stayed on the step, the cold air and gentle snowfall cooling my heated cheeks. I was doing too much mental juggling. Duncan was too appealing and too complicated. Though he claimed not to want to take care of Celia, the way he handled her reminded me that he'd done this before.

He could do it again.

I sucked in a chilly, bracing breath, then returned to the house.

Duncan was sitting on the bench in the porch, looking down at Celia, and I caught a fleeting glimpse of longing on his face, compounding the sense of rightness.

"I hate to wake her," he said, brushing her hair away from her face with a surprising tenderness. Then he frowned and pulled a toy out of Celia's hand. I noticed it was a small plush puppy dog.

"Was that Tasha's?" I asked.

Duncan didn't look up, but his features hardened. His eyes narrowed, his lips pressed together and I knew I should have kept my question to myself.

"Please don't talk about her," he said, setting the toy aside.

"I'm sorry," I said, reaching for Celia. "I'm sorry. I shouldn't have said anything."

Duncan's gaze was fixed on something behind me, his features crumpled, as if he were looking into a painful past. Then he blinked and seemed to return to the present. "No. I'm sorry. That was out of line."

He handed Celia to me then, shifting her carefully. The little girl's head lolled to one side as I took her, and she dropped her doll. Duncan picked it up, and set it down on the bench, releasing a harsh laugh as he looked down at it.

"Does she take this silly thing everywhere?"

"She's very attached to Jane and everything she wants goes through the doll," I said as I sat down beside the doll, carefully threading Celia's floppy arms through the sleeves of her jacket. "I play along, though I feel dumb talking to a doll, but it's the only way I can communicate with Celia."

I made myself stop. I knew I was talking too much, and I blamed it on my scattered emotions and Duncan's presence looming over me—tall, broad-shouldered.

As I pulled Celia's toque over her ears, her head moved, she blinked slowly, then scrunched her face as she straightened, pushing away from me. She looked around, as if trying to orient herself. Then she spied her doll and snatched her up, holding her close. She yawned, then looked up at Duncan, giving him a slow smile.

"Hi, Dunkle. I'm having a birthday party here, and you're taking me for a ride on your horses."

"We're giving you and your friends a sleigh ride," he corrected, taking a step back, as if needing both physical and emotional distance between him and his niece.

"But can I go for a ride on one of your horses?"

Duncan shrugged. "I don't know."

"We'll see, right?" she asked. Then she turned to me. "Jane wants to go for a ride on one of Dunkle's horses."

I looked at her and felt a momentary confusion. She had talked to me through Jane, but had addressed Duncan directly, just as she had in church on Sunday. When she had gone running up to Duncan to show him the dress her doll was wearing.

I looked over at Duncan, who stood apart

from both of us, his hands shoved in his pockets, a frown creasing his forehead. I could see that he was uncomfortable with the connection that Celia seemed to have with him.

But nonetheless, I felt a tiny glimmer of hope. If I could capitalize on it, make Duncan see this, maybe he would realize he really was the best person to take care of Celia.

CHAPTER 6

*P*aper plates decorated with pictures of horses and smeared with traces of neon-glo icing were strewn over the oversized wood table that dominated the dining room. Remnants of said neon icing were also pressed into the cloth covering some of the chairs.

Not that it mattered. The pink simply blended in with some of the other stains. I knew I should clean them, but it would have to wait. Progress on the house was slow. I had finally restored order to the pantry, and was now working on Celia's room. Next up, Jerrod and Francine's.

One thing at a time, I reminded myself.

Girly, high-pitched squeals came from up-stairs, accompanied by questionable thumps.

After they devoured the cake Celia took her friends, Laine, Savannah and Tiffany upstairs. Cora was with them now, so despite the chaotic noises, I could only assume she had things in hand.

"That went well," Esther, Duncan's other sister, said, as she cleared up the last of the paper plates. "Though it does seem rather cruel to leave the horse so massacred."

Esther was tall, like Duncan, but had the body of a dancer, lean and willowy. Her blonde hair was clipped short, emphasizing her narrow features.

She looked pointedly at the legs and mane that were all that was left of the horse-shaped cake that Celia, via Jane, had admired with breathless awe. An edible *My Little Pony* in pink and purple.

"It does look rather pathetic, now," I said, with a laugh. I took a stab at the pink icing on the chair and quickly gave up, wondering once again why my sister-in-law had bought white-cloth covered chairs, when she couldn't seem to keep them clean.

"Celia seemed happy," Esther said, as she carried the plates to the kitchen. "I'm glad you decided to have the party."

"I felt we should try to carry on as normal as possible," I said, as I followed her with the cake platter. "It helped that she got all excited when your mother suggested we have a horse-themed party."

"I'm sure my mom spent one afternoon on Pinterest and another in the city, looking for decorations and ideas."

"She did a great job." Floating balloons with horses printed on them were anchored to the table by ribbons tied to horseshoes. Banners made of horse images were draped across the wall behind the table. The girls had all received cowboy hats, as did the dolls that had accompanied some of the girls.

My mind was still reeling at all the work Cora had to have done to accomplish this in such a short time—and how much it must have cost.

Esther dumped the paper plates in the garbage, then turned to me. The blue turtleneck she wore, which exactly matched the shade of her eyes set off her blonde hair. "And how are you doing with this all? I'm sure it's difficult living here in Jerrod's house?"

"I'd never visited them here, so at least I don't have those memories."

"Did Jerrod ever talk to you? About how he and Francine got along?"

I shot Esther a puzzled look. "What do you mean?"

She shrugged, a vague gesture combined with lack of eye contact that raised a flicker of concern.

"I was just wondering. I know that money was tight for them. What, with buying this house and all. Francine had to have the best. I know they fought about it."

I was surprised that she would talk about her own sister that way. Though I had often thought the same, as the sister-in-law I would never have voiced my opinion.

"I didn't know that."

"So Jerrod never said anything to you about their relationship?"

"Jerrod was never one to talk about his feelings. Or talk a lot, period." After the adoption, we'd kept contact to a minimum. It had hurt, but I only wanted what was best for Celia. I understood his concerns, I felt them myself. But Esther's pointed questions puzzled me. "Why are you asking me about them?"

Esther looked down and I saw pain twist her features. "Doesn't matter," she said, her voice quiet. "It's not important. He's gone now…they're both gone…" her words faded away as her voice broke.

I reached out to console her, but as I did, she shifted her stance.

It was a small movement, but it was definitely a movement away from me.

"So what have you been doing about Francine and Jerrod's things?" she asked, changing the conversation.

"I just started on Celia's things. I'll probably get to Jerrod and Francine's after that." I paused then gave her a concerned look. "Are you sure you don't want to help?"

"I thought I could come and take care of the office." She gave me a piercing look. "You haven't been in there yet, have you?"

"No. It's locked and I haven't been able to get in."

"I have the key. I had been helping Jerrod with his accounting," she said, her tone softening. "I know what is what so I'll go through it when I'm home for the holidays."

"That sounds fine to me." I had no intention of going through the office anyway.

Cleaning up Jerrod and Francine's other things was difficult enough. This morning, I had found an old hockey jersey in the laundry that I had given him for Christmas one year. I sat for a long time in the bedroom, tears rolling down my cheeks, as I remembered that bright and happy time in my life.

And now, Christmas was coming again and I was dreading it.

"I'm glad you understand. I feel bad that you are taking care of all of this. I just know it would be too hard for Mom, and I don't have time until school is over. And it would be so difficult—" her voice broke and I struggled to keep my own emotions under control. "This really sucks, doesn't it?" she said finally.

"In many ways."

"As well, when I come to clean the office, we need to talk about you and Duncan's...situation."

I wanted to ask her what she meant by that but was interrupted by the thunder of feet descending the stairs, and voices laughing. Any attempt at further conversation was obliterated.

"I think we should get these girls dressed," Cora called out as she came down the stairs last, following the girls who were running to the porch in a squealing mass.

She stopped at the bottom, glancing from me

to Esther. "I'm sorry, were you two having a heart-to-heart?"

"Just getting to know Jerrod's sister," Esther said, in what sounded like a falsely bright voice. She pushed herself away from the counter and as she passed me I caught a shining glimpse of tears in her eyes.

I felt a sympathetic clench of my own heart. It was a hard time for everyone, I thought, quickly cleaning up the rest of the mess, then hurrying to join Cora and Esther in the porch.

But even as I helped put the girl's clothes on I couldn't help but think why she mentioned Jerrod more than Francine.

A few moments later we had all the girls all dressed, though Celia insisted that her Oma help her and not her aunt Esther.

I was thankful that Laine and Savannah brought their dolls as well and suspected Cora had something to do with that. This way Celia and Jane didn't stand out as much. The last thing I wanted was for her to be teased on her birthday.

I took Celia, Laine and Savannah in the SUV, Cora and Esther took Tiffany. But in spite of only having three little girls in the vehicle, the sugar-induced noise level as we drove toward Duncan's place was deafening.

"Is Celia's Uncle Duncan a cowboy?" Laine asked.

"He has horses," I said. I had never thought of him as a cowboy, but no sooner did the idea enter my mind than I imagined him in a cowboy hat, his usual plaid shirt, blue jeans and cowboy boots.

It worked. Too well.

I gave my head a shake and concentrated on the happy chatter in the vehicle, thankful that, for now at least, Celia seemed to be smiling and enjoying herself. She was my priority, I reminded myself. Not the fact that her uncle Duncan would probably rock a cowboy hat and boots.

"So how much sugar did these little angels get?" Duncan asked as he lifted the last of the giggling girls into the cutter.

Miriam laughed as she shook the snow off a mitten one of the girls had dropped.

"Blame your sister. I fed them a well-balanced meal of chicken fingers and fries. I'm sure it was the two inches of icing on the horse cake that tipped them into crazy-land." Miriam helped one little girl shove her hand into the mitten, then pulled her own out of the large pockets of her down-filled coat.

"Good thing Bonnie and Clyde are bombproof," Duncan said, eyeing the horses standing patiently in the harness. Clyde shook his head, the bells on his shoulder jingling, signaling his desire to get moving, but ever since he'd hooked them up to the sleigh, they'd been the picture of patience and good training.

He looked over his shoulder to where his mother and sister stood, their heads bent, glancing his way once in a while, as if sharing secrets like teenagers.

"Are you coming along?" he called out.

"There's not enough room in the sleigh," Esther said, hunching her shoulders against the cold. "Besides, it's too cold."

"Cold? It's barely freezing."

Indeed, it was a picture-perfect day for a sleigh ride. The snow sparkled below a benevolent sun hanging in a bluebird sky. Not a breath of wind stirred the air.

"You go ahead," his mother said, waving him off. "We'll stay behind and keep the home fires burning."

He could have guessed they weren't coming. In all the years he'd had his horses, they'd never expressed any desire to either ride them or go out on the sleigh with him.

"Looks like it's you and me," he said with forced heartiness, as he turned back to Miriam, who was tugging on her own mittens.

The tentative smile she gave him settled too easily in his heart.

His practical side reminded him that she'd brushed him off before. How was he to know she wouldn't do it again?

But his lonely side returned the smile, and for a moment they stood like two statues, watching each other, and as he looked into her eyes, the old attraction flickered.

Dangerous territory, he told himself, and yet, he couldn't look away. He was about to help her into the sleigh when she scrambled up on her own.

She settled between Celia and one friend, across from the other two girls who were bouncing up and down on the seat. "Girls, you'll have to sit quietly," he warned them, dragging his attention away from Miriam. "We don't want to make the horses nervous."

"Dunkle, will you go fast?" Celia was asking.

"No. We'll be going on a trail through the bushes so we'll go slow." He pulled out a couple of blankets and handed them to Miriam. "The girls might want these covering their legs. Just to keep them warm."

She took them from him, giving him another cautious smile. But this time, he forced himself not to give in to his changing feelings. She would leave. Again. And he'd be stuck by himself.

Again.

He didn't have the emotional reserves to deal with that.

He unhitched the horses from the rail, then hauled himself onto the front of the cutter and unwound the reins from the post, threading them through his gloved hands. "Everyone okay?" he asked.

"Yes. Let's go, Dunkle," Celia called out, giddy with excitement.

With a cluck and a 'gee', the horses started out, lifting their feet high in anticipation as Duncan kept the tension on the reins to hold them in. They immediately got the hint and leaned into the harness, settling into a steady walk.

He looked back to make sure everyone was okay.

The girls had settled down a bit. Miriam had her arms around the girls beside her.

"This is fun, isn't it?" she asked, her own eyes

bright, her smile genuine and wide, the cool air making her cheeks rosy, the sunshine catching auburn glints in her hair.

Duncan dragged his attention back to the horses, who had settled into a solid rhythm. Other than the giggling girls, the only sound was the horses' huffing breaths, the muffled tramp of their hooves, and the hissing of the sled's runners over the snow. Being with his horses created a welcome pocket of peace in a life that had too much chaos.

He pulled in a deep breath then exhaled, as if releasing an ever-present tension.

A constant by-product of the logging. Though he knew why he kept it up, part of him was growing weary at the endless movement, busyness and work it created.

"I think we should sing a sleighing song," Miriam said.

"*Jingle Bells*," one of the girls called out.

"That's a perfect song. Because Christmas is coming." She started singing and soon the girls had joined in, yelling on the 'hey' parts, and substituting Bonnie's name for Bobtail in the song.

He glanced back surprised to catch Miriam looking at him. She was smiling, her cheeks red, her eyes bright.

She looked gorgeous and for a moment he couldn't look away. Then a jerk on the reins made him focus on the horses. But as they rode around the field he was as aware of the woman in the sleigh behind him as of the horses in front.

They headed toward the trees and down the narrow trail, his horses still pulling steady. He smiled, gently adjusting the tension on the reins, always working with the horses, paying attention to their reactions.

He really needed to do this more often.

And why can't you? Why can't you leave Les in charge the operation more? Spend time doing what you like?

All by yourself?

The question came with a flare of loneliness and once again his thoughts shifted to Miriam and how eager she was to come along.

He glanced back again. "You girls doing okay? You warm enough?"

"Going good," Miriam said, flashing him a mittened thumbs up. Her smile seemed to take over her face. She was really enjoying this.

"I'll head down this trail for another ten minutes, then swing back if that's okay."

She nodded and for another moment their gazes held. He was the first to look away.

Twenty minutes later he was pulling the horses up and they came to a stop close to the barn. His mother and Esther were waiting.

"We've got a fire going," Esther said as she walked to the sleigh to help the girls out, his mother right behind her. "Come and warm up and have some s'mores."

Before he could get down to help, Miriam was handing the girls to Esther and his mother who quickly ushered the girls toward the fire. Miriam held back a moment looking from Celia who was walking beside his mother, back to him.

"Do you need a hand with the horses?" she asked.

Her question surprised him. He didn't think she'd be interested. But unhitching the horses was more complicated than hitching so the help was welcome.

"That'd be great. Do you know anything about horses and harnesses?"

"Only from what I've seen of Wagon Train reruns and a few glimpses of the History Channel." She returned his smile and he felt again that quiver of connection, and beneath that, a desire to find out more about her.

"Then you're well prepared. I first need to unhitch the horses from the wagon. Can you hold the lead lines while I unhook the trace chains?"

"Oh those," she said with mock authority.

"You don't have a clue what I'm talking about do you?" he asked as she clambered into the box.

With a casual wave of her mittened hand she dismissed his question. "Any idiot knows what trace chains are."

He laughed again as he handed her the lines.

A few moments later he had the trace chains off, then released the tongue from the neck yokes, slowly lowering it to the ground.

"You can hand me Bonnie's lines," he said, walking back to the cutter. "But hang onto Clyde's for now. I'll come back for him."

He took the lines from her and walked behind Bonnie as she walked into the barn and directly into her open stall. She nosed the trough then looked at him as if wondering where her treat was.

"You'll get it soon enough," he said with a chuckle, clipping a lead rope to hold her in place. Just as he got the lines loose he heard Clyde's heavy footfalls and he spun around, heart quickening. Had he gotten loose from Miriam?

But she was behind him, grinning as she drove him into the barn.

"Where does he go?"

He jerked his chin toward Clyde's stall but the horse was already moving in that direction.

"Guess he knows where home is," Miriam said with a chuckle following him.

"There's a rope attached to the front of the stall. Clip it to his head collar."

He watched a moment to make sure Clyde was okay, then worked quickly, unbuckling and easing the heavy harness off Bonnie. Bells jangled as he sorted the straps and traces, then hung it up with the rest of the tack.

Miriam was talking to Clyde, stroking his nose, looking entirely calm.

"You seem pretty comfortable with horses. You been around them much?"

"Not really. Life has taught me to be a quick learner and to adapt." She returned his smile over Clyde's neck as he worked, and he felt again that faint quiver of connection, and beneath that, a desire to find out more about her.

"Are you talking about life with your mother?"

"Amongst other situations."

"Living in Jerrod's home?" he asked slipping the straps and loosening the breeching.

"Not at all. Jerrod's parents were the only reliable people in my life."

She was petting Clyde when she said that, her mouth still holding that soft smile, as if she were somewhere else. Somewhere solid and secure.

"And the other lessons?" With a grunt he slipped the rest of the harness off.

She seemed to pull herself out of wherever she had gone. Her features settled into the same ironic look they usually held, as if she herself was holding her own secrets in. "Where I learned the other lessons is not worth mentioning." He hung up the harness and returned to the stall, stroking Clyde, sighing in the silence that fell between them.

But suddenly, he wanted her to do precisely that. Mention them. Fill in the blanks between that last date they had together and now. Answer the questions that bothered him as he had tried to contact her.

He was surprised that after all this time, and all that happened to him, that this still mattered.

"You can give him a treat now," Duncan said, pulling himself back to the present. "The oats and pail are in a bin at the end of the alley. Unless you want to join the girls," he added hastily.

"I don't mind. I'm sure your mom and Esther can manage." She paused a moment, however, looking suddenly pensive. "I wanted to ask you a question anyway. About Francine and Jerrod. Did she ever talk to you about their relationship?"

Duncan thought back to that moment when he had tried to convince his sister not to go on the sledding trip. How she seemed to be pleading with him to leave it be. That she needed to do this.

"I'm sure they had their difficulties. I mean, what couple doesn't?"

"I can vouch for that," she said with a humorless laugh.

He heard pain in her voice and wondered what caused it. "What do you mean?"

Miriam blinked as if she suddenly realized what she was saying. Then she took a step back. "Maybe I better see what the girls are up to after all."

And then she left him with his confused thoughts and a curiosity about her past relationships.

CHAPTER 7

*T*he fire snapped and crackled and I crowded as close as I could, trying to roast a marshmallow I promised Celia I would make for her. My feet were freezing in my unsuitable boots, and my mitts were like two blocks of ice, and deep inside I felt a growing confusion.

Seeing Duncan with the horses, looking so relaxed and at ease showed me another, far too appealing side. For the first time since I'd come to Holmes Crossing I caught a glimpse of the man I met all those years ago.

"Stop that. Jane doesn't like that."

Celia's distressed cry pulled my attention from the marshmallow skewered on the end of my roasting stick.

Celia, hugging her doll, sat hunched on a bench beside Tiffany, a young girl with long, dark hair, brown eyes and a taunting smile.

Tiffany was tugging on Jane's boot, but her narrowed eyes were fixed on Celia. I'd seen that look too many times in my life and now, as it did then, made my skin crawl.

"Stop," Celia called out, pulling her doll to one side.

"Your marshmallow's burning," Esther pointed out to me from across the fire where she was assembling a s'more for one of the other girls.

I glanced back at the flaming black ball at the end of my stick and sighed at the charred and gooey mess. I stuffed the stick in the fire in a gesture of surrender and got up to see what was going on between Tiffany and Celia.

"What's wrong?" I asked, crouching down in front of the girls.

"Jane is angry," Celia said, glowering at her friend. "Tiffany is being mean to her."

"Her doll can't talk," Tiffany said. "She shouldn't lie."

"Celia's not lying," I said, trying to find a balance between soothing hurt feelings and keeping the peace. "She's talking about Jane."

"But she says stuff and says that Jane says it."

"Jane only talks to me," Celia insisted, shooting a frown at Tiffany. "She won't talk to you."

"How come I can't hear it?" Tiffany's voice held a note of disgust that no five-year-old should have so perfected.

I watched the two, feeling completely out of my depth and puzzled that Celia had invited this girl when, it seemed, there was this antipathy between them.

"Jane is a special doll," I said to Tiffany, putting my arm around her and gently easing her away from Celia, removing her from the situation. "And you're a special little girl, so why don't I make you a special s'more?"

Tiffany shot a disdainful look at my roasting stick still sitting in the fire as I escorted her to a bench closer to the grate. "You don't make good s'mores."

My smile shifted to fake sincerity, and I felt bad that I was growing to dislike this little girl. "I've never made s'mores before," I said. "I'm still learning."

"You've never made s'mores?" Esther asked as she slipped her perfect marshmallow onto a graham wafer. "I thought Jerrod's family went camping all the time."

"Only until he was twelve. I didn't move in with the Carpenters until he was thirteen." I pulled the stick out of the fire and found a napkin to wipe the sad remains off. Then I dug in the bag for another marshmallow and skewered it onto the stick.

"Oh. Right. I forgot. His father died a year after that."

She handed Celia's other friend, Laine, her s'more. "Here you go, sweetie. Celia do you want me to make a s'more for you?"

"I don't want you to," she snapped, still in a funk.

"Celia," Cora reprimanded. "That's no way to talk to your aunty."

But Celia hunkered further down, her attention on her doll.

I wanted to intervene but knew that Celia would come around in her own time.

"Tiffany, why don't I make you a s'more?"

"No. I don't think so," she sniffed, gravitating to Esther.

I gave up, set my stick aside and pushed myself to my feet just as Duncan came out of the barn. He looked around and caught my eye, and then that little jolt he created in me happened again.

"Got the horses done?" I asked, hoping I sounded more casual than I felt.

"They're in the pasture now." He gave me a careful smile and the jolt settled into a faint buzz.

Gregg, my old boyfriend, taught me well the dangers of letting people close. But the sight of this man's smile and the way his eyes crinkled pushed at the barriers I had built around my heart.

Then, I heard Celia muttering to her doll, and with a start, I realized I had been ignoring her. I excused myself and was about to go and sit with Celia to comfort her, but Mrs. Tiemstra beat me to it. She drew the little girl onto her lap and Celia drooped against her, her head resting on Cora's shoulder as her grandmother stroked her arm, talking quietly to her.

My heart folded at the sight. Celia had never sat so pliant in my lap. Had never nestled her head into my neck or put her arms around me.

That should be me. I should be the one she connects with. I should be the one with the power to comfort her. I'm her mother.

I held my breath as I waited for the storm of emotions that were slowly roiling in my chest to still. I couldn't let the selfish feelings out. Cora's lap was Celia's proper place.

I turned abruptly away, walking around Duncan, joining Laine and Savannah, who were playing with their dolls, making them talk to each other. The sight made me feel a bit better about Celia and her ventriloquist dummy act. Maybe it was more normal than I thought.

"So, tell me about your dolls," I asked, settling down beside the girls. "What are their names?"

But while Laine and Savannah chattered, part of my attention was pinned to the man who was now approaching his mother and Celia.

"Dunkle, that sleigh ride was so fun," I heard Celia exclaim. "I wish we could do it again."

He was crouched down now, talking to her, and once again I was puzzled by the fact that Celia spoke directly to him, not via the doll.

Then I felt a light tap on my shoulder.

"Can I talk to you a moment?" Esther asked. "I'd like to finish up our conversation from before."

I didn't want to but I sensed she wasn't going to quit until she had said her piece.

"Sure." I tore my gaze away from Celia, who was talking animatedly to Duncan, making eye contact, her hands waving as she spoke.

"Away from everyone," Esther added, jerking her head toward the barn behind us.

"Will you girls be okay?" I asked Laine and Savannah. They nodded.

Tiffany had joined Cora on the bench, eating the perfect s'more Esther had just finished. Celia was still talking to Duncan.

Esther had gone ahead of me and opened one of the side doors of the barn I had just been in with Duncan a few moments ago, waiting for me to go inside.

She flicked a switch and a watery light from a bare light bulb cut the gloom. I had to blink to adjust my eyes from the bright sunshine outside to the dim light inside.

"I wanted to talk to you without Celia overhearing," Esther was saying, walking over to a square bale of hay and dropping onto it. "This may be a bit awkward, but I was wondering if you noticed how Celia doesn't talk to Duncan through that doll of hers."

I nodded, still feeling the faint pangs of jealousy at that action of hers.

"It seems to me that Celia isn't that close to you," she said.

Her blunt statement was like a body blow. Though I knew it myself, hearing her spell it out so starkly made it more real and painful.

She's my daughter, I wanted to cry out. *I carried*

*her for nine months. Gave birth to her. I would have
kept her if I could.*

"I think it's because we barely know each other," I said, struggling to keep my tone even and
unemotional, drawing on older, seasoned skills. "I
haven't seen a lot of her as she was growing up."

"I understood that you weren't involved for
most of her life. Jerrod said there were...reasons."

My heart jumped at her hesitation. Did she
know my past? My dark secret?

But as I stilled my own panicky thoughts, I realized she was probably talking about my role as
an aunt.

"I was living far away," I said, realizing how
she could see that as a feeble excuse.

"Which raises the question why my sister
named you as Celia's guardian. And why Jerrod
named Duncan."

"I think my brother originally wanted your
parents as guardians," I said not sure how to get
through this awkward conversation. It had been
difficult enough to see Duncan's reaction when
the lawyer stated Francine and Jerrod's choices.
Listening to Esther's skepticism only added to my
insecurities. "And he probably changed it after
your father's accident. As for Francine, who
knows?"

"She probably had her own twisted agenda," Esther muttered, looking away.

"What do you mean?"

She pulled her attention back to me and quickly shook her head. "Sorry. Just thinking out loud."

But her comment made me even more curious what she meant. Plus, I sensed she was dancing around the edges of where she really wanted to go.

"You think Duncan should be Celia's guardian," I said, heading her off at the proverbial impasse.

Esther's eyes grew wide and her mouth slipped open in an O of surprise. But she recovered quickly, then gave a decisive nod. "Yes. That's exactly what I think."

Even though I knew where Esther had been headed, and though I had already discussed this with Mrs. Tiemstra it still hurt to be reminded of it again.

I pushed my own changing feelings aside, trying to be dispassionate about the discussion. However, that didn't mean I didn't have my own questions.

"Why do you think your sister named me guardian?" I asked.

Esther shrugged. "I don't know why. I mean, Celia isn't even related by blood to you."

She's my daughter.

You can't think that, I reminded myself. You gave up your rights. You gave those up when-

"But she's not related by blood to Duncan either," I pressed.

"No, but he's family at least."

I let that slip.

"And given your situation – I mean you live far away and I understand that your employment situation has been, well, erratic."

And how did she know that? Had Jerrod and her been talking?

Regardless, I was getting tired of her pointed comments.

"If you're trying to get to the point where you ask me if I'm willing to give up my rights to Celia..." I paused there, the words choking me even as I spoke them "...then you may as well know that from the beginning I also thought Duncan should be her guardian. In fact, when he told me he couldn't or wouldn't take on the responsibility, I was upset. Your mother and I discussed this when we planned out Celia's birthday party."

Again, Esther did her impression of a dead

fish, and again, she pulled herself together. "You talked with my mother already? You agree with me?"

"I know my situation better than you seem to, and while I know that while your parents can't take care of Celia, with Duncan she'll have some semblance of a family. Whereas with me..." I let my sentence fade away as I felt my throat thicken.

This was ridiculous. I had to stop this feeling sorry for myself. I knew my reality.

It was just that every minute I had spent this past week with Celia had become more precious. Every moment drew out maternal feelings I couldn't indulge in yet couldn't ignore.

Neither could I ignore the differences between what Duncan could give her and what I could. That cozy house with its cheery fireplace, the space and freedom this yard could offer her, horses that she loved. Grandparents, an aunt. Family. Community.

I couldn't even come close with my cramped apartment and lonely life.

"I'm surprised your mother didn't say anything to you," I continued. "I had exactly this conversation with her in the café. As we were planning this birthday party."

Esther bit her lip. "My mother and I don't talk

a lot, and we haven't had much opportunity since I came back." Then she leaned back against the wooden wall behind her, stroking her chin with her fingers, as if plotting. "But if what you say is true, the only obstacle is Duncan. We need to find a way for him to take over his guardianship of Celia."

It was dizzying how quickly she accepted what I had said.

She stood, smiling at me, a co-conspirator in her plans. "So if you agree, then we need to come up with a way to get Duncan more involved."

I simply shrugged, not trusting myself to speak, angry at the unexpected emotions crowding up my throat.

"I know he's busy," Esther continued, not noticing my silence as she stared at the ground, thinking. Planning. "He's got a lot going on, but we'll just have to make him see how important this is." She looked up at me then. "You need to find opportunities to bring him and Celia together. If you could let him know that you think it's best if Celia be with him and if I work on him from my end, explain to him that we're all behind him. And you may as well know, though I haven't told my parents yet, I'm taking some time off school. Coming to help take care of Celia until

Jerrod and Francine's estate is all settled and, hopefully, Dad gets a bit better."

Her declaration should have assured me that Celia would be in good hands. Instead, it only underlined how little I could do for my daughter.

"Well, that would help," I said. "And that's quite a sacrifice. To put your schooling on hold."

Esther shrugged. "Not so much. I need to take some time off and figure out where I'm going. It's been...been a bad year. Too many other things going on."

She sounded sad, and again, I had to remind myself of what she'd lost as well.

"You've had your own sorrows too," I said. "I'm sure this has been especially difficult for you."

"What do you mean, especially difficult?" she asked, her voice taking on a surprisingly sharp tone. "What do you know? What has Jerrod told you?"

Her defensiveness puzzled me. "Your sister. You just lost a sister," I said.

Her expression grew confused and then she nodded, looking suddenly relieved as if she had been talking about something else. "It's been a crazy few weeks." Esther dragged her hands over her face, then she looked down, her eyes closed. She stayed that way a moment, then looked over at me. "So, you're okay with this?" she asked. "Helping us to sway Duncan to do what he should?"

I'm not okay with this, I wanted to say. *I want to be able to take care of my own daughter.*

But reality was not my ally, so I simply nodded. "I want what's best for Celia," I said quietly. Obediently. The good girl trying to make up for the mistakes she'd made.

* * *

"DID YOU HAVE A GOOD TIME TODAY?" I asked as I toweled Celia off.

She had smelled like wood smoke and horse and outdoors. When we got back to the house I suggested she have a bath. She had protested at first but I told her that Jane also wanted a bath. This netted me a skeptical look, but I spoke with authority gleaned from desperation, so she gave in.

"I did. Riding in the sled was so fun. I love the horses. I wish I could ride them myself. And the s'mores were good and it was nice to be with Oma." Her words spilled out in an enthusiastic rush, her eyes bright as she looked up at me.

I felt a melting deep in my soul, a wavering of

my own convictions. This was the first time we had made eye contact and she had addressed me directly since the funeral. Her eyes holding mine was a gentle incursion into the place I had shut off ever since I handed her over to the social worker that dark dreary day.

"I want to go to Dunkle's again," she said, then, as if she knew what she was doing, she looked down. Away from me. "Jane wants to go to Dunkle's again."

So did I.

I quashed that thought, recognizing it for the foolish thing it was.

But for a moment, a brief snatch of time, my daughter had acknowledged me. Had been animated and excited and talking to me. Making eye contact with me.

I tried not to latch on to it. Instead, I picked up the hairbrush and handed it to Celia, so she could brush her hair herself. I'd found out the hard way the first time I bathed her that she didn't like me touching her hair.

"What was Jane's favorite part of the day?" I asked, even though the words choked me. I wanted her to keep talking, and if it had to go through this inanimate creature, then so be it.

"She didn't like it when Tiffany teased me and

told me that having a doll is dumb. That made Jane sad."

"And that made you sad too?" I asked, trying to draw her own ideas out.

All I got from her was a curt nod as she dragged the brush through the tangled mat of her hair. I was itching to grab the brush and help, so instead I expended my energy on cleaning up the toys she had in the bathtub.

"And I didn't like it when Aunty Esther wanted to make me a s'more," she said with a deep frown.

This surprised me. I thought there would be a stronger connection between Celia and her aunt.

"Aunty Esther really likes you," I said carefully.

Celia's frown deepened, clearly unwilling to talk about her aunt.

Curious.

I drained the tub, wiped down the taps and counter with the towel. I gathered Celia's clothes and tossed everything into the laundry basket tucked in a closet behind a door, taking a moment to appreciate the order I had marshaled out of the sticky chaos that had been the bathroom. I felt like I was slowly putting my own stamp on this beautiful home.

Celia was struggling to get her nightgown on,

and once again I stayed back, letting her figure it out herself. She got it on backward, her hair snagging on the buttons, crying out when her hair got tugged. Once again she pulled, still crying.

I couldn't stand it anymore.

"I think Jane would want me to help you," I said, keeping my voice quiet and unobtrusive.

To my surprise, Celia nodded.

I gently loosened her hair from the buttons then got the nightgown turned around. Then I took Jane and put her matching nightgown on as well.

"Should I brush Jane's hair?" I asked and when Celia nodded her assent I felt like I had caught a glimpse of a shift in our relationship. I sat down and under Celia's guidance, carefully brushed Jane's hair. I managed to French braid one side of Jane's hair, then blended it into a regular braid, pulling it all to one side and tying it off with a brightly colored ribbon.

"That looks pretty." Celia took the doll, examining the hairstyle from a few different angles. Then she stood on the little stool in front of the sink and frowned at her own still-scraggly hair in the mirror. "Can you make mine look the same?"

Don't rejoice. Don't draw attention.

"Yes. I can," I said pleased with my restraint.

And as she clutched her doll, I carefully worked my way through the damp snarls of her hair. This is what mothers do, I thought slowing my movements, savoring the moment.

Fifteen minutes later, I was finished, and Celia was grinning as she turned her head this way and that, looking from her reflection to Jane. "We look exactly the same," she said, a slow smile spreading over her face. Then she turned to me, her smile growing. "Thanks, Aunty Miriam."

I returned her smile, my own heart pounding with a mixture of affection at the fact that she had addressed me personally, yet my joy was blunted by a ragged feeling of dissatisfaction.

I don't want to be Aunty Miriam. I want to be Mom.

I caught myself, my heart stuttering in my chest.

You had your chance I reminded myself. You did what was best for her.

But I didn't have a choice.

I stilled the voice, remembering what the social worker I had been working with to arrange Celia's adoption had told me. That my choices had brought me to where I was and to do what was best for my baby.

Part of me had always wanted to protest that I didn't know all the dark secrets of my boyfriend's, Gregg's life.

But at the same time I knew that I had made my own choice to stay with Gregg even after I caught a glimpse of part of his double life. The drugs. The parties.

I pushed those memories far down. No need to resurrect that part of my past. I had promised myself that God had forgiven me.

However, that didn't stop me from stroking my daughter's hair, letting my hand linger on the sweet softness of her cheek. Allowing myself these few moments of connection.

"You're welcome, little girl," I said.

"Can you read me a story?" she asked, and then, as if realizing what she had done, dropped her head, clutching her doll close. "Can you read Jane a story?"

"I'll read you both a story," I said, recognizing the small progress we had made tonight. "Let me know what Jane wants and I'll read it to both of you."

We went to her room, and to my surprise, she pulled out one of the books I had illustrated off her extensive bookshelf. She dropped it on the bed, and as I glanced at the dustcover, the sight of the dancing princesses I had painstakingly worked over all those years ago created a surprising longing in me.

"Shall I read this one first?" I asked, holding it up. The corners were dog-eared and the ripped dust jacket had streaks of what looked like chocolate on it.

It looked well loved.

"No, this one comes first." She handed me another book.

The princess on the cover of this book stood on a hill, her head thrown back, arms out, her crown almost falling off her head as the wind teased her dress and hair.

As I looked at the picture my mind sifted back to a happier time in my life. A time when I thought I was on the cusp of a new career and opportunities.

And then Gregg happened and my life spun around and down.

"It's about a princess who doesn't want to be a princess anymore," Celia told me, hunkering down beside me, clutching Jane. "And she runs way and finds 'ventures, and helps save a bunny and a toad and other things." She stopped, her eyes fixed on the book as I opened it.

It felt like coming home, I thought, as I cleared

my throat and began reading. So easily I pictured myself sketching out the princess, crouched down by her father's throne. Pouting. The joy I had felt as the picture came to life. The layering of the colors bringing dimension and color to the sketch.

As I read, I touched the pictures, as if connecting to that joy again. And suddenly, my fingers itched to draw and paint again.

"I like that story," Celia said, as I closed the book at the end.

I wanted to ask her if she liked the pictures, the artist in me needing the affirmation, but she took it from me and plunked the second one on my lap. Then, to my surprise, as I read she moved closer. A few minutes later, Celia leaned against me. Her warmth, the curve of her body fitting into mine, created a gentle ache.

But with it came a tenderness and an urge to protect this child from all harm. To keep her close.

I swallowed and kept reading, allowing myself to recreate that magical time in my life when all was well. When the future beckoned as brightly as it did to the princesses I drew.

Four books, one lullaby, and a recitation of "Now I Lay Me" later, Celia lay tucked in the sheets of her beautiful bed, the pink princess duvet pulled up around her chin. She gave me a sleepy smile, rolled over onto her side, and as I watched her eyes drift closed, her lashes settled into a delicate fan on her rosy cheeks.

I lowered myself to the carpet beside the bed to do my nightly surveillance.

I pulled the gauze netting of the canopy around the front of her bed, waiting as her breaths grew heavy and even. Then, when I thought she was fast asleep, I gave in to an impulse and gently stroked my hand over her warm, soft cheek.

Was that a smile?

"Mommy," I heard her whisper.

My heart jumped, and I struggled not to pull her into my arms. Instead, I satisfied myself with laying my hand on her shoulder so if she woke during this in-between time, she would know I was there.

"Please watch over her, Lord," I whispered. "Heal her broken heart. Take care of her lonely soul."

As I prayed, my thoughts strayed to Duncan, the man who Esther and I had both agreed should take care of her. Would he do this for her? Would he guard her while she slept?

I looked around the beautiful room, with its white, Pottery Barn furniture, the tasteful prints on the walls, the bookshelf with its vast collection of books and Jane's furniture—almost as expensive as Celia's. As I stretched my legs out on the pink, lush carpet I knew I could never have given my daughter even one quarter of this.

Would that matter? Did it matter to you?

I couldn't help thinking of the tiny room I lived in at the Carpenters' house. It was barely large enough for a single bed. I didn't even have a dresser. All my clothes fit in a drawer I slid under my bed. The house itself was a jumble of box-sized rooms and garage-sale furniture.

But to me it was a sanctuary. A home.

Would Duncan provide that for her? He said he couldn't do it, but would that change if Esther got involved? And why did she want to be? Why would a single girl want to tie herself down with a child? Help her reluctant brother take Celia in?

I closed my eyes, trying to still my troubled thoughts. Reluctantly returning to the place where I was when I first made that hard decision.

I let Celia go for a good reason. For her own sake.

I just had to do it again.

CHAPTER 8

uncan stood at the back of the church, wondering as he did every Sunday what he was doing here. Why he had bothered getting up this morning to come to church?

Out of need and out of custom.

The words of an old hymn ran through his mind, as he shoved his hands in his back pockets.

Well, today it was custom that brought him here. This morning, as he had for many years, he'd gotten up and the first thought through his mind was, *No.*

But, as had happened before, custom kicked in, and he went through his Sunday routine. Clinging to routine got him through those dark days after Kimberly and his little girl's death. It would now get him through these gray ones.

So he got up, had breakfast, fed the cows and horses, showered, changed and got in his truck. But this morning, though he was hesitant to pay it too much mind, something else had pulled him here. A tiny anticipation, a hope that Miriam would come.

But he hadn't seen Jerrod and Francine's SUV in the parking lot, nor could he see Miriam and Celia from his vantage point back here.

He felt a curious letdown. His mother had texted him, saying she and his father wouldn't be coming. He may as well go. He was about to do exactly that, when the doors of the foyer opened, and Jack and Terra came into the church. And now he was too late. Leaving would create questions he wasn't about to answer, and Terra was never hesitant about asking them.

His friends joined him at the back of sanctuary, nervous smiles and sympathy wreathed on their faces. Jack clapped him on the shoulder and Terra gave him a quick hug.

"How was the birthday party?" she asked as she pulled away.

Duncan shot her a frown. "How did you know about that?"

172

"I heard Laine's mother talking about it at the diner after she dropped her daughter off."

He should have known. Terra's diner was like a gossip black hole. All it took was a drink of hot coffee, a bit of tangy lemon pie, and every secret tucked away in your brain was sucked out.

"The party was good." Spending time with Miriam was even better.

"Is that a smile I see on your face?" Terra asked, nudging him in the side.

"I'm just happy to be in church," Duncan parried easily, not giving her an inch.

Terra held his gaze, her lips quirking into a curious smile, but he didn't so much as glance away. She was the first to give in, turning to Jack. "We should go sit down."

Then, just as he was celebrating his victory, the door of the foyer opened and in walked Miriam and Celia.

Celia had her doll tucked under her arm and was frowning at Miriam, yanking at her coat to pull it off, muttering at her. Miriam's hair was pulled back in a complicated knot at the back of her head that gave her an exotic look. Set off the upward tilt of her eyes.

Terra looked back at the same time. "Well,

well, well. Look who's here," she said in a knowing voice.

"Yeah. My niece." Duncan ignored her as Celia tried to unbutton her coat. Miriam looked as if she was urging Celia to keep it on. Not that he blamed her. If Celia was wearing the dress she wore last week, the poor kid would freeze in church.

"She's pretty, isn't she?" Terra continued.

Duncan dragged his attention back to Terra and Jack, catching the mischievous quirk of Terra's lips, but didn't take the obvious bait. "Celia is, as always, adorable."

"And I think we've overstayed our welcome." Jack gave Duncan an apologetic grin. "We'll be leaving you alone now. Come on over some time when things slow down in the bush. I've got a horse I wouldn't mind some help with."

"I'll do that," Duncan said, flashing his friend a smile, thankful for the reprieve.

Then he heard Celia call out his name, and he knew he couldn't avoid the inevitable.

"Dunkle. There you are," Celia called out, pulling away from Miriam and running toward him.

Though her coat had stayed on, he could see that, once again, she wore the same unsuitable dress she had worn last week. The dress Esther had convinced him to buy for Celia, because it came with a matching one for the doll. And sure enough, the doll wore the exact same dress again too.

Celia grabbed his hand, grinning up at him. "Hi, Dunkle. I had fun at my birthday party," she said.

Her enthusiasm was infectious, and he couldn't help but smile, happy to see her in good spirits. "That's good. But you still have some chocolate from your s'mores on your face."

But Celia just grinned at his obvious teasing. "No, I don't, silly. Aunty Miriam washed my face all clean. I had a long bath and I had bubbles." She patted her hair. "And aunty Miriam made my hair pretty. Just like Jane's. And yesterday we cleaned up my room."

Then Miriam joined him and a different emotion took over. Her hair shone in the overhead lights and her dark lashes framed her brown eyes.

"Good morning, Miriam," he said, swallowing down a visceral reaction to her beauty.

"Good morning to you," she returned, a gentle smile on her lips.

And for a moment he couldn't look away, nor did he want to.

"Dunkle, I want to sit with you," Celia announced, grabbing his hand.

Duncan's initial reaction was to pull back. But though his usual retreat was for his own protection, he knew he had to put that aside for the sake of his niece. So he kept her hand in his and tightened the grip ever so gently, and a familiar emotion seeped into his soul as she leaned into him.

"Well, let's go find a place, then," he said, his voice sounding strange in his ears. Less harsh. Softer.

He looked over at Miriam and caught a peculiar expression on her face. Her smile seemed to waver and in her eyes he caught a puzzling melancholy.

"Are you okay?" he asked.

Miriam blinked quickly, her gaze focusing on him, then gave a tight nod. "Yes. I'm fine."

"Let's go sit down," Celia announced.

But as Duncan let Celia take the lead, he shot another glance at Miriam, and in spite of her quick reply, he caught a troubled expression on her face.

Mystery upon mystery, he thought as he came to an empty pew and stood aside to let Miriam and Celia sit down.

The musicians at the front had played a

couple of songs already, and Duncan sat back, looking up at the lyrics on the screen, but part of his attention was on the woman sitting beside Celia.

He gave himself a mental shake, and forced his full attention to the song the group was singing.

"His heart was broken for the brokenhearted, as he brings us now to the heart of life. He feels our pain and takes it on, and calls us now, arise."

Duncan felt an answering throb of pain at the lyrics that so closely echoed his own experiences. He hadn't even completely dealt with Kimberly and Tasha's deaths, and now he was faced with more loss.

He swallowed down a sudden burst of anger with God, who had taken so much away. Had God been brokenhearted? Did He know loss?

But no sooner were the words formulated when he felt a small, soft hand slip itself into his, wiggling its way past fingers pressed against a palm.

He looked down at Celia, who was grinning up at him.

Every time he saw her, it was like another wound, another nick on his soul, but right behind that came the words of the song's chorus—*"He feels our pain and takes it on and calls us now, arise."*

A challenge to let go? A reminder that he didn't have to carry it all?

He wasn't sure what to do with this knowledge, and he sucked in a breath, trying to calm his racing heart. Trying to find his bearings.

And as he did, his eyes, as if seeking a homing place, landed on Miriam, only to find her looking at him.

Their eyes met and held, and in that moment, he caught a glimpse, like a ray of light, of a possibility.

Then the pastor arrived and as the service began a faint echo of it haunted him. With every passing minute, sitting with Celia and Miriam, he felt as if he were shifting between present and past.

He forced his attention back to the pastor, who was talking about sorrow. Duncan knew he was referencing the deaths of Francine and Jerrod. He knew their deaths had affected the community, and the presence of their orphaned daughter in the sanctuary underscored the tragedy. The occasional pitying glances back at them showed him how the rest of the congregation felt.

"...we can pretend it doesn't exist, but as C.S. Lewis says, 'Pain insists upon being attended to.

God whispers to us in our pleasures, speaks in our conscience, but shouts in our pains; it is His megaphone to rouse a deaf world.' And whether we want to admit it or not, it is in the hard, dark places of our lives that we draw closest to God. That we cry out to Him the hardest."

Duncan was tired of pain and grief and longed for ordinary.

Then Celia shifted, leaning against him, her hand slipping into the crook of his arm, and he felt as if a crack opened in his grief-hardened-heart.

He looked down at the little girl, who was swinging her feet with the obliviousness of youth. He knew she was also grieving, but it seemed she was more willing to take things as they came.

Then he glanced over at Miriam, who was looking at the minister, her features twisted, as if she was fighting her own internal battle.

He gave in to an impulse, reached across the pew, and laid his hand on her shoulder. He let it rest there a moment, let their shared grief act as a bridge between them.

Her eyes shot to his, and for a moment he wondered if he had overstepped a boundary. But then she smiled, and then reached up and covered his hand with hers, strengthening the connection.

They sat that way through the next hymn. The longer they stayed connected, the more reluctant Duncan was to let her go. At all.

* * *

I STIFLED a yawn as I pulled a bag of cookies off the shelf in the grocery store, flipping it to one side to read the ingredients, but the tiny letters blurred before my eyes. I really needed more sleep, I thought, feeling as if I was on the verge of tears.

Too many conflicting emotions. Too many confusing thoughts.

Yesterday, in church, I had felt a few moments of peace. Hearing the pastor talking about God meeting us in the dark places brought me back to the darkest place and time I had ever been - after I gave up Celia.

And yet, I knew that in that place, in that darkness, I found the God I had turned my back on. And in that unlikeliest of places, I found peace.

I clung to that peace and when Duncan put his hand on my shoulder I felt, for the first time in years, that I had someone beside me.

But all that fell apart when Celia found out, as

we were leaving church, that Dunkle wasn't going to be at Oma and Opas for lunch. So she wasn't going either.

The harder I pushed, the harder she fought back. So I drove home with a hostile child and my own puzzlement at Duncan's decision. I had to admit to feeling let down as well. I had to admit to a sense of anticipation of spending time with him in a family setting.

When we came home, Celia fell asleep on the couch and woke up in a funk, insisting that I get her *boughten* cookies. Which I didn't have, because we were still working our way through the baking we got from the funeral.

Then, she sat up most of the night, unable to sleep, getting herself all worked up about the cookies though I knew it had as much to do with Dunkle as it did with the cookies.

Mrs. Lansing wasn't at work today so I couldn't talk to her about the counselor appointment. So, after dropping Celia off at kindergarten, and staying a few moments to make sure she was okay, I hied myself to the grocery store to fulfill her majesty's demands. The only reason I did it was because the request had come from Celia herself, and not Jane.

So here I stood trying to decipher cookie packages and failing.

"I can save you some trouble," a voice said, making me jump. "Buy the ones with the most sugar and trans-fat if you want them to get eaten. Buying the healthy ones only makes you feel better. The kids won't touch them."

Surprised, I looked up to see a woman with short dark hair, wearing scrubs, and pushing a cart half-full of groceries. She looked familiar, but I couldn't separate her face from the myriad countenances I had seen since I came to Holmes Crossing.

"Excuse me?"

She held her hand out. "Sorry to be such a know-it-all. I'm Leslie VandeKeere. We've met a couple of times, but you probably don't remember me."

"I'm sorry. I don't."

She waved it off. "No worries. You must have met over a dozen people already. It can be overwhelming. Trust me, I know." She laughed and pointed to herself. "Recent import. Still learning names and connections, and trying not to gossip about an aunt to her niece."

Then she grabbed a bag of sugary, chocolate-covered cookies off the shelf and dropped them in my cart. "Celia will thank you. And I absolve you of any guilt."

I laughed, enjoying her breezy manner. "That makes everything so much better."

Leslie settled her elbows on her cart, as if getting ready for a chat. "Have you gotten through all the food yet? From the funeral? I know my sister, Terra, said you were drowning in lasagna, soup, and chocolate cake."

"I froze a bunch of the casseroles."

"Good thinking. So, you getting settled in?"

I lifted my one shoulder in a vague shrug, hoping she would interpret it as a positive. I wasn't really 'settling in', so to speak, because I hadn't counted on staying here.

The thought hit me deep and hard, but I ignored it. Stick with the plan, I reminded myself.

"This must be difficult for you," Leslie continued. "Being stuck here and not knowing anyone."

"I've managed to keep myself busy," I said.

"It can still be lonely. So, in light of that, I was wondering if you would be interested in joining me at my sister's café. A group of us ladies usually meet there Monday mornings. I'm just coming off of night shift, and they're just coming off the Bible study, and you're welcome to join us."

I hesitated, not sure I would fit in with Bible

study ladies, but the thought of visiting with other women held an appeal.

"We're ordinary women," she continued. "All trying to find our way through Pinterest boards and Facebook lives." Her grin was infectious, and I figured, why not? Wasn't like I had a full social calendar.

"Sure. I can do that."

"I have to finish up, and I'll meet you there. Do you know where the Holmes Crossing Café is?"

"Just off Main Street, by the bakery?"

"You got 'er." She flashed me a smile, then grabbed a couple of bags of the cookies she had just put in my cart and put them in hers, then gave me a broad wink and left.

Ten minutes later, I parked on Main Street and was walking down the sidewalk, my shoulders hunched against the cold, head down in an effort to keep warm. A nasty wind was zipping down the street, swirling snow and knifing through my jacket.

I slipped into the café, shivering in the sudden warmth. In the far back, I saw a group of women gathered around a couple of tables they had pushed together. A few of them dandled babies in their arms, a couple of toddlers sat by the table, playing.

Then I saw Leslie wave to me, calling me over.

I took in a deep breath, then walked toward them, feeling a raft of second thoughts as I approached the group who, from the laughter and myriad conversations, all knew each other well.

"Girls, this is Miriam. Jerrod's sister," Leslie said as I joined the ladies, who all looked up at me with curiosity.

This created an immediate moment of silence, sympathetic faces, then murmurs of 'I'm sorry', 'so sad'. The woman closest to me, a heavyset young woman with long, red hair pulled back in a thick braid, caught my hand and squeezed. "That is the saddest thing ever," she exclaimed, then looked around at the rest of the girls. "Isn't it? I just cried when I heard about those two."

I tried to gently extricate my hand, but she would have none of it. "You just sit down here, girl. We're going to have a quick prayer for you."

I wasn't sure how to deal with this. Was it right to turn down prayer? But she pulled me down close to her in a one-armed hug.

"My name is Rita, by the way. You'll meet the rest of these lovely ladies in a minute." Rita looked around, her smile taking in everyone there as I sat down. "I know we've already prayed a bunch, but I think we could do this one more time?"

Everyone nodded, as if this was the most normal thing to do in a café. Rita caught my one hand and, as Leslie took the other one, everyone bowed their heads.

"Dear Lord, we don't know Miriam well, but You know her heart and her needs. You know she is hurting now. You are watching over her all the time. Be with her as she takes care of her niece. Give her strength and courage and mountains of love. Help us to support her with our prayers and a hug now and then."

Everyone muttered a low Amen and then, after a beat, the conversation began again.

"So I heard that my girl, Laine, had a great time at Celia's birthday party," Rita told me as she peeled the paper from the oversized muffin on her plate. "It was all she could talk about. Her favorite part was the sleigh ride. She said it was just like a Christmas card."

"I'm glad she had a good time."

"I'm a bit jealous," one woman said, setting her baby on her shoulder and patting its curved back, brushing a light kiss over its soft cheek. "Spending time on a sleigh ride with Holmes

Crossing's most eligible bachelor. And best-looking."

"Oh, Sandy. It's not like your Gerard is fish bait," one of the other girls teased.

"He's not. I think he's majorly hot, but he's not eligible, now is he?" Sandy returned with a sly wink. "And Duncan, with his rugged good looks, is."

I tried not to flush, thinking myself of Duncan's very appealing qualities.

"I imagine taking care of Celia has turned your life upside down," Rita put in, saving me from myself. "What did you do back in Vancouver? Did you work full-time? Has it been hard to get away? Have you lived there long?"

Her questions came at me hot and heavy, and Leslie muttered a gentle protest.

"Oh, you don't have to answer them all," Rita said, folding the muffin paper and setting it aside. "I thought I would give you a bunch to get things started."

"I work in a hotel," I said, trying not to think too much about my life in Vancouver. Last night, I talked to Christine, and she had gently probed as to when I would be back. Gillian, my boss was making noises about how long I'd been gone, too, saying something about being unsure how long she could hold my job. "As for what I do all day, somehow the days fill up."

"Don't they always?" Rita said, with a shake of her head. "That work without a name. If you ever need a break from your own company on Monday mornings, you can come and join us for Bible study. It's not hard stuff. Just women who love Jesus trying to figure out how we can serve Him and our families."

Her description made me smile. "That sounds encouraging."

"Have you been to Bible study before?" Rita continued.

"Please don't feel pressured," Leslie broke in, touching my arm. "I know when I first came I wasn't too comfortable with the idea."

I shot her a surprised look. "Really? I can't imagine that."

She must have sensed my surprise, because she gave me a smile. "We all have our own stories," was all she said. "All had our stumbles on our journey to God."

Which made me think of my own stumbles. I looked around this group of women and wondered if they would understand how gullible I'd been to believe Gregg's lies. Why I couldn't have caught the clues of his double life.

Just then a tall, slender woman, her hair a tumble of red curls around a faintly freckled face, came by with a pot of coffee. "Hey, sis," she said, nudging Leslie with one elbow as she filled outstretched mugs with the other.

"Terra, have you met Miriam Carpenter?" Leslie asked, looking up at her sister.

"Actually, it's Bristol," I automatically corrected, as Terra offered her free hand and I shook it.

"You're Jerrod's sister, aren't you?" Terra asked.

"I was his foster sister."

"Same diff. Family is family," she said with a grin that made me immediately like her. "Nice to meet you. Hope that you're managing through all this nasty stuff you've had to deal with. As Les—Duncan's partner—says, this sucks."

"Terra," Leslie reprimanded. "That's no way to talk."

"Les Greidanus may be a bit crude, but I have to agree with him. Poor little Celia. And poor you and Duncan," she said, giving me a sympathetic look.

Her pairing of our names gave me a start and created a flush of warmth that, I was sure, everyone noticed.

Then my cell phone rang, and with an apologetic

look I fished it out of my purse, the name on the call display sending my heart racing. It was the school.

"What's wrong, sweetie?" Rita asked, clearly not missing a trick.

"You can take it in the hallway down there," Terra said, pointing to a secluded spot just off the main area of the cafe. "I'll make sure you're not interrupted."

I shot her a grateful glance, then got up from the table, trying to ignore the curious expressions of the women watching me.

"Miriam here," I said, as I hurried to the place Terra had shown me.

"Sorry to disturb you, but I was wondering if you could come to the school." It was Miss Abernathy, the kindergarten teacher. My heart immediately went into overdrive.

"Is Celia okay?" I asked.

"She's fine. I think we need to talk face-to-face."

This didn't sound promising. What could have happened between me dropping her off only an hour ago and now?

"When do you want me there?"

"It can wait..."

But from the tone in her voice, I guessed it

would be better if I came sooner, rather than later.

"I can come right now, if that's okay."

"That would actually work well."

I said goodbye, my face hot, and my head pounding. I needed a few minutes to contain myself. Seriously, if all it took was a call from the school to raise my blood pressure then this being a guardian was certainly not for me.

And I was suddenly angry with Duncan.

He should be helping me with this, I thought.

I came back to the table to collect my purse and once again all eyes were on me.

"Everything okay?" Leslie asked, frowning at me.

"That was the school. I need to see Miss Abernathy."

"Oh, honey, that's no fun," one of the women said. "My son is in her class. She's a good teacher, but a bit dramatic."

That helped. A bit.

"We'll be praying for you," Rita said. "You're not alone."

As I hooked my purse over my shoulder I caught her words and held them a moment.

Not alone.

I felt an opening sensation in my chest. An expanding moment of happiness.

"Thanks. I appreciate that." I gave all the women a smile and received one from each in return.

"You just don't get pulled into the theatrics and you'll be okay," one of the women said.

"Take care," Terra said, patting me gently on the shoulder.

I nodded and left. But as I drove away, I couldn't help an inkling of dread.

CHAPTER 9

"$\mathcal{I}$'m sorry I had to call you in today, but we need to talk about Celia." I could see a tension around Miss Abernathy's mouth that told me today had not been a good day for Celia.

Or for Miss Abernathy.

We were sitting in the classroom, perched on the tiny chairs more suitable for five-year-old behinds than mine. Miss Abernathy was a petite thing, barely reaching five feet, so the chair wasn't a problem for her. I, however, was barely holding on to my perch.

The children were outside for their noon-hour playtime, which meant that Celia sat in one corner of the playground with Jane, ignoring her fellow students and the teacher on supervision.

"Is she okay? Has Jane been causing problems?"

As soon as the words popped out, I realized how they sounded. Like I was entering the same place Celia was occupying.

"I meant, has Celia taking her doll to school been a problem?" I corrected.

"Unfortunately, one of the boys was teasing Celia about her doll, and she lost her temper. She gave him a push and he fell down." She sounded so outraged I was tempted to ask if Celia had drawn blood with this 'push', but I knew how inappropriate this would be. I thought of what one of the women had told me as I left the café. Not to get drawn into the theatrics.

"How badly was the boy hurt?" I asked, trying to sound reasonable. This was a girl. Pushing a boy. Maybe not optimal, but hardly the rumble Miss Abernathy was making it out to be.

"He wasn't hurt. But he was very upset."

"I'm sorry about that—"

"This is the fourth time Celia has had an outburst, and that's just today," Miss Abernathy continued. "She had a number of them last week that Mrs. Lansing asked me not to discuss with you.

But I see an escalation I'm not comfortable with. And while I know Mrs. Lansing said we would deal with this step by step, I'm thinking, for Celia's sake, it might be better if she spend some time at home until Christmas."

A bubble of panic rose up at the thought of taking care of Celia every day. On my own until Christmas. It was hard enough doing this every other day.

"That seems a bit extreme," I said. "I mean, we're not talking about a teenager dealing drugs."

Miss Abernathy's frown told me that she didn't appreciate my feeble attempt at perspective. "I feel it might be best if Celia receive some quality time with you." Miss Abernathy continued.

"What about the counselor Mrs. Lansing was talking about? Has he or she been found yet? Any appointments set up? Maybe if we could start with that it might help Celia cope."

"I'm not sure. You'll have to discuss this with Mrs. Lansing when she's back. But for now, I think Celia would benefit from some time away from school."

"Do you want me to take her home now?"

Miss Abernathy seemed to consider that, then nodded slowly. "I don't want her to think that we are singling her out. That could cause some difficulty for her. However, we need to find a way to avoid potential for future outbursts."

"So that would be a yes." I couldn't help the sharp note in my voice. Too many words. Too much talking.

"Correct," she said, her frown deepening.

Thankfully, I didn't have any big plans for the day. I wanted to talk to a real estate agent about listing the property, just as a fallback. Then I spoke with Phil about some of the bills that had come up, and he had mentioned a recent claim made against Jerrod and Francine's estate by a contractor Jerrod had done some work for. And that he would need access to Jerrod's office sometime soon. But Jerrod's office was locked and I thought it would be better if Duncan asked Esther for the key.

Duncan again. He really needed to get more involved.

"Okay. Then I'll get her from the playground," I said, fighting down my frustration.

"I would suggest waiting until the children return and you take her then. It would create a better flow."

Whatever that meant.

I just nodded, my head growing tight as I tried

to visualize what to do with Celia all day, every day.

Then my cell phone trilled, and as I glanced at the screen I had further reason for dismay.

It was my boss. Gillian.

"Excuse me please. I have to take this," I murmured.

I connected the call as I walked out of the classroom and into the empty hall.

"Miriam. How are you doing?" Gillians's overly cheerful voice didn't cheer me. Her quiet demeanor hid a steely determination and a ruthless personality. Cheerful usually meant she was performing an unpleasant job.

"I'm okay."

"This must be a difficult time for you." She paused, but I wasn't sure where this conversation was going, so I let her take the lead. "I know you asked for four days off, and I don't need to tell you that we're well past that, now. I'm sure you can do math, too." Her forced laugh made me even more nervous.

"There have been some complications," was all I could manage past the growing constriction in my chest. It had taken me months of applications and rejections before I got this job. And I only got it thanks to Christine vouching for me. "In fact, I was hoping to call you and ask for a few more days. I was named guardian of my niece and the situation, well, it's complicated."

Please, Lord, please let her understand.

"So I understand from Christine, and I'm sympathetic, but you must realize I can't go this long without an assistant. You're a great worker and I've been thrilled with your dedication, but—"

And there it was.

"Are you letting me go?"

"I don't want to. That's why I wanted to check in with you." Her quiet sigh ignited the faintest spark of hope. "Tell you what. If you can guarantee me that you'll be back after Christmas, I'll hold your position for you."

Though I was thankful for the reprieve I didn't know if that was enough time. But neither would I tell her that. I know I was lucky to get this job. Gillian was an exacting boss, and because of my record we had an unspoken agreement that she expected me to prove myself worthy of her trust.

"Thank you so much," was all I dared say for now. "I really appreciate your kind consideration. I will try my best to make it up to you." I was careful not to lay it on too thick, but she needed to know I understood what would be waiting for me on my return. Longer hours and lesser pay. And I was fine with that. If it meant keeping this job.

She said a polite goodbye. I did the same and I ended the call with trembling fingers. I waited a moment to pull things together, then returned to the classroom just as the bell sounded.

One thing at a time I reminded myself.

But as the outside doors opened, letting in a blast of cold air and a herd of noisy, red-cheeked children, I knew what else I had to do.

Whether he liked it or not I had to get Duncan involved.

* * *

"IT JUST QUIT WORKING. Don't know why," Anton was saying, his too-large hard hat wobbling on a tiny head perched on a skinny neck. His coveralls overwhelmed his narrow body and he kept pushing up the sleeves.

"Seriously? You don't know why?" Duncan could only stare at his least-useful employee, as a nasty winter wind whistled down the cut block and right down the neck of his jacket. "I saw you ramming that skidder over that log deck even though I told you yesterday and the day before and the day before that to stop being so hard on the equipment. What did you think would happen?"

"It's a tough piece of equipment. It can take it." Anton's goofy grin made Duncan even angrier.

"No. It can't. Something's gonna give when you're always that rammy." His voice rose on every word, as the frustration he'd been pushing down the past week surfaced. He caught himself then took a breath as Les joined them.

"What's up?" Les asked.

Duncan jerked his chin toward Anton, not trusting himself to speak, his gloved hands clenched at his sides.

"Skidder broke down," Anton said, shifting himself to move closer to Les, as if he needed his protection.

"What were you doing when it happened?" Les was asking, thankfully taking over.

Duncan hunched his shoulders, frustrated with his own lack of control. He knew the value of keeping frustrations in check, something he learned from watching his father blow up every time something went wrong. But today, he felt as if he'd used up all his restraint. He felt as if stress was piling on his shoulders and he didn't know where to put it.

Stop clinging to what you don't need to carry.

So what didn't he need to carry? All this? This work that sucked more from him every day? Work that took up every winter for the past six years since he married Kimberly and discovered a part of her he hadn't seen before?

Kimberly had expensive tastes, which required more income, which necessitated more work. So, against his will and against his better judgment, Duncan had partnered with his father in a business he never cared for.

A business, which was almost giving him ulcers. But what could he do, now that his father was disabled and unable to run the business himself? And the irony of it was, it was working here, in the bush, that his father got hurt working an unstable log pile on a snowy day.

He fell, the logs rolled and he got pinned.

Now he was in a wheelchair and Duncan was going crazy.

"Duncan? Are you with us?"

Les' voice broke into his spinning thoughts.

"Sorry. Other things on my mind." Duncan adjusted his own hard hat, wishing he'd put on a toque. His ears were freezing.

"I get that," Les said giving him a sympathetic

look, which quickly faded as practicality took over. "So what do you think the problem is?"

Les and Anton were looking at him as if he had all the answers. And suddenly it was too much. "I don't know. What do *you* think?" His question came out harsher than he intended, but he didn't care.

"Okay. Fair enough," Les said. "I'm thinking hydraulic hoses."

"Then start with those." He was about to say something more when he heard Will, one of the truckers, calling his name just as his cell phone rang.

He glanced at the phone, frowning at the unfamiliar number.

"Tell Will to wait," he said to Les. "I've got to take this call."

He had no clue who was on the other end, but right about now, even talking to their lawyer, Phil, about Jerrod and Francine's tangled estate was preferable to dealing with one more breakdown, or slow down, or question.

"Duncan here."

"Sorry to bug you at work."

Curious how the sound of Miriam's voice could immediately lift him from his funk.

"That's okay. What can I do for you?"

"I need to talk to you."

Take a number, he felt like saying, but he didn't, because talking to Miriam was preferable to anything else right about now.

"I just came back from the school," she continued. "Celia's teacher asked if we could keep her home from school until Christmas."

"What? Why?" The snow squeaked under his heavy boots as he made his way to the lunch trailer parked farther down the logging block, trying to suppress his disappointment.

What? You thought she called to tell you she missed you?

"Apparently she's been causing problems in school," Miriam was saying. "I'm not going into details on the phone, but Duncan, I need your help with this."

"What can I possibly do?"

He stepped into the trailer, shedding his grease-stained jacket one-handed, and grabbing his Thermos to pour himself a cup of coffee.

"I can't keep taking care of Celia on my own. I'm sorry, but you need to be more involved."

He stopped in front of the large map hanging on the wall, laying out the cut blocks for the logging season. They were supposed to have five done by now, but instead, were still working on number three because of added restrictions placed on them by the company they logged for.

Frustration wrapped relentless fingers around his gut. This business was grinding him down. Never caught up. Never on top of things. Always pushing reluctant employees, fighting inflexible deadlines, and trying to keep swimming against a relentless flow.

Now this.

"I don't see how I can help. My parents can't, and Esther is still in school."

Between his parents and Esther pressuring him to get involved with Celia, he felt like he was getting shoved into a place he had been fighting tooth and nail to stay far away from. He thought he would have been done after the birthday party, but apparently, it had only given Miriam a taste of what she might be able to expect from him.

"I understand that you're busy and you have work," she continued. "And I'm truly sorry, but I can't do this on my own anymore. This is too much for me." The desperation in her voice created another surge of guilt. How could he be too busy to take care of his own niece?

He dragged one hand over his face, trying to shut down the chattering in his brain.

"Can you give me a day or two to figure

something out?" Maybe he could talk to Esther. Have a family meeting. If they wanted him to take on the responsibility of Celia, they would have to help.

"Of course. I'm sorry, I know I shouldn't have called you right away, but I needed to talk to someone." Was it his imagination or did he hear a break in her voice?

He heard Celia calling in the background, and a flicker of pain licked at his soul.

"It's okay," he said. "I'll...I'll figure something out to get you some help."

"Thanks. I should go. Jane is hungry." She released a light, wry laugh, which made him smile, but also raised other concerns about his niece's mental well being.

"We'll talk later," was all he could say, and then she ended the call.

He slipped his cell phone in his pocket, looking once again at the map and all the work it represented. He thought of the sacrifices he'd made so Kimberly could have the life she wanted and so his father's legacy could carry on.

And what was the point? His father was in a wheelchair because of this business, and his wife and daughter were gone.

Stop clinging to what you don't need to carry.

The door of the trailer opened, letting in another gust of chilly wind.

"Problem solved," Les was saying. "It was a hydraulic fitting that blew loose."

Duncan pulled himself into the present and the difficulties he had just been dealing with. "Thank goodness for small miracles," he said. "I thought we'd need to run in for parts, the way he was driving that thing."

"So, what's your problem?" Les asked, peeling his gloves off and tossing them aside as he poured himself a cup of coffee. "You're grumpier than usual."

"I know. I'm sorry. I'll apologize to Anton in a minute." Duncan dropped into a chair and eased the kink in his neck.

"No need. Guy needed a bit of an attitude adjustment, anyway. Doesn't hurt to put some fear into him. So, what was your important phone call about? Did our part for the generator come in?"

"No. That was Miriam. She needed help with Celia."

"So you're going, right?"

"Are you kidding? There's no way I can go."

"You should. She's seriously hot."

"Stop talking like that."

"Well, she is, and you should spend more time

with her. You liked her once before, why not see where it goes this time? Besides, when's the last time you were on a date?" Then he snapped his fingers. "Wait, I know the answer to this one. Never."

Duncan turned back to the map. "Near as I can figure, we'll be done this block by the end of the week. Maybe we'll get caught up by Christmas, if we can keep the guys motivated."

"I don't know why you're pushing to get more production."

"Skyline is talking about issuing a few more blocks. If we get these done, we can get first dibs on them." But even as he spoke he felt a clutch of futility.

"And why would we want to do that? We're on tap to make more than we did last year, which is more than we made the year before." Les sat down across from Duncan, tilting the chair back on two legs. "What's your deal?"

"You know what my deal is. I want to get the company debt paid down."

"And then what?"

"Just keep going." He had never thought too much past that. When he partnered with his father he discovered that his father wasn't a very good manager and the company owed way too much money. But now that Duncan had taken over the operation, paying down the debt was a real possibility.

If they could keep up the production at the levels Duncan had expected.

Les rocked his chair back and forth, his gaze holding Duncan's.

"You sound beat, man. What's going on?"

Duncan leaned forward, his elbows resting on his knees as he swirled his coffee around the stained mug that held the words *Sawdust is Man Glitter*. He had gotten the mug from Les when he started working because, according to Les, everyone needed their own mug at coffee time.

"Drank a lot of coffee out of this mug," he murmured, taking another sip of the lukewarm brew as he sidestepped the question.

"Swapped a lot of stories, too."

Duncan set the mug aside then he sighed, reality dropping on his shoulders like a stone. "You asked what's going on. Trouble is, I don't know. I'm tired. I don't know why I'm doing half of the things I do. I feel like I'm on some kind of hamster wheel. Working to keep my dad's business going, and I don't know why. I don't have a wife. I don't have a kid—" he stopped himself from going down that dark hole in time. "Seems pointless."

For a moment, the only sound was the muted growl of equipment outside the trailer.

"You know it's only been a couple of weeks since your sister died," Les said, his voice quiet. "You haven't taken any time off. Not really."

"I did on Friday."

"Hardly a day off. Packing around a bunch of kids on a sleigh. That can't have been fun."

Duncan thought of the few moments he had shared with Miriam that day. "I wouldn't say that," he muttered, setting his mug aside.

"I think you need a break. Take a week. Just kick back. Things are going fine in spite of that fake deadline you've got us under. Maybe if you take some time off you won't be such a grouch." Though Les was smiling as he said the words, Duncan heard a veiled warning in his partner's voice.

"I'm sorry. I know I've been touchy. I shouldn't have blown up at Anton like that."

"You already apologized, and it's not that big a deal, but it's not you. You're not the cranky partner. That's my job. Look, you lost your sister and your brother-in-law, and I know there's a bunch of crap to deal with because of that. Take some time off. I've got things under control here."

"I suppose I should catch up on the books," he said, pushing himself up from his chair.

"And see if you can give this Miriam chick a hand," he said. "How hard can that be?"

Harder than you think.

"I'll think on that."

Then Les got up and dropped a hand on his shoulder. "Just go. For Anton's sake, for Will's sake. For mine."

Duncan chuckled at that, then nodded. "You're right. I need to give everyone else a break, too."

He grabbed his mug and rinsed it out in the sink, setting it on the wooden shelf with the other mugs. And as he stepped out of the trailer he saw Anton's skidder driving out to the block. A bit slower than usual, so that was a plus.

It would be okay, he told himself as he got into his truck. Everyone could manage without him for an afternoon. He'd talk to Miriam, but first he was stopping at the café.

Then, as he drove away, he was surprised at the feeling of relief he felt. And, even more surprising, that the guilt he also felt wasn't even enough to stifle it.

CHAPTER 10

*T*he smell of fresh Saskatoon pie wafted through the café as Duncan dropped into a chair by the window. The café was almost empty this time of the day, a fact that Duncan had been counting on. The only other customers were a couple of older women sitting in one of the far corners.

Helen the other waitress was chatting them up, her hands planted on her ample hips, her gray bobbed hair swinging as she laughed at something one of them said.

"Well, well, what brings you to town today?" Terra stopped by his table, dropping a laminated menu in front of him. Her auburn hair was pulled back in a ponytail, and with her black turtleneck and black pants, she looked more like an undertaker than a waitress.

He didn't need to feel guilty at her question. Les had told him to take a breather, but old habits were hard to break.

"I'm taking the afternoon off."

Terra dropped her hand on her chest, her eyes going wide with fake shock. "What? Duncan Tiemstra is slacking off?"

"I'll be doing books," he protested. "Later. I didn't have lunch, so I thought I'd come here."

She gave him a patronizing nod. "Of course. Good choice. What will you have?"

"Soup, grilled-cheese sandwich, and some of that pie for dessert."

"We'll start with the soup and sandwich, and if you eat all your crusts, you can have some pie," she said with a smirk.

"Thanks, Mom," he returned, cupping his chilled fingers around the mug of coffee, inhaling the comfort that floated through this café. It was like another home to him. He released his breath, as if shedding his edginess.

The bells above the door jangled, and two older men came in, stamping snow off their boots and shedding their coats. One man wore fluorescent-orange suspenders, straining over a green shirt tucked into faded khakis. He looked like an escapee from a construction crew. His companion wore a priest's collar and dark slacks.

Father Sam and Cor DeWindt. Jack's father.

Cor saw him, waved a greeting and headed directly toward him.

"Hey, Duncan. How are you doing?" he asked.

"I'm good."

Cor looked directly at him, his expression one of disbelief. "Aren't you usually in the bush right about now?" Cor asked.

Again, he had to push down the self-reproach. "I'm taking the afternoon off."

"That's great. Good idea," Cor said, pulling the chair beside Duncan away from the table and dropping into it. "You work too hard."

"Are you sure Duncan wants company?" Father Sam asked, hesitating.

"Of course he does," Cor said. "Sit down. Maybe you can squeeze a confession out of him."

"That's not how it works," Father Sam said with a wry note, as he did exactly what Cor suggested.

"So, this has been a hard time for you," Cor said, folding his arms over his chest, leaning back in his chair. "Now, tell me how you are really doing."

Duncan shrugged, weariness washing over him, and suddenly, he was tired of hiding and faking it. "I'm exhausted," was all he said.

The door of the café opened again and Cor, with his indefatigable curiosity, turned to see who it was.

Perfect, Duncan thought taking another sip of his coffee as Jack paused in the entrance, looking around. The gang was all here.

"Over here," Cor called out, and with a quick nod of acknowledgment, Jack ambled over. His twill shirt and blue jeans showed that he was off-duty today. As he sat in a chair beside Duncan, Terra arrived with Duncan's lunch.

"Hey, my dearest man," Terra said, dropping a quick kiss on Jack's lips before delivering Duncan's food. "Miss me already?"

"Helen texted me that the Saskatoon pie was almost ready," he said, grinning up at her.

"So it's all about the pie."

"Only reason I married you."

She flicked her hand over the back of his head, then turned to Father Sam and Cor. "The usual?"

"Not if you're making Saskatoon pie. I'll have some of that, instead," Father Sam replied.

"I'm sticking with lemon pie."

"You old Calvinist you," Father Sam mumbled. "Torturing yourself with tartness."

"What about your sugar levels?" Jack asked.

"Stop fussing, you old hens." Cor shot them each a sharp look.

Duncan grinned at the give-and-take, suddenly not minding the company.

"You here because you had an equipment breakdown?" Jack asked, resting his elbows on the table, looking sideways at his friend.

"Taking a break."

Jack looked as surprised as Terra did.

"What? A guy can't take a break from work?" Duncan asked.

"A guy can, but that guy isn't often you," Jack returned. "But hey, this is a good thing. You should do this more often."

"I did on Friday." Duncan shook some salt in his soup. "Took Celia and her friends for a ride in the sleigh. For her birthday."

"That's good, too. You work too hard."

"I don't work any harder than anyone else." Duncan didn't feel like rehashing the conversation he'd had with Les. He bent his head and started eating.

"Actually, not true," Jack said. "You work in the

bush all winter and then you hustle all summer
with the cows and the haying."

"I like the cows and the haying," Duncan
muttered.

"There's something idyllic about that," Father
Sam put in. "I can understand."

"Not much idyllic about logging," Cor added.

"And you know this, how?" Father Sam asked.

"I did it for one season. Noisy and busy, and
too much equipment to break down. And you
only have a few months to get everything done.
No, thanks." Cor pointed to the fat, heavy flakes
of snow gathering on the vehicles parked in front
of the café and the sidewalk. "Plus, you have to
deal with all of that. Every time it snows. And the
cold and the hassles."

"I sense you didn't enjoy your stint working in
the bush," Father Sam said with a grin.

"Not as much as I liked working for the Van-
deKeeres in the summer."

Duncan finished his soup, while Father Sam
and Cor discussed the merits of running cattle
versus logging and how hard it could be to do
both. The casual dissection of his life sounded
depressing.

"What do you have planned for the rest of the

day?" Jack asked as Duncan started in on his sandwich.

Duncan thought of Miriam and her plea for help and pushed the thought aside. Later. He told her he would deal with it later.

"I've some paperwork to do."

"I thought you hired an accountant to do your books?"

"I have to actually bring in the books for her to do them and I haven't had time to get the receipts and bills together."

"So do that today."

"I don't need more advice," he snapped then immediately felt bad. What was wrong with him?

Cor and Father Sam stopped talking, glancing over at Jack and Duncan.

"Sorry," he said, feeling really low. That was twice in one day. "Too much going on."

"Of course there is," Cor said. "You've been pushing yourself way too hard the past few years."

"I've just been working."

"You've been going like a banshee ever since Kimberly died. It's like you've been trying to fill the emptiness in your life."

"I don't think Duncan needs a psychoanalysis of his life, Dad," Jack warned.

"Probably not," Cor said with a shrug. "But sometimes the truth needs to be told."

"Maybe not in a coffee shop," Father Sam said. "With other people present."

"You sound like you agree with him." Duncan turned to Father Sam.

"You don't need my advice." Father Sam gave him a gentle smile. "But I can offer you my prayers. I think you've had some difficult things fall on your shoulders, the past while."

Somehow his words hit him harder than Cor's admonitions did.

"I'm thankful for the prayers," was all Duncan could say.

"It's a small thing, but God knows what you need."

"And speaking of what you need, now you've got your niece to take care of," Cor put in. "And I think that could be a good thing. Maybe help you get over the loss of your own little girl."

"Dad. Seriously. Stop. Now." Jack's voice held a slight edge.

"What? That's some big secret?"

Jack gave Duncan an apologetic look and a shrug, as if telling Duncan that he had tried his best but it was out of his hands.

"It's no big secret," Duncan agreed. "But I don't

think taking care of Celia will help with...getting over what I lost."

"Maybe not, but it could give you some purpose."

"I have a purpose. I'm currently taking a break from it."

"That's not a purpose," Cor snorted. "That's a burden, and I'm pretty sure you would agree, if you thought about it long enough."

Jack sighed his frustration with his father, but a small part of Duncan, the part that slithered into his mind whenever work stress felt over-whelming, did have to agree. His work was a burden that grew with each loss in his life. And now, with his sister and brother-in-law gone, fu-tility dug its relentless claws even deeper.

"It keeps me busy," he muttered feeling like he had to make a last-ditch defense.

Cor lowered his voice and leaned forward. "Trust me, my boy. You can't out-busy sorrow. Sometimes you need to face it."

His words seeped into his soul, and the sorrow Cor accused him of outrunning crawled up his throat.

Thankfully, Terra came at that moment with Cor and Father Sam's pie, and he had a momen-tary reprieve.

"So Duncan, enjoying the company and the advice?" Terra asked, clearly not missing a beat, as Cor picked up a fork, thankfully now occupied.

"It's…stimulating," was all he said, as he handed her his empty bowl and plate.

"I'm sure it is. And I see you ate your crusts, so you get pie." She turned to her husband. "More coffee?"

"Sounds good."

"Coming up."

The easy smiles they exchanged made Duncan envious of their easy relationship. He knew Terra had a hard past. But thankfully, she and Jack had found each other, and as Terra's hand gently and unobtrusively stroked Jack's arm, he wondered if he would ever find the same.

"Boy, it's sure coming down out there," Terra said, glancing past them through the large, plate-glass window. Duncan glanced outside just as a woman and young girl hurried past.

Then, the bells of the café jangled again, and he felt a mixture of guilt mingled with happiness when Miriam and Celia stepped inside.

Miriam brushed the snow off her coat, flakes sticking to her thick, wavy hair. Her cheeks were an attractive pink, and her eyes bright. As she tugged Celia's toque off, the little girl's blonde curls bounced on her shoulder, her rosy cheeks enhanced by her red sweater. Celia held up Jane and Miriam removed her toque and coat as well, handing the doll back to Celia and stroking down the girl's mussed hair. She made it all look so easy and so natural, and when she gave Celia a warm smile, his heart constricted.

Then she looked around, and when their eyes met, her smile shifted and faded away.

There he was, she must be thinking. The big disappointment.

"Dunkle," Celia cried out, finally spotting him. She raced toward him, her eyes bright, clutching her doll under one arm. She reached their table and then stopped, frowning at Jack. "Jane says you're in my way," she announced.

"Celia, I don't think that's the way you should talk to people," Miriam said.

"Jane said it," Celia said, still looking at Jack.

"Doesn't matter who said it, we need to be more polite." Miriam's voice was firm, but Duncan caught a glimpse of weariness in her expression.

"Please excuse us," Celia said, still clutching Jane.

Jack stood up and Celia wiggled past him, her good humor restored.

"Can I please sit on your lap?" she asked, holding one arm up, fully expecting him to comply.

He swallowed, wondering once again why this girl was so attached to him, when he had done so little to encourage her.

But when he lifted her on his lap, he felt a melting deep in his soul. Then, in spite of the pain in his heart, he slipped one arm around her to anchor her fast.

"My name is Cor, by the way, and this is Father Sam, and my son, Jack," Cor said to Miriam, taking over the conversation.

Duncan's own throat was thick, heavy with fluctuating emotions, and he didn't trust himself to speak as Celia laid her head on his chest, her hair tickling his chin.

This little girl. His niece. So close to Tasha in age.

And yet, he found that each time he saw her, she became more Celia and less a reminder of his own little girl.

* * *

I LOOKED AROUND THE GATHERING, nodding at each introduction. Then Jack got up and grabbed a chair, pulling it close so I could join them. An automatic protest rose to my lips, but I caught myself in time. I had only come to the café because I promised to give Celia a treat, and she insisted on a milkshake at the café. I'd had no intention on barging in on anyone else's coffee time.

"Well, here you are again, Miriam." Terra stopped by the table with a pot of coffee to refill mugs. "You must really like it here."

"It's the pie," the man named Cor said.

"Would you like some?" Terra asked.

"Just coffee." I wasn't hungry after my morning adventures. "Celia, do you still want a milkshake?"

"Jane wants a milkshake," she insisted, shaking her doll to make her ponytail bounce. A ponytail I had spent an inordinate amount of time putting in.

"Strawberry, vanilla or chocolate?" Terra asked.

"Jane likes pink," Celia announced.

"Strawberry it is." Terra cleared off the empty pie plates, and then left.

The café was quiet this time of day, but already it felt familiar. It should, I thought. Twice in one day. No wonder Terra had given me a funny look.

"So, Miriam, how are you doing?" Cor was asking, his expression intent, serious. "Are the people of Holmes Crossing being good to you?"

"Very much so."

"I'm sure you've had a lot to deal with the past while." Cor put a gentle hand on my forearm. "You need to know that we pray for you. And for Duncan."

More prayers. Was that all the people here in Holmes Crossing did?

"Thank you," I said, very sincerely. "I do appreciate that."

"So you and Duncan are responsible for this little girl," Cor continued. "That's an interesting situation."

"Okay. Dad. Now you really have to stop." Jack turned to me. "My father has a problem with boundaries, and I apologize for that."

I waved off his comment. I actually wouldn't have minded following through on the subject, but I guessed, from the frown on Duncan's face, this wasn't the time or place.

"And why is this little girl not in school?" Cor continued. He turned to Jack with a questioning look. "I'm allowed to talk about that, right?"

Jack just rolled his eyes, which made me chuckle.

"I don't like school," Celia said from the safety of Duncan's arms. "Jane doesn't either. But now I can't go back until after Christmas," Celia continued.

"Why not?" Father Sam asked.

Celia sat up, looking up at Duncan. "I pushed Bradley Holwyk. He was fighting with me and yelling and talking mean to my doll—to Jane. I got mad and shoved him away, and now I'm a bad girl."

I was about to protest her comment when Duncan laughed, which was hardly an appropriate reaction. "Don't worry, Celia. Bradley comes from a long line of yellers," he said. "Didn't his dad used to try to push you around?" Duncan directed his question to Jack, who shrugged.

"Tried. Failed," was his concise reply.

"His brother wasn't any better." Duncan turned to Celia. "Did you start the fight?"

"No. He was following me around," Celia said matter-of-factly. "And he wouldn't leave me alone."

"Then you did the right thing." Duncan held my surprised gaze and grinned at my muffled protest. "If she walked away and he followed her, she had every right to deck him."

"She hardly decked him," I protested. "More like a push."

"She should have decked him."

I wasn't sure I liked the way this conversation was going. Certainly not with Celia present. On the way to the café I had talked to her about controlling her anger. I'd seen my biological mother's temper too many times and seen the havoc it created. Though I knew the underlying cause of Celia's anger, I also knew her genetics. And it made me nervous.

"I'm sure you would tell her to turn the other cheek," Duncan said to Father Sam, a faint gleam in his eye.

"I'm supposed to be impartial, but I think there are times when it's better to give to a Holwyk than to receive," Father Sam said.

This elicited chuckles all around, and started Cor on a story about his own experience with a member of this Holwyk family, which reminded Jack of a story that he subsequently related.

Terra came by with Celia's milkshake and another round of coffee, good-naturedly grumbling about the campers at table eight. No one seemed inclined to move, however, and, truth be told, I was content to stay and listen to the stories. All that waited at home was more work, and with Celia around, I would have to hold that off.

Plus, I needed to check in with my boss. A conversation I preferred to hold off on as well.

"So, Miriam, we've been rather rude," Father Sam was saying, leaning forward and smiling at me. "Sharing stories of Holmes Crossing. I understand that you live in Vancouver. How do you like living there?"

I glanced around the table, uncomfortable with being the center of everyone's attention. "Um, I like it. Though it's rainy season in Vancouver, now. Not the best weather."

"That's Vancouver," Cor said with a shake of his head. "My sister lived there for five years. Came that close to a nervous breakdown." He indicated how close with his finger and thumb an inch apart.

"Are you sure it wasn't this close?" Duncan said, reaching over and pushing Cor's fingers closer together.

"Smart aleck," Cor returned.

"And what do you do there, if you don't mind my asking," Father Sam asked, ignoring both Duncan and Cor.

"I work for a hotel. In the administration department." That was a bit of a stretch, but somehow, with Duncan watching me, I didn't want to say that all I did was help the floor manager do her job. Nor did I want to say that I was borderline unemployed.

"Nice that you can take this much time off to take care of your niece," Father Sam said.

I simply nodded, not sure I wanted to embellish my small evasion in front of a priest.

"Miriam also works as an illustrator," Duncan put in. "She's done a couple of children's books. Celia has them."

He said that with a touch of pride that surprised me.

"Really? That's intriguing," Father Sam said

"I haven't done that for a while," I said. At least with this I could be straight up.

"Why not?"

So much for straight up, I thought as I dug around, looking for a diplomatic way to avoid telling him the less-savory details of my detour in life. I tried to avoid thinking about it at all.

"I needed to make a living," I said, looking down at the mug of coffee that Terra had just refilled. "A person doesn't make that much as an illustrator, and I had bills that needed to get paid."

Legal bills and damage deposits and living expenses while I tried to find an employer willing to hire me with my record.

Which made me think of Gillian and the axe hanging over my head.

"That's too bad. Do you think you might ever go back to it?"

I shrugged, thinking of the sketches and watercolors Christine insisted I try and sell. "I'm not sure. I think I would need to be inspired."

"And what better place to be inspired than Holmes Crossing?" Cor asked, pointing out the window to the snow collecting, softening the green of the spruce trees in the park across the street, the old brick post office flanking it on one side, and the brick façade of the Co-op on the other. "I bet that's prettier than the rain you'd be seeing in Vancouver right about now."

"It is pretty," I agreed. And he was right about the rain. Though this would have only been my second winter in Vancouver, I hadn't been looking forward to the overcast skies and the steady drizzle that I'd experienced last year.

"Well, now that you're taking care of Celia, are you settling down here?" Cor asked. "This is her home, after all. Her grandparents and her uncle all live here."

"Again, Dad, not our business," Jack said, a

stern note in his voice that seemed to surprise his father. "Especially considering who is here." His head tilted toward Celia, but his eyes were on his father as he sent a wordless signal.

Thankfully, Cor caught the hint and gave me an apologetic smile. "Sorry," he whispered.

"I think Holmes Crossing is a good place," I said, cradling my mug. "My brother seemed to think so. I'm sure that's why he moved his family back here."

Unwittingly, my eyes cut to Duncan surprised to see him looking at me. For a moment our gazes held, and I read confusion in his eyes.

As if he agreed, but didn't know what to do about it.

"And Celia, I heard it was your birthday a few days ago," Cor turned back to Celia. "Did you have fun?"

"Jane and me went on Dunkle's sleigh," Celia murmured, finger-combing Jane's ponytail. Then she sat up, grabbing Duncan by his chin. "You said at my birthday party that you would give me a ride on your horses. Can I do that now? I don't have to go to school."

"I have to ask your Aunt Miriam first."

He shot me a look of entreaty, as if he hoped I would help him out.

"You know, I think that's a fabulous idea," I said. "I can go back to the house, get some warmer clothes and we could meet you at your place. It could be an adventure."

"So, today?"

"No time like the present," I said, keeping my tone light, joking, knowing he couldn't weasel out of this commitment. Not with witnesses.

But as my eyes held his I felt it again. That frisson of awareness and connection that seemed to tremble between us.

Neither of us looked away, and for a moment I felt as if we were the only people in the café.

Be careful, a warning voice told me as I finally jerked my eyes away, my cheeks warming. *You are treading a fine line.*

I knew it, but at the same time I didn't have much choice. If I wanted to get Duncan more involved, I would have to work alongside him.

It's all for Celia, I told myself. I can do this if it means Celia will end up in a safe and secure place.

I just had to make sure to guard my heart.

CHAPTER 11

*T*his was a mistake. This was a mistake.

Duncan repeated the words over and over as he drove back to his place, wondering how he had gotten roped into taking Celia riding at his place.

A little girl who made him feel guilty, that was how.

He rolled his neck, trying to ease a growing tension, still struggling with the idea that he was here and Les was managing his operation in the bush. Trying to figure out what he was supposed to do to help Miriam with Celia, both of whom were slowly worming their way into his life.

He used to be able to compartmentalize the

parts of his life and store it in little boxes. Keep it all separate.

But since Francine and Jerrod's deaths, he felt as if the boxes were coming apart and things were bleeding into each other.

He pulled himself back to the moment, focusing on thinking about which horse Celia would ride.

Maybe Abby. She was his old faithful. A bit of a plug.

He parked the truck and walked through the snow that had fallen since he left this morning. He grabbed the snow shovel standing beside his back door and made quick work of clearing a path. Tonight he'd have to start up his tractor to clear the yard.

Back inside the house, he re-stoked the wood stove and did a quick man-clean of the house. He shoved everything on the counter into the dishwasher. Bread and toaster went in a cupboard. Books and magazines were gathered and dumped in the oversized ottoman that Kimberly paid way too much money for. He gathered up the laundry he'd been planning on putting away and dumped it on the unmade bed in his bedroom.

This is why the good Lord made doors, he told himself as he left the room.

He shot a critical glance over the house, trying to see it through a woman's eyes. Kimberly always accused him of not being able to see the mess.

She was probably right, but he couldn't see anything else that needed to be done.

Just in time, too, he thought, as he heard a vehicle pull up. He grabbed his coat and walked down the walk, waiting until Miriam shut off her SUV. He opened her door just as she reached for it, which netted him a puzzled smile.

"Aren't you the chivalrous one?"

"You've met my mother," he said matter-of-factly.

Her smile grew, and the gleam in her eye showed him that she knew exactly what he meant.

"I should help Celia," she said, sliding down out of the vehicle.

He half-hoped she would lose her balance so he could help her again, but she was fairly nimble and managed to slam the door shut and stride around the SUV in the snow and not slip once.

Too bad.

Celia sat in her booster seat, dandling her doll on her lap. Then she glanced over at him, and her serious expression was blasted away when she grinned at him. "Dunkle."

And, as always when she called him that, he tried not to cringe. Whenever she used that name, he imagined some twinkly-eyed, jolly man with a beard who whittled toys out of wood and kept candies in his pocket.

And yet, the nickname was oddly endearing.

"Hey, Celia."

"Where's my horse?" she demanded, as Miriam unbuckled her seat belt and helped her out of the vehicle.

"I just got here, Miss Demeanor," he said with a gruff laugh. "Give me a few minutes."

"I'm not Demeanor, I'm Celia," she said, missing his joke.

But he saw Miriam grin. She was his target audience, so he was happy.

And now you're trying to entertain the ladies.

He pushed the thought aside, and waited as Miriam reached into the vehicle and pulled out a bag. "Food," she said, when Duncan shot her a puzzled glance.

"You think I don't have any?"

"Whatever you have, I can see you and raise you six casseroles," she said. "I figured I may as well share the wealth if I'm getting you to help me."

"A bachelor never says no to food," he said as they walked down the shoveled path toward his house.

Celia danced ahead of them, bouncing like a kangaroo, clearly happy.

"She seems perky."

Miriam nodded, but Duncan could see that she looked troubled. "She is now," she said.

"Much as I know you probably don't like the idea of her not attending school, it might end up being a good thing for her."

"It might," Miriam agreed. Then she shot him a solemn look. "But like I said, it will mean I need more help from you. I haven't had a chance to talk to Mrs. Lansing yet about setting up an appointment with a counselor so for now, it's you and me and your family. And, hopefully, eventually, just you and your family."

Duncan held her gaze her words creating another feeling of unease. "One of these days you need to tell me exactly why you won't take care of her."

"It's not that I won't," she said, stopping as if to gather her thoughts.

"So what is it?"

"I can't give her what you and your family can." Her eyes cut to his house as if to underline her defense. "I can't give her a place like this. And I don't think it would be fair to move her away from here to Vancouver."

It all sounded so practical but still a part of him wanted to protest. "She hasn't lived here that long," he said, still trying to marshal his own arguments. "I don't think she's that attached."

"Really? She calls you Dunkle. She goes directly to you every time she sees you. You're the one person she doesn't talk to through that crazy doll of hers. She's crazy about you."

Each one of her comments landed and clung. "I don't know why," he muttered. "I haven't encouraged it."

Miriam's expression softened. "And I understand why you don't want to be with Celia. And..." She eased out a sigh. "You may not want to hear it again, but I'm sorry for what you lost in your past. But this is the present. Celia has lost much, too. Right now she needs you. Besides, her grandparents are here," Miriam continued, as if she needed to make it abundantly clear why he needed to do this. "The more time I spend here, the more I know I'm right. She has family and community here, all things I can't give her. Plus, she barely knows me."

"I got it," Duncan said. "But I still don't know how this will work."

"We'll take it one step at a time," Miriam said as she started walking back to the door. "Usually the best way to make major life changes."

"You're wise," he said giving her a crooked smile.

"I've learned my own life lessons the hard way," she said.

Again with the oblique reference that he wanted to find more about, but Miriam had opened the door to the house and was going inside.

When Duncan joined Miriam in the porch, he spotted Celia's boots and coat in a heap on the floor. Miriam bent over to pick them up just as he did. Their hands brushed each other. Duncan yanked his hand back, then felt immensely stupid as he did.

Miriam stopped at the island and set the casserole on it, frowning as she watched Celia, who had plunked herself down on the floor. She was chatting with her doll, her voice animated.

"I can't get over how happy she is when she's here," Miriam said. Then she turned to Duncan, her expression concerned. "She doesn't sleep well at home. Most every night she sits hunched on her bed and cries."

"About what?" Duncan asked.

Miriam shrugged. "She just says that it's noisy. One time she said something about Aunt Esther making her angry and that was why she couldn't sleep. But I have no idea what that was about."

"I can't figure why she'd think it's noisy. The house is far from town. It's quiet as the grave."

"In more ways than one," Miriam murmured and Duncan realized how unsuitable his comment sounded.

But Miriam was already walking toward Celia. She bent down and said something to the little girl, her voice low. Then she reached out and brushed her fingers lightly over Celia's hair.

Though Miriam's arguments against taking Celia back to Vancouver with her were difficult to dismiss, he still felt Miriam was exactly the right person for Celia. She was obviously attached and clearly knew what to do with her. He sensed there was a deeper reason she didn't want to take Celia but assumed Miriam wouldn't give up her secret easily.

"Are we going riding now, Dunkle?" Celia

asked, her eyes suddenly bright as she jumped up and ran toward him.

"I have to get the horse ready."

"Can Jane come too?"

"As long as she doesn't scream and scare the horse," Duncan said, playing along.

Celia chuckled and shook her head. "Jane can't scream, silly."

Duncan thought of what Miriam had told him about.

"I'll head outside," he said, taking a step back. "I'll come and get you when I'm ready."

"Do you need a hand?" Miriam joined them, slipping her hands in the back pockets of her blue jeans. The gesture made her look young and vulnerable, and as she tossed her long hair over her shoulder, he felt a nudge of sympathy for her and the situation his sister had created for her. "Celia and I can help."

"I think I can get one horse ready."

"Just one?"

He caught her surprise. "Yeah. For Celia. I'll be leading her."

"Oh. Of course." She sounded disappointed.

"Did you want to ride, too?" He felt a moment of surprise. None of the women in his life were the least bit interested in horses, let alone riding.

"Sorry. I just thought..." she let the sentence slip away and he guessed he was right.

"I can easily saddle one up for you as well."

She waved off his offer. "You'll be leading Celia and I'll just get in the way."

"I can saddle one up for me as well. It's no big deal."

She shook her head and he wanted to offer again but figured this could go on all afternoon. "Okay, meet me outside in about fifteen minutes by the barn."

"Sure."

He could see her smile was forced, and he was tempted to offer again. He wanted to erase the faint disappointment she had tried to hide.

And as he walked to the corral, he figured he would just go ahead and saddle a couple more horses. He could lead Celia and they could ride all together.

* * *

THERE WERE three horses tied up by the corral.

As we came nearer, the snow squeaking under our feet, a small flash of excitement flickered through me. I was going riding, after all.

When Duncan had said that he was just saddling one horse, I knew that this trip was strictly for Celia, but I had nurtured a secret hope that we would all go riding.

Now it looked as though my wish was happening after all, in spite of me trying to be all polite.

Duncan was tightening the cinch on the last horse as we came near. He looked up, his eyes shaded by his cowboy hat, but not his smile. And my previous flicker hummed into a faint glow.

This guy...

Was trouble, I reminded myself. I couldn't get distracted. My focus was Celia, not flirting with this ruggedly handsome cowboy.

"This one is for Celia," Duncan was saying, as he pointed out a dark-brown one. "Her name is Thistle."

"Not a promising name," I joked, deflecting my ever-changing feelings around this guy into lame jokes.

"She's called that because she was born by a patch of thistles. I spent weeks pulling leftover prickles out of my legs and arms after we found her." This netted me another lazy grin, which only served to stoke the glow.

"She's beautiful," Celia said, her voice full of

the awe that young girls everywhere seem to hold for horses.

"I'll help you on." Duncan reached down for her.

Celia wasn't light, but Duncan grabbed her by the waist and settled her on the animal as if she weighed no more than thistledown itself.

"Just hold onto the saddle horn," Duncan advised as he helped her feet into the stirrups.

"That's a little saddle." I was surprised that it fit her so well.

"Used to be Francine's." A light note of melancholy tinged his voice, and I felt an answering thrum of sympathy.

"I imagine we'll keep bumping up against that over and over," I told him, brushing his arm in a gesture of empathy.

He released his breath on a sigh that echoed my own sorrow. But when he looked at me I saw something else in his haunted expression. Something that hinted at a deeper pain.

"Are you okay?" I asked.

But he simply shrugged off my question, patted Thistle, and looked up at Celia.

"You feeling good up there?"

She nodded, and the wide grin on her face made me thankful we had decided to do this. She looked happier than she had since I first saw her, eyes bright and cheeks already pinking up in the chilly winter air.

"I'll help Aunty Miriam on her horse, and then we can get going," Duncan said.

Celia nodded, one mittened hand on the saddle horn, the other clutching the ever-present Jane.

Duncan ran his hand over the horse's rump as he walked to where another one was tied up, next to Thistle.

"This one is Abby," he said, pointing to the palomino. "Climb on and I'll adjust the stirrups."

"She's awfully large," I said, a thread of concern tightening around my chest. I had ridden before, but I was sure the horses at my foster mother's farm were a lot smaller.

"She's older, but steady."

So, trusting in Duncan's judgment, I lifted my foot up to a stirrup that seemed to be at least at chest height, got my foot in, reached up for the saddle horn, and tried to launch myself as discreetly as possible. I had no intention of scaring this huge creature.

But my underdeveloped thighs couldn't make the leap and I fell back, foot still in the stirrup, hands slipping from the saddle horn.

I was ready to try again but then Duncan grabbed me by the waist and lifted me up. The unexpected help surprised me, and with the extra momentum I was nearly launched over the other side. Thankfully, I managed to catch the other stirrup with my foot and recuperated quickly, catching the saddle horn and settling in, feeling all cowgirly and pleased I hadn't made an idiot of myself.

"Sorry. You're lighter than I thought." Duncan gave me an apologetic grin. "At least the stirrups are the right length."

"Good guess. Was this Francine's old saddle, too?"

Again, a shadow slipped over his face. "No. It belonged to my wife."

"Sorry. I didn't...didn't think..."

He waved off my apology, then untied the horse and handed me the reins. "Doesn't matter. She didn't use it much." Then, before I could dig myself in deeper, he walked over to his own horse, tied up beside Celia's. In one easy motion, he swung himself into the saddle, settled in, leaned over, and took the reins of Celia's horse.

His horses stood quietly, ears flicking but not moving at all and my fluttering nerves settled into anticipation. It had been years since I'd ridden. And even though there was a winter chill in the air, the sun in the blue sky above brightened the day and gave a sense of warmth.

"Everyone ready?" Duncan asked, turning to look from Celia to me.

"Let's go," Celia said, kicking Thistle in the ribs. My heart jumped, but Thistle didn't. She simply stood there, seemingly oblivious.

"Maybe don't kick her, sweetie." Duncan spoke quietly, but his deep voice held a firmness that made Celia stop immediately.

"Sorry, Dunkle," she said, hanging her head.

"I forgive you. And so does Thistle. She knows what she has to do." This was accompanied by a faint smile, then with another glance my way, he clucked to his horse, turned it with one hand, and we were off.

The horses' hooves squeaked over the snow as we walked out of the yard, around the corrals then through an open gate.

"I thought we would ride through this field and then through the trees along the river," Duncan called out.

"Sounds good," I called back, as if I had even the faintest clue what he was talking about.

"Is my horse a girl or a boy?" Celia was asking, rocking with her horse's movements.

"A girl," Duncan replied.

"Has she had babies?"

"A few."

"Do they live here, too?"

"No. Some of them are at VandeKeere's place and I sold one to another family for their little girl." This was spoken with a gentle smile and their interaction gave me hope.

The rocking motion of the horse, the warmth of her body, and the bobbing of her head as she walked lulled me. I felt a peace suffuse me and drew in a large, satisfying breath.

Then coughed as the winter air chilled my lungs.

The snow was up to the horses' knees out here in the pasture, but they didn't slow down, and as we walked I saw our tracks from the time we took the sleigh.

Another memory to store away when I left.

The thought dug like an icicle in my soul.

I let my eyes wander over the open fields, rimmed by trees, the blue sky like a bowl above us. The utter quiet, broken only by the swish of the horses' hooves in the snow, or the occasional question from Celia, eased the stresses of the past few years. I looked over at Celia.

My daughter.

Why couldn't I stay?

The question snaked its way through the fortress I had put around my heart since she was born. A fortress I had been building brick by brick since Jerrod told me to stay away from Duncan because he was too good for me.

This I knew but to hear it from my own brother cut me to the core. When I met Duncan I allowed myself possibilities. But deep down I knew Jerrod was right.

I looked away from Celia, my emotions in flux. Every minute I spent with her, every minute I crouched beside her as she cried silently in her room, every moment I caught a flash of joy in her eyes, every errant smile slanted my way—I felt her presence encroach in my life.

And I started to really think I could be a mother to her.

I looked past her to Duncan—solid, broad, his hat pulled low on his head, his hair hanging below. He looked at ease with his horse as he led Celia's.

It was an apt metaphor, reminding me of Duncan's life, which was such a sharp contrast to mine.

Family.

Alone.

Connected.

Untethered.

"We'll be heading down the trail ahead," Duncan called out, pointing with a gloved hand to the break in the dark line of spruce and pine trees. "Then it's just a short ride to the river trail."

I simply nodded.

"You okay?" he asked, still looking back.

"I'm fine," I said with a casual wave of my mittened hand. "How about you, Celia? How are you doing? Are you warm enough?"

I couldn't read her expression but she nodded and I saw Duncan grant her a faint smile.

He was the right person for her. I had to trust my brother's judgment. Jerr obviously knew me better than I knew myself. Knew what I had lived and experienced. The poor choices I'd made.

The trail closed in as we entered it, the light of the sun, hanging winter-low in the sky now diffused by the forest we entered.

"It's like magic," Celia said her voice holding a tinge of awe as she looked around the branches frosted by sparkling snow. "Like a princess land."

I had to agree, the chill of breeze in the open field gone in the shelter of the woods. I couldn't stop looking around, feeling the same wonder that Celia did.

This place was amazing.

I wanted to capture it. Translate it to lines and colors on paper.

We rode a little farther, and then the trees opened up, and suddenly we were on the edge of the world. Trees fell away, a green and white carpet down to the frozen river below us. The white field on the opposite bank flowed toward treed hills that created a large, open valley.

Duncan reined in his horse, and mine came up beside his. I pulled gently on the reins, and Abby thankfully stopped. "Those fields on the other side of the valley belong to my family as well," he said, pointing across the river.

"What do you do with them?"

"It's rich, river-bottom land, so we crop it. Last year it was canola, this year we'll be doing wheat."

"Wow. You really are a Renaissance man," I said. "Cowboy, logger and farmer."

He shrugged off my comment as if it were inconsequential. "I like to keep busy," was his laconic reply. "You still okay, Celia?"

She nodded, her eyes shining, her cheeks pink with the cold. Her toque had slipped off to one side, and her coat wasn't zipped all the way up, but her grin warmed my heart. And every doubt I had about bringing her here was erased.

Duncan was leaning forward, his forearm resting on his saddle horn, his hat pushed back on his head. A smile played over his well-shaped lips. In profile, sitting on that horse, his eyes narrowed, creating a fan of wrinkles at the corner of his eye, he looked even more appealing than he had before. He looked peaceful. At one with nature. And my own foolish heart gave another, heavy, thump of appreciation.

Then he looked over at me, his blue eyes meeting mine. For a long moment neither of us looked away.

This is getting dangerous. You can't let yourself be pulled into this. This is not your place. This is temporary.

I dragged my eyes away, forcing myself to look at Celia. Then she, too, glanced over at me, and her smile dove into my heart.

The two of them were a force that threatened the very foundations of my life.

"We should get going," I said, turning my horse away. I had no clue where I was going so I had to depend on Duncan getting the heavy hint.

Thankfully, he did, and we rode on.

But I felt that I had, for a brief and wonderful moment, been offered something amazing.

Something I couldn't accept.

CHAPTER 12

"You horses did good today," Duncan said, dumping a forkful of hay over the fence for them.

Abby just munched on the hay and Thistle snorted, as if to tell him that this was all in a day's work and nothing to get all sentimental about.

Trouble was, he did feel sentimental. And a few other things as well.

Spending the afternoon with Miriam on horseback, his favorite place to be, had put him in a good mood.

And Celia?

He tested the thought, as if touching a bruise. To his surprise, having her around today hadn't brought back the same sorrow it did the other

times he'd seen her. It was as if the steady expo-
sure to the little girl showed him that she was
simply Celia, a young girl, lost and alone.

But take care of her? Could he do it?

He shoved the fork into the hay bale and took
a moment to rub Abby's nose, smiling as she
dropped her head over the fence as if asking for
more.

"So what do you think of Miriam?" he asked,
lifting her head. "She's pretty enough, isn't she?"

Abby tossed her head as if in agreement, and
Duncan eased out a sigh.

"And why am I asking you?"

Because he wasn't about to talk about
Miriam with Jack or, worse, Les, or any of his
fellow workers. He knew exactly what they
would say.

Go for it. She's a catch.

The words weren't as easy to dismiss as they
might have been a few weeks ago.

You cared for her once.

And she brushed me off then, too.

He pushed the fresh snow off the rail fence
and leaned on it a moment, watching the horses
as they ate, baring their teeth at any of the others
if they came too close to their particular pile.
They had their pecking order well established,

and guarded it with bites and kicks if there was any hint of incursion.

His mother had, at one time, accused him of doing the same. Keeping people away, especially other women, to guard his heart. To some degree it might be true, but what his mother didn't know was that it was more complicated than that.

He drew in a deep sigh and pushed himself away from the fence. Miriam and Celia were waiting in the house.

As was the casserole Miriam had brought. Maybe she would join him for dinner?

Warning bells pealed at the thought, but in spite of them, he hurried his steps over the snow-covered drive and up the walk to the house.

Inside, warmth enveloped him, and right behind that came the teasing scent of supper cooking.

He shivered, shaking the snow off his coat, then hung it up.

Miriam's worn boots sat neatly beside Celia's, and the sight gave his heart another hitch. It looked the way the porch of a house should look. Other people. Other boots and coats.

And it would have been that way, had things been different.

He sent up a quick prayer for strength and

stepped into the kitchen.

Miriam was bent over by the open oven door, poking a fork into a dish inside the oven. She straightened when he came in. "I was just heating up the casserole for you. Thought that was the least I could do before we leave."

"Thanks. I appreciate that."

Her cheeks were flushed, some of her hair had slipped from the complicated braid she'd twisted her hair into, and her smile created a crimp in his heart. "The horses okay? You seemed to be out there awhile. I was waiting to say goodbye."

Just needed to get myself centered.

"Had a few other things I needed to do," he said, glancing past her frowning. "Where's Celia?"

"She was playing on the couch, but then she went upstairs. I hope that's okay."

"I guess." The idea that Celia was up in the bedroom didn't bother him as much as it did the first time.

Baby steps, he figured. Slow incursions into protected places.

He paused at the kitchen island as Miriam tucked her hair behind her ear and set the oven mitts she'd been wearing on the counter. "So you're leaving?"

It was on the tip of his tongue to ask her to

stay awhile. Stay for dinner. The thought of eating by himself, though he had done it countless times before, suddenly seemed depressing and pathetic.

"I should go. Celia needs to get to bed on time. I'll get Celia, and then we'll be out of your hair." She walked around the island, and his feet seemed to move of their own accord, taking him closer to her. She stopped as well, and for a breathless moment, they stood facing each other. Expectation hung between them, and Duncan's breath quickened. He wanted to touch her. To connect.

She didn't look away, either, and then before he could stop himself, his hand lifted, touched her cheek.

He saw her throat work as she swallowed.

Did he imagine her leaning in?

But then she lowered her eyes, took a step back, and walked away from him and up the stairs.

He pulled his hand over his chin, trying to get himself back to center. Miriam was leaving. He felt he had to remind himself of that.

And you've got your own stuff.

He busied himself, tidying up the living room, waiting. But Miriam didn't come down. A few more minutes passed and then, curious, he went upstairs.

He found them in Tasha's room.

As his eyes adjusted to the gloom his breath quickened and his heart began a slow, heavy thudding. Miriam was crouched on the floor beside Tasha's bed.

And Celia was sleeping in it.

No. This was wrong. No one slept in that bed.

He wanted to hurry over and snatch Celia out of the space that had been his daughter's.

His breath caught in his chest as he calmed himself. It was just a bed. And Tasha was gone.

He clenched and unclenched his hands, composing himself as Miriam glanced back.

"She won't wake up," Miriam said.

He swallowed down another knot of pain as he came closer, looking down at Celia sprawled out on the bed, her one arm curled around her doll, the other laying stretched out, palm up.

And he remembered what Miriam had told him the last time they found her here in this room. How poorly Celia slept at her home. She looked so peaceful and he knew he couldn't wake her, no matter how much it bothered him. She had as much right to be there as his memories did.

"It's okay. She may as well sleep awhile," he said.

"Maybe if you carry her down the stairs?" Miriam asked, giving Celia another shake.

"Let her sleep. I'm sure she can use it." And from the dark rings under Miriam's eyes, she looked like she could, as well.

For now, however, he was hungry, and the tantalizing scent of the casserole was wafting up the stairs.

"If she's sleeping anyway, you may as well stay for supper."

"The casserole won't be ready for half an hour or so," she said.

"Then let's sit downstairs and wait. If she wakes up in the meantime, then you can leave."

She looked at Celia, as if hoping she would magically get up, then nodded and got up. As he followed her down the stairs, he felt a flicker of anticipation. It had been a long time since he'd had female company for an evening.

Slow down. She's only here because Celia is sleeping.

"I'll check the casserole," he said as they came to the bottom of the stairs. "You go sit in the living room."

When he came back into the room, Miriam

was standing by the wood stove, her arms crossed, and a frown furrowing her brow.

"May as well sit down. It's not done yet," he said.

She gave him an awkward smile, then dropped onto the couch by the stove, tucking her legs under her.

Duncan looked over at his recliner, but knew if he sat down there he'd be asleep in minutes. The love seat was covered with books of parts for the buncher and limber. The only place left to him was the other end of the couch.

Would it look weird if he sat down there?

Stop overthinking this.

So he dropped into the opposite corner of the couch, and put his feet on the coffee table in front of him.

The silence was surprisingly comfortable, and he eased out a sigh.

"Thanks again for the horse ride," Miriam said, wrapping her arms around her knees. "I enjoyed it."

"I'm just glad the horses behaved," he said.

Another moment of silence followed, punctuated by the sound of wood snapping in the wood stove.

"This house? How old is it?" she asked, looking

around the large, open room.

"My Uncle Bert built it but I'm not sure exactly when. He and Aunt Amanda moved away about five years ago."

Miriam nodded. "Do you have any other family here?"

"My mom used to be a Greidanus so we're tied in with that family. Jim Greidanus is my cousin."

This netted him a puzzled look from Miriam.

"Jim. He's married to Kathy. They've got two kids. They were in church on Sunday, sitting a couple of pews ahead of us? He's tall. Reddish hair. She's got this short, spiky, black hair and a bunch of studs in her ears. Sat by Leslie and Dan and their kids."

"I've met Leslie but I don't remember Jim and Kathy."

Duncan laughed. "Sorry. I've lived here so long I forget that when new folks like you come to town, you don't actually know everyone like the rest of us do."

"Nope. I don't speak Holmes Crossing," she said with a wry grin.

"Anyhow, Jim's brother, Lester, works with me in the bush. If that helps. And I can see from the growing confusion on your face it doesn't."

"Drawing yet another blank."

"Les is my partner. We've been working together for years now."

She nodded, her intertwined fingers locked around her knees as she looked back at the stove.

The silence fell again between them, the fire snapping and crackling in the stove. Duncan got up and tossed another couple of logs in, closed the door and sat down again.

Miriam was chewing at her lower lip, her frown even deeper as she watched the fire through the stove's tempered glass window.

"What's wrong?" he asked.

She looked up at him, and then shook her head. "Nothing. It's just...nothing."

"Doesn't look like nothing. You look sad."

"I was just thinking about Jerrod." She caught the corner of her lip between her teeth, resting her head on her jeans-clad knees, strands of hair slipping around her face. "I still can't believe he's gone."

His own heart gave an answering pang. "Were you close?" he asked, preferring to talk about her sorrow. His brought out too many other memories.

"At one time we were. But since Celia...well, since they adopted Celia, I haven't seen a lot of him. I wasn't around much, mind you, but over the past year we'd been texting and emailing more. I was hoping to see him more and now..." Her voice trailed off as she fought back a yawn.

"And now you can't." Duncan rested his head against the back of the couch, weariness pulling at him, creating a fuzzy feeling in his head. Her yawn triggered one of his own. "I know what you mean. I had a fight with Francine just before she and Jerrod went out. Before she died." He released a mirthless laugh. "Can't believe that's the last thing she heard from me."

"What did you fight about?"

Duncan stifled another yawn, his jaw cracking with the effort. "Them going on that snowmobiling trip. I thought it was irresponsible for them to do something so risky. They weren't familiar with the mountains and just got those high-powered machines. The one time in my life I didn't wish I was right."

"If it's any consolation, I thought it was irresponsible, too, and if I had been able to talk to Jerrod before they left I would probably have said the same thing."

Her response made him feel somewhat better.

"Francine was fairly emphatic," Duncan said. "She told me that she had to do this. That it was important for her and Jerrod to do this together,"

Duncan said. "Would you know what she meant by that? Did Jerrod say anything to you?"

"I didn't know they went out on this trip until I was told they'd died."

He had hoped she might have been able to help him. Ever since Francine threw that statement out at him, a hint of desperation in her voice, it had stayed, skulking at the edges of his thoughts, making him wonder if he shouldn't have pushed harder.

"The last year, I got the feeling that things hadn't been that great between them," he said. "Maybe she thought the trip would help." He rubbed his eyes, fighting down the weariness washing over him.

"Francine struck me as an intense person. Am I right?"

He wondered what triggered the question.

"Actually, yeah. She could really lay it on when she was ticked about something. Never really held back."

"Jerrod is…was the same way." Miriam sat up, pushing her hair back from her face, her expression suddenly intent. "Were she and Jerrod having difficulties in their relationship? Is that what she meant when she said it was important for her and Jerrod to take the trip?"

"Could be. But I didn't visit a lot with them after they moved here. I meant to. It just didn't happen." He could still feel guilty about that as well. "As for the difficulties, I'm not surprised. I'm sure they overextended themselves. Once the lawyer finishes settling the estate, we'll know for sure."

Duncan didn't want to think about the repercussions of that situation. The last time Phil spoke to him, he'd said that a previous partner of Jerrod's was making a claim against the estate for work he had done and not been paid for. On top of that the insurance company had been balking at paying out, given what Francine and Jerrod were doing when they died. Which meant that the house might need to be sold to pay the mortgage off.

"Just trying to put some things together," Miriam said. "Celia hasn't been sleeping well at night. She's always talking about voices. How noisy her mommy and daddy are. That they keep her awake. I'm just wondering if Jerrod and Francine were fighting in the house, and if Celia was hearing that."

Duncan frowned, trying to process this. Put it together with what he knew about his sister. "Esther's made some comments about Francine too.

What a witch she could be. How she didn't appreciate Jerrod enough and was always making ridiculous demands. I just thought it was jealous sister stuff. Esther and Francine didn't always get along, which made it seem kind of weird when she got all excited that Francine and Jerrod were moving closer. I thought it was because of Celia."

"I don't want to put down people who aren't here to defend themselves, but I just want to figure out what's causing Celia to sleep so poorly. I wonder if some friction between Jerrod and Francine could be the reason."

"Well, she's sleeping really well here."

Miriam gave him a smile that slipped too easily into the empty and lonely spaces of his life. "And for that I'm thankful. I know you're not comfortable with the idea of her in your little girl's...the bed," she hastily amended. "I don't know why she decided to sleep there—"

"Maybe she knew her mother slept in it."

"Francine slept in it?"

"That bed has been in the family for years. My dad's father made it for him. My dad slept in it, as did my Uncle Bert. I did, Francine and Esther did, as well. Francine asked for it when they adopted Celia, but Kimberly and I had counted on using it for..." He stopped a moment, his throat thickening, but he swallowed and pushed through. "We figured on using it for Tasha." The memory brought about the familiar ache and sorrow, and he struggled to push it down.

"I think it's amazing to have an heirloom like that," Miriam said, her voice quiet. "I'm sure...I'm sure it was hard for you...to see it empty."

Her voice held such a plaintive note that it created an answering twang in him. It was as if she understood exactly what he was dealing with.

He would have asked more, but he was hanging on to his own control by a thread.

It was the situation, he told himself as he fought to regain his equilibrium. Alone with an attractive woman who seemed to genuinely understand what he had been dealing with. The fire, the low lights, the smell of supper in the oven all combined to create an intimate atmosphere.

A sense of home.

He shifted to get up, to create a distance between him and Miriam, when he felt her hand on his arm.

He swung his gaze to her, curious.

"I never met your wife or little girl, but I'm sorry for you. Sorry for the emptiness I'm sure you've had to deal with."

The melancholy tone in her husky voice, her

trembling smile, the way her eyes seemed to drift into his soul all wore at his already flimsy defenses.

"It was a while ago," he managed.

"But not enough to lose the pain. Three years isn't that long ago."

Duncan expelled a harsh sigh. "You're the only one who doesn't think so. I keep hearing that I have to move on."

"To where?"

"Exactly. Especially hard to find a place to go when I feel like God has abandoned me."

"It's hard to see His hand in our lives when we're stuck in the dark and can't see ahead."

He acknowledged her comment with a tight nod.

"But I know from my own experience that no matter how large the turmoil in my life, God is larger than that," she continued. "And that even though my life didn't turn out the way I thought it should, I could still feel God's provision. His care."

"That's quite a confession to make," he said. "I wish I could share your conviction."

"It's not mine," she said, resting her chin on her knee as she glanced beyond him, as if looking into her own past. "The conviction comes with the reality that though my life may change and be tossed around, God is still faithful. His love endures. He's the only constant in my life."

The certainty in her voice caught his attention as much as her words did.

"You really believe that," he said, his own empty soul longing for what she had.

"I do. And I think, deep down, you do as well. I know you were raised as a Christian. It's hard to walk away from a relationship with Jesus once He's been a part of your life."

"It's not as much a matter of walking away as figuring He just doesn't care."

"He's never promised us a life without problems," she said, turning her sincere gaze back to him. "This is still a sinful world. But He does promise that we can count on God's extravagant love for us. He knows loss and pain. He went through it, too."

Silence followed that statement, and Duncan felt a stirring in his soul. An old desire for an old relationship with the God she spoke so easily of.

"Tell me about your wife and daughter," she said, suddenly, tilting her head to one side, the gesture inviting his confidences. "Tell me about Kimberly and Tasha."

Miriam spoke softly, as if recognizing how

carefully she had to ask.

Duncan was about to shake off her probing and leave the memories buried.

But a sudden and unexpected weariness dropped on his shoulders. He had been fighting down thoughts of his family for so long. He looked over at Miriam and caught the sympathy in her look. Caught a puzzling shimmer of tears in her eyes.

And he sensed here was someone he could confide in.

* * *

IT WAS the haunted look in Duncan's eyes that made me gently prod and push.

I wanted to talk to someone who knew. Who understood the loss of a child.

"Kimberly and I were high school sweethearts, though we'd known each other most of our lives," Duncan was saying, laying his head back against the couch, his long hair framing his rugged features, a bright contrast to the dark leather. "We'd dated since we were in grade ten. We were a walking cliché. I was on the football team. She was a cheerleader." He gave me a brief wry smile. "Except I was something like third-string running back, and she was just a backup. But we figured we had it all. Even went to prom together."

I sat back against the armrest of the couch, wrapping my arms around my legs, listening to Duncan's story with a mixture of envy and curiosity. To have been so settled in life that you married someone you knew so well. To be so ingrained in a community.

What was that like?

As he spoke, his features seemed to take on a curious hardness. As if he was still fighting his own emotions.

"She got a job here, and I helped my dad on the farm with a plan to take it over. Had life all figured out. But we had a huge fight." He emitted a harsh laugh. "She wanted to move. I wanted to stay. So we broke up. Then Jerrod and Francine got married, and I met you…"

"So I was the rebound," I said with a light laugh though the thought bothered me.

He grabbed my hand, squeezing it as his eyes delved into mine. "No. You weren't that at all. I was genuinely attracted to you. You were fun and easy to be around. I thought you felt the same but…" Then he shook his head, pulling his hand away, breaking the momentary connection. "I guess that wasn't meant to be, either."

His words made my heart hurt. I wanted to explain, but knew that meant revealing more than I was ready to.

"Anyhow, I got back together with Kimberly at my mom's urging. Then Tasha was born, and I discovered a whole new meaning to the word love."

I couldn't stop the stab of jealousy. The 'what ifs' that had often plagued me when Jerrod had texted me after the wedding. Warning me away from Duncan. Telling me that maybe I wasn't good enough for him.

What if I hadn't believed him? Would I have answered Duncan's texts? Would I have ended up not dating Gregg and getting caught up in the mess of his life?

I thought of Celia, sleeping soundly upstairs, knowing that she would never have been born.

And I wouldn't have experienced the bitter-sweet pain I was feeling now.

I pushed my feelings down, looking back at Duncan. "What was Tasha like?"

"She was a sweet little girl," Duncan replied. "I know all fathers think that, but she really was. Slept easy. Ate everything. Cute as a button..." Duncan's voice cracked a moment, and I wondered if I had pushed him too far.

But I could tell from the way his face softened that the memory wasn't entirely unpleasant.

And behind that came a look of relief.

"She had thin, sandy-brown hair that stuck out in every direction. Kimberly kept trying to twist it up into ponytails or pigtails, but it would always slip out." He gave a choked laugh. But he took a breath and continued. "She was such a ragamuffin. Never clean. My mom was forever buying these cute dresses for her, but she always found a way to get them dirty or ripped. She was clumsy too."

"Do you have any pictures of her?" Though I tried not to appear nosy, I didn't see any in the usual places. Living room wall, mantle above the wood stove.

"A few. Mom and Esther took them down after the funeral. I let them, because I didn't want to be faced with the loss."

"Do you know where they are?"

"I think they're in my bedroom. I haven't gone looking."

I understood. After I let Celia go, Jerrod and Francine didn't send me pictures. I didn't want to see her growing up without me. Much easier to pretend she was still this tiny infant that I held for a few, brief seconds before she was taken away.

Duncan closed his eyes and drew in one shuddering breath, then another.

My own loss blended with sympathy for this man and before I could stop myself I moved closer and put my hand on his shoulder.

To my surprise his other hand came up and covered mine with his own.

"Sorry. I haven't talked about Tasha much. My family...we don't talk about our feelings." He opened his eyes and his haunted look wound icy fingers around my own wounded soul. "And now we're doing the same with Francine and Jerrod."

"You've never talked about Kimberly or Tasha?"

"My parents, especially my mother, prefer to deflect. Detach. They're good people," he hastily added, his voice husky. "They just don't talk about feelings or emotions." He drew in another breath and gave me a forced smile. "I get it. I don't like it either."

"Because it hurts and we don't like to face hurt. We don't like being vulnerable or out of control."

"You sound like you understand."

"I've had my share of things I'd sooner forget,

but I know loss."

"What have you lost?" He didn't look at me, his face still looking upward, but his hand on mine kept the connection warm. I felt my secret hovering, waiting to come out. I wanted to tell him. Lay my claim on my daughter.

But if I did, he wouldn't take Celia. I knew it. He seemed like an honorable man. And, knowing he was avoiding his own pain by keeping Celia at arm's length only made it harder to give him another reason to.

"Every time I went to Jerrod's house I lost a part of my biological mother," I said instead, deflecting the question to a situation I thought he would accept. "She would leave me abandoned and I would call 911 and I would lose a bit more of her."

"That must have been hard."

"I spent a lot of time crying in Sally's arms. My foster mother always said that each grief has its quota of tears. They will come out one way or the other and that I may as well get them out of the way."

"I have hardly cried since Tasha...since..."

I saw his Adam's apple shift up and then down as he swallowed, and for a moment I regretted pushing him to this moment of confession.

He pressed the heel of his free hand to his head, hiding his face and when he lowered his hand I saw moisture at the corner of his eyes.

He pulled his hand off of mine, scrubbing at his face as if hoping to stop whatever I had started.

"Sorry," he managed, leaning forward, his face buried in his palms, elbows planted on his shaking knees. He was quiet a moment, then he lifted his face, looking out over the living room. "I know I said I haven't cried, but I didn't feel I had the right."

"What do you mean?"

"The day they died...Kimberly and I had a fight. Things had been difficult for Kimberly ever since Tasha was born. I had just taken over the logging business from my dad. I was trying to make a living for us. It made me busy and stressed. I spent long days away from home, so it seemed like all I was doing was working, fighting with Kimberly who never had enough and sleeping. She wanted to move and knew I wouldn't so she started spending money. Then, one morning, before I left for work, Kimberly told me that we needed to talk. I didn't have time. I'd had an equipment breakdown the day before, and we were behind..." He released another harsh laugh.

"Seems like the company was always lagging." He sucked in a quick breath. "Anyway, I brushed her off. Told her we'd talk that night. Then…then at noon, I got a call. There'd been an accident, and Kimberly and Tasha—" He stopped there, his hands clenched on his knees.

He didn't need to say anything more. His head and shoulders lowered as if the burden of the sorrow he'd been secretly carrying was pulling him down.

"It was my fault," he whispered. "I should have listened to her."

"What do you mean?"

He pulled in a shaky breath. "She came from a wealthy family and was used to nice things. I knew she wanted this house to be bigger. I know it's not a palace, but I thought it was okay." He looked around his home as if apologizing for its shortcomings.

"I think it's cozy. Welcoming."

He gave me a smile that wavered. "Thanks. But Kimberly was right. It did need some work. But what she wanted to do cost money." He stopped, waving his comments away. "I shouldn't talk like that. I should have taken the time to listen to her. Really listen to her. If I had maybe…maybe…"

Then his voice broke again, his hands clutched his head and a sob burst forth. Then another.

His sobs were deep and wrenching, bursting out of him. The ugly crying of a man in the depths of an unthinkable grief.

My heart folded in sympathy. I had cried those tears. Had carried that burden.

But my daughter was still alive. Sleeping in his daughter's bed.

I couldn't stand the harsh sound of his grief any longer. I shifted closer and slipped my other arm around his broad chest, wishing I was larger, stronger, so I could hold him up.

His arms caught me close and together we supported each other as his body shook and tears flowed.

Hearing the cries of this burly man was devastating and soul shattering. It upended everything in my life. To see such strength become so weak made me have to fight my own tears.

Slowly, his tears subsided, as I knew they must. Sorrow had its ebb and flow, and as his receded I could feel him relaxing. Spent by the emotion.

"I'm sorry," he murmured as he drew away. "I shouldn't have—"

"I'm not," I said, the connection we had just

shared tearing away any boundaries between us. "I think you needed to do this."

He closed his eyes, his tears glistening in the half-light. "I don't like feeling this weak."

"Nobody does," I said, taking a chance and reaching out to stroke his hair. To try and give him some small comfort. "Is this the first time you've really cried since your wife and daughter died?"

He shifted, moving away from me slightly, but he kept his one arm around my waist, as if keeping himself anchored.

"Not like this." He breathed in slowly, then released his breath as if expelling his grief with it.

"Raw grief is never pretty," I said, remembering my own tears shed after I gave up Celia. How lonely I was. Until I started attending a Bible study. And I found a faithful God who carried me through.

Duncan drew in one last shuddering breath and then pulled completely away. I felt a moment of loss as he straightened, swiped at his eyes and sniffed.

"So will this make things better?" he asked, a hitch in his voice.

"No. But it will help you move on the path to healing."

"Sounds airy-fairy to me," he said, giving me a tremulous half-smile.

"We women specialize in airy-fairy. That and delusional flights of fancy on unicorns." The moment had been so heavy, so hard, I needed to lighten the atmosphere.

"I can't see you believing in that," he said, his smile strengthening, settling on his well-shaped lips.

The low lights cast his face into intriguing shadows. Highlighted his strong features. Made his eyes glow.

"I didn't believe in unicorns. My mother did," I said, fighting my sudden breathlessness.

"Sally?"

"No. My biological mother. She believed they were magical and would someday come and whisk us away to some imaginary fairy land where everything would be better." I wasn't able to keep the bitter tone out of my voice.

"When we first met you said she was dead?"

"When I was sixteen. I remember hoping that Sally would adopt me, but by the time I turned eighteen, I was on my own anyhow."

"You sure have had your own sorrows," he said, his hand suddenly resting on my shoulder.

He didn't know the half of it.

"Everyone has," I said. "Everyone's life has its share of grief. Difference is, I shed my tears along the way."

"Did you really?"

Then, to my shock and dismay I felt my own eyes filling at his piercing question.

"And you're shedding some now," he said, touching my cheek.

I wasn't going to look at him. We were both in such a vulnerable place. And yet, I couldn't stop my head from turning, my eyes from meeting his.

He didn't look away, and I wasn't sure if it was my imagination or my own lonely heart, but it seemed to me that an awareness arced between us, tangible as a touch.

The moment trembled as time seemed to slow and old emotions blended with new.

He moved his head a fraction as he caught my hand in his callused one, then he brushed a kiss over my fingertips. I touched his lips, tracing their shape, feeling their warmth.

Then, as if it was as natural as breathing, we each moved closer. I slipped my arms around his neck, he caught me by my waist.

I felt as if I had been holding my breath for years, and was finally able to release it. As if all the emptiness in my life was filled in this moment.

Our breath mingled, his face grew indistinct, and then our lips met. Warm, soft, inviting.

His mouth moved over mine, I slipped my hand through his hair, anchoring him as he pulled me against his hard, broad chest.

Our kiss deepened, lengthened. I felt a curl of warmth, deep in my soul. And for the first time in many years, I felt a sense of coming home.

He kissed me again and then, slowly we drew away as if to regroup and examine.

He slipped his rough finger down the side of my face, his eyes following its delicate path, as if he was trying to memorize my features.

His lips parted as if he was about to speak and I put my finger on them. I didn't want to hear another apology. I didn't want him to voice any regrets.

But he simply kissed my fingers, his hand tangling in my hair.

Then he leaned back against the couch, pulling me with him.

I tucked my head into the crook of his neck, laying my hand on his chest, measuring his breaths.

"I hope you didn't let me kiss you because you

felt sorry for me," he murmured, his voice a low rumble under my hand.

"I do feel sorry for you," I whispered, toying with the flap of his shirt pocket, surprised that this felt so right. So normal. "But that's not why I kissed you."

He breathed in, then out, and I sensed some tension leave him.

He turned his head to look to me, giving me a slow smile, a gentle curl of his lips that shifted the equilibrium I struggled to find. "Something about you invites confession." And then he brushed another kiss over my forehead. "And something else."

There it was again. That connection I was having a hard time ignoring.

"Sometimes I feel so guilty because I feel worse about losing Tasha than I did about losing Kimberly," he said, his fingers making slow circles over my head, slowly erasing my resistance to him.

"Burying a child is one of the most unnatural events in life," I said. "Sally told me that when a friend of hers lost her child. She said it went against everything God set out in life."

"It was...difficult. Heart wrenching. Soul destroying. I didn't trust God after that. Still have a hard time with Him. I got tired of hearing that this was God's will and I had to trust Him."

"Do you think it was His will?"

"Do you?"

"I don't know how God works," I confessed. "I don't know if things are His will or not. But I do know that in the dark places of my life, God has provided. He's given me a reason to carry on. Given me the blessing of His presence and love. I think we have so many of life's mysteries figured out that we don't know what to do with the mystery of God and how He works in our life."

His expression grew serious. "You're an astute person. I'm assuming you're speaking from the difficulties of your own life."

The only thing I could give him was a quick nod.

"I get the feeling you won't tell me."

I gently pulled back, giving him what I hoped was a casual shrug. An attempt at rebuilding a boundary I'd let erode. "It's not that interesting."

"Does it have to do with your mother? Your natural mother? Were you sad when she died?"

I latched onto that, telling myself that it was partly true, even if it was a small deflection. "It was hard, but the one thing I felt was that she couldn't disappoint me anymore."

"And she had?"

"I try not to think about that anymore. I was blessed to be brought into the Carpenter family. I'll always be grateful to God that He gave me that home."

And the thought that I'd lost Jerrod, the last connection to that home, made my own lips tremble. I blinked my tears away, just as Duncan reached over and brushed the errant moisture from my cheek.

"It's hard, isn't it?"

I nodded, reason returning alongside my grief. I pulled away from this amazing and good man, reminding myself that he was still grieving the loss of his wife and child. A woman who he had known most of his life. A woman who was a part of this community.

I knew I couldn't give him what he needed or deserved. My past was too ingrained in me. Along with that, I had my own plans, and they couldn't include this momentary dream I had allowed myself to give in to.

Maybe you should tell him something of your life so he'll know beyond a doubt why you can't take care of Celia?

And which part?

Finding out, the hard way, that your boyfriend, the father of your daughter, was a drug dealer? And how the consequences of that changed your life? Got you in trouble with the law?

But I was innocent. I didn't know he had stashed those drugs in my car.

The judge hadn't believed me. I didn't know if Duncan would and I wasn't about to take that chance. Not after what we just shared. Not after feeling, for the first time in a long time, that I was important. That I was valuable.

As I felt the heat of his gaze, the safety of his arms, I knew I couldn't. I didn't want to see the rejection in his eyes. Didn't want him to be the first to withdraw.

Then the timer went off on the oven, and other realities intruded.

"I think the casserole is ready," I said, giving me a reason to move away, though I did so unwillingly.

"Right. I forgot about that," he said with a crooked smile.

I felt my resolve waver as I rose from the couch.

Yet even as I reluctantly left that momentary haven, I knew we had shared something I would not forget. Something that created a bond I would not easily break.

* * *

Duncan watched the vehicle holding Miriam and Celia leave, its taillights winking in the dark as Miriam braked, then made the turn out of the yard.

He'd offered to bring her home, but she refused. It wasn't far, she'd said and though she was right he still felt wrong to let her go. He wanted to spend some more time with her. Wanted to figure out where to put his changing feelings for her.

He waited until he couldn't see the lights of her vehicle any longer, resisting the urge to follow her. The roads were good, the moon was out. And he got the feeling she wouldn't appreciate it if he followed her.

He walked back to the living room, the house feeling even emptier now that Miriam and Celia were gone. He and Miriam had eaten supper together, silently, and yet, it felt comfortable. It was as if neither wanted to break what had happened between them. When Celia woke up, she ate some of the casserole and then demanded to go home.

He grabbed the remote and turned on the television, flicking through the channels, trying to find a place to land.

Kimberly often accused him of having a short attention span, saying he was going to make their daughter just as unable to focus as he seemed to be.

His heart turned at the memory of his wife and daughter, but somehow the pain didn't create the usual dull ache. Had crying, literally, on Miriam's shoulder shifted his focus? Diluted the emotion?

And once again, he replayed that moment after his breakdown when he pulled Miriam close. Kissed her.

He wished he could simply pawn it off on the fact that his guard was down. He'd finally shed tears that he'd held back for so long he thought they had dried up. But he knew there were more.

He'd been attracted to Miriam the first moment he saw her, and his lonely heart had been drawn to her. And now it seemed that maybe he had a second chance with her.

He flicked off the television and tossed the remote aside as he stood. Miriam had insisted on cleaning up after their meal, so he didn't even have that to occupy himself. He yawned, the weariness from before falling on him like a blanket.

He slipped into bed, flipped off the light, and was suddenly wide-awake, the night's events replaying in his mind. He flipped onto his side, but that meant looking at the clock glowing on his bedside table. He dropped onto his back again, staring at the ceiling.

Shouldn't have done it, he told himself over and over. Shouldn't have kissed her.

And yet, and yet...

It hadn't felt wrong.

And what was he supposed to do about that?

He sat up, shoving his hair back from his face and flicking on the light, giving up on sleep. He pulled open the drawer beside his bed, looking for a book he was sure he'd put there. But all he saw was his Bible. The one his parents had given him and Kimberly when they got married.

He pulled it out, flipping past the flyleaf with his and Kimberly's names inscribed inside. Paging through the Bible he saw notes here and there, scribbled in the margin.

Kimberly's handwriting. He knew she read her Bible from time to time. He just never knew she read it this much.

His heart flipped slowly over, and he stopped

on one page and took a moment to read her comments.

"Struggling today. Trying to find comfort."

He read the Psalm she had made the notation beside. Psalm 77. *"I cried out to God for help; I cried out to God to hear me. When I was in distress, I sought the Lord; at night I stretched out untiring hands, and I would not be comforted."*

He re-read the passage once again trying to understand what was going through Kimberly's mind.

Was the disappointment that dogged the last few years of her life hanging over her? Was she seeking escape from her life and unable to find the comfort God held out to her?

Once again, he was hounded by the regret that he hadn't been able to give her what she needed or wanted.

At this point, all thoughts of sleep were out the window, so he got up and walked over to the bedroom closet. Deep in the back, on the top shelf, he found the box. A shoebox from yet another pair of expensive shoes that Kimberly needed so desperately. The shoes had disappeared in a methodical cleaning expedition taken on by his mother and sister. They had been ruthlessly efficient, but they'd missed this.

He opened it and pulled out the letter that Kimberly had written to him before she left this house. Before she, in her distraction or sorrow—Duncan was never sure what it could have been—made a bad turn, spun out of control on a patch of black ice, and ran her car into a deep gulley close to the river. Tasha hadn't been in her booster seat—

Duncan stopped his thoughts there. He'd imagined too many times what had happened to his daughter that horrible day. Wondered why Kimberly hadn't buckled her in to keep her safe. He had to leave it be.

He pulled the envelope out of the box, his name written on the front in Kimberly's deliberate script, and debated whether or not he should read it again, or just throw it away.

He was about to slip it out of the envelope when his cell phone, lying beside his bed, rang.

He set the letter aside and grabbed his phone. It was Les and guilt, his steady traveling companion, reared its familiar head. He had promised Les he would call him to go over their plans for tomorrow.

"So, today went well," Les said when he answered the phone. "Even though you weren't around. How was your afternoon and evening?"

Surprising, Duncan wanted to say, still not sure how to process everything that had happened. It seemed like weeks ago he'd left the logging block instead of only half a day.

"It was good. Took Celia and Miriam out for a ride on the horses."

"Excellent. This is good progress. Spending time with the luminous Miriam. And what are you doing tomorrow?"

"Coming back to work."

"This is not progress. Look, I told you to take a break. So take a break. A real one. Things went just fine today without you around. Go do something else with those girls tomorrow."

"Are you trying to shut me out?"

"No. I'm hoping to buy you out." Les was silent for a beat. "Kidding."

Les had made this casual comment before, and Duncan had always brushed it off with a laugh. But now, Duncan wondered how much of that comment was kidding, and how much of it was serious.

"I don't know what to do with Celia, anyway," he said.

"And Miriam?"

Duncan's cheeks burned at the thought of the kiss he had shared with her. It had been a mistake. And yet, something about it felt right in spite of how quickly it happened.

"Christmas is coming up," Les was saying. "Take them shopping. Go to the city. Chicks love going to the mall."

"I think I'd sooner be fixing hose fittings in minus-forty degree weather than head to the mall in December."

"Yeah, but you'd be with Miriam," Les said. "And Celia of course, but, hey, let's be real."

"Why do you keep harping on Miriam?" The question came out sharper than he intended.

It was the guilt that made him touchy. That, and the feeling that the kiss they shared had shifted them to a new place. And he couldn't go back.

"I just think it's time you start looking at other women. Start thinking about dating again. I know you went out with her before. Something happened then, build on that."

"Maybe," Duncan said, testing the thought of him and Miriam. Wondering if she thought the same.

She kissed you back.

"Not maybe. Yes. Anyway, I don't want to see you tomorrow. You need to buy me and the crew presents, anyhow."

Duncan smiled at that. "Probably should. Make up for the way I've been ragging on everyone lately."

"So, I'll see you later this week." Then Les said goodbye before he could protest.

Duncan set his phone beside the bed, then walked over to the window. The snow had stopped falling, and the clouds had dissipated. A fat, full moon cast a watery light over the snow-covered land. Spring was a long time in coming yet. Spring with its fresh grass, new calves and a life that he much preferred. He wanted to expand the farm, but couldn't right now. Not until he was free from the debt of the company.

You would be if you sold it.

He wanted to immediately dismiss the thought, but behind that, came Les' half-joking comment about buying him out.

If he sold the business, he could expand his herd. Buy the Peters' farm that he'd had his eye on for the past year.

It was your father's business, he reminded himself, as he looked out over his yard. *And it brings in good money.*

For whom? And at what does that 'good money' cost you?

He dismissed the malignant thought. It wasn't

because of the logging business that Tasha and Kimberly died. It was because of Kimberly's choices and her inability to adjust to the changes in their life.

Changes that occurred when Tasha was born.

Kimberly had fallen into a depression and had never come out of it. He had put it down to baby blues. Had done some research on it. Apparently it went away, but it took time. Only with Kimberly it never did.

He sat down on his bed and withdrew the letter. Kimberly's writing was a confused scrawl of words, indicative of her distress. Guilt stabbed him again, as it usually did when he read the first few words of the letter.

You won't listen, so I need to write this down. I can't do this anymore. I never could. I tried to tell you before that I didn't think I could take care of our baby, and I can't. I have to go. Have to leave. You won't listen. The rest of the letter was a litany of complaints that, each time he read them, made him realize how little he had known what was going on in his wife's mind. How much she had held back. She said that she was leaving him and Tasha. She didn't want to be a mother. Had never really wanted kids. That Tasha was a mistake.

The letter ended with a goodbye and a note to

tell him that she was bringing Tasha to his parents' place so they could take care of her until he came back from work.

But neither Tasha nor Kimberly ever made it to his parents' place.

His heart jerked in his chest, pulling again on the emotions he'd buried since that bleak, soul-destroying day.

Then a tear slid down his cheek. He blinked, and a few more followed. A sob crawled up his throat, and then another. He crumpled the letter in his hands, pressing it against his forehead, as tear followed tear, sorrow followed sorrow.

Many moments later, spent from the grief that washed over him, he lifted his head, sucking in a deep, hard breath.

His bleary, burning eyes fell on the Bible that he had dropped on the bedside table. He grabbed it, suddenly hungry to find any kind of spiritual nourishment from it.

He turned to the passages Kimberly had marked, ignoring her notes, reading the passages for himself. Seeking the comfort that had eluded him the past three years.

His trust in God had been sorely tested and tried, and he dared God to show him that He still cared.

"Where can I go from your Spirit? Where can I flee from your presence? If I go up to the heavens, you are there; if I make my bed in the depths you are there."

Duncan let the words settle on his bruised, lonely soul. He thought of what Miriam had said only a short while ago. How we could count on God's extravagant love. The words sounded so lofty and wonderful. Too good to be true.

But as he read the rest of the Psalm, he felt an old emotion. A whisper of conversations he had before Kimberly and Tasha died. Before he consigned their bodies to the ground and guilt and sorrow took their place in his life.

"When I awake, I am still with you."

And, he knew, it went the other way as well. That God was still with him and would guide him through his life. He wasn't sure where to put those emotions right now but as he sat quietly, as he let the words settle in his soul he felt the beginnings of an old certainty.

He could ignore God all he wanted but that didn't negate His reality. God was and is and in this moment he felt God's very presence.

He prayed then, pouring out his soul, letting God back into his life. Back into his soul.

CHAPTER 13

J tied up the strings on the garbage bag I
had just filled from Francine's and Jerrod's closets, thankful to finally be done with this
difficult job.

I wasn't surprised that Francine had so many
clothes. She loved shopping. I was just amazed at
the amount my brother had amassed.

"Can I have some juice?" Celia stood in the
doorway, clutching Jane, frowning as I dragged
the bag into the main bedroom. Celia had been
downstairs watching a movie after breakfast,
even though I had offered to play a game with
her. When she refused, I hadn't pushed the issue,
then wondered if I was being a bad parent.

It was exhausting, this taking care of Celia,

wanting to lay my claim to her, yet needing to keep my distance. I just hoped Duncan took seriously my request to be more involved. It was getting more difficult each day to imagine leaving.

"Of course you can have some juice, honey." I dropped the bag in the corner, just as I realized Celia had addressed me directly.

One small step for Celia, one giant leap for normality.

"What kind of juice do you want?"

"Orange. Jane likes orange best and so do I."

"Orange it is." I grabbed the other bags by the strings and dragged then down the thickly carpeted hallway that still held vacuum marks from my house-cleaning spurt this morning.

"Are we seeing Dunkle again?" Celia asked as she followed me down the stairs and into the front foyer where the other bags I had just packed lay. I wasn't sure what to do with them. Duncan's mother didn't want them. But Esther said she was coming next week to clean out Jerrod's office. Though she hadn't answered any of my texts asking her what she wanted me to do, I thought it might be best if I waited before making a final decision. She might want some things from her sister.

"I don't know," I said, wishing the thought of seeing Duncan again didn't make me blush.

"Call him. Jane wants to go horseback riding again," she demanded as we walked back into the kitchen.

"I think it might be too cold to go horseback riding."

She frowned as if absorbing this information while I poured the juice into two cups. One for her and one for Jane. At least Celia's appetite was returning. This morning, she had eaten two pancakes and a sausage, while Jane had passed on the plate of food I put out for her. And nothing ended up on the floor.

"Do the horses like it when we ride them?" she asked climbing up on the stool by the eating bar and taking a drink from the cup I set in front of her.

"I think the horses like that we are spending time with them." I stood beside her, the smell of her shampoo teasing my nose, her smiling face turned up to me.

I wanted to pull her close. Hold her forever.

A dull ache grew in my heart as I gave into an impulse and stroked a strand of hair back from her face. She didn't flinch or pull back, just accepted my gentle touch.

How could I walk away from her? I thought, as my fingers stroked her silky curls. How could I leave her alone again?

Why don't you stay?

Duncan's suggestion of yesterday pushed past my questions.

I rested my elbows on the counter, watching Celia, a memory of myself when I was that age jumping to the fore. A dingy motel and my mother, drunk, laughing too loud as she watched television. The smell of onions and hamburgers from our supper the night before. A feeling of un-settledness and, even larger than that, a fear of what the next few days would bring.

That was my legacy, I thought, straightening, as if pulling away from her. I may put my mother down, but at least she didn't end up in prison.

"Stop clinging to what you don't need to carry."

I tested the words and held them as if to see how I could make them work.

Help me, Lord, I prayed, as I watched Celia finish her juice then give me a smile that pierced my heart as surely as one of Cupid's arrows.

The ringing of the doorbell broke into the moment, and I pushed myself away from the counter. Cora had said she might stop by, it was probably her.

But when I pulled open the door, clutching my sweater around me against the sudden blast of cold air, my heart jumped in my chest.

Duncan stood on the step, his hands shoved in the pockets of a down-filled jacket, a cowboy hat perched on his head.

"Hey there," he said, giving me a cautious smile as if checking where things were between us.

"Come in." I stood aside as he stepped into the foyer, stamping the snow off his feet, filling the space with his presence.

"Thought I would stop by. See if you needed me to shovel snow for you, but I see you did it already."

"First thing this morning."

He nodded and stood towering over me, making me feel inconsequential. "And how's Celia? She sleep okay?"

"Not fantastic, but better." She'd only been up twice complaining about her mom's and dad's loud voices. Then she said something about Aunt Esther though I wasn't sure. Her words were a confused mumble. "I think her nap at your place helped."

Duncan looked at me then, his eyes holding

mine, and once again that sense of awareness anchored us.

"And you?" His question came out in a hoarse whisper that sent a shiver spiraling down my spine. He cleared his throat and tried again. "How did you sleep?"

"Not bad. And you?" I wanted to do a face-palm. *Really? After all that happened last night, this is what we are talking about?*

"You know, I slept good." He stayed where he was and I had to fight the desire to reach out and touch him. To make physical the connection that hovered between us. Then he bit his lip and I saw a shadow of regret in his eyes. I knew what was coming. "About last night—"

I put my hand up to stop him. "First off, that's about the most clichéd thing you could say. Secondly, I don't know if we should discuss what happened last night."

"Maybe not, but we can't pretend it didn't happen."

What was he trying to say? I couldn't help the anticipation that hummed through me, but I stopped it, trying to get a grip on reality.

"You're right. We can't, but I don't know if we should repeat it." Even though it was wonderful and thrilling, and for a moment I felt like a woman someone wanted.

Until he finds out everything about you.

He held my gaze, nodding slowly as if in agreement. "You're probably right."

"I'm not always right, but when I am it's usually all the time."

He grinned at that, and the comment seemed to ease the tension that had suddenly sprung up between us.

"Duly noted." He shrugged off his coat. "So, mind if I come in?"

"Of course not." I pulled open the closet and fished out a hanger, holding my hand out for his coat.

"That closet looks a lot emptier than the last time I saw it," he said, taking the hanger from me and threading it through his coat himself.

"I cleaned up." Then I felt a flurry of guilt. "And I'm sorry. I should have talked to the family."

He waved off my comments as he hung his coat up in the now-empty closet. "I doubt anyone wanted anything from here."

I walked into the kitchen Duncan right behind me.

"Dunkle. You're at my house," Celia said, popping up from behind the couch where she'd been hiding. She came running toward him, her arms out.

She collided with him, wrapping her arms around his legs.

"Why are you here?" she asked, leaning back to look up at him.

Duncan smoothed his hands over her hair in a gentle gesture. "You know, Christmas is coming, and I noticed that you don't have a tree and neither do I, so I was wondering if you wanted to come with me to get one."

"Now?" I asked.

"Sure. We could drive out to the bush. I need to check on operations after being gone yesterday and it gives you a break from...well...stuff. If that's okay with you?" He looked over at me, his crooked smile making my knees feel just a bit trembly.

My brain tussled with the wisdom of spending time with Duncan, yet if I wanted him to take more responsibility, this was how it would look.

"That sounds like a great idea," I said, secretly loving the idea of cutting down a Christmas tree with this very rugged man. "Very country."

"It's how we roll. Every year for as long as I can remember we went out to the bush to cut down our own tree." He looked down at Celia and gave her a kind smile. "And now we can do it together."

I'm sure the word didn't mean anything, but the way he said it was as if he was linking us all.

A pretend family carrying on a family tradition.

The thought made me want to smile and cry at the same time.

* * *

"Do I get to pick out the Christmas tree when we get there?" Celia piped up from the back seat of Duncan's pick-up truck. She had refused to sit in her booster seat in the truck, but thankfully Miriam had insisted, and now she seemed happy.

"You sure do," Duncan said, looking at her in his rear-view mirror, grinning at her enthusiasm. This was the most animated he had seen her since the funeral, which justified his decision to stay away from work another day.

Plus, it gave him another chance to see Miriam.

This morning he had gotten another call from Les to make sure he stayed away from work. He wanted to, but couldn't bring himself to stay away completely, so he hit upon the idea to take Celia and Miriam out to the bush to cut down a Christmas tree. That way he could stop at the block, make sure everything was okay.

"Can we have two trees?" Celia asked. "Can I have one in my bedroom?"

"That's up to Miriam," Duncan said, glancing over at her again.

"I think that's a great idea," Miriam said, looking back at Celia, smiling gently. She looked cute with her bright-pink toque, a happy contrast to her tawny hair, a puffy, down-filled jacket, blue jeans, and those same flimsy boots she'd worn each time he saw her outside.

"Are your feet warm enough?" he asked, cranking up the heat a bit more.

"I'm good." She grinned, and he couldn't help but return it. He thought being around her would be awkward, especially after last night, but somehow it wasn't.

"But they might not be so warm once we start tramping through the snow. Did you try any of Francine's—" he choked off the question, before he could finish it.

A shadow of pain flitted across her face as, once again, they both stumbled up against their loss.

"I'm sorry," he muttered.

"It's fine. I did try some of them on, but none of them fit." She kept her voice down, as if talking about Francine's boots in front of Celia made her feel guilty.

"You should have told me. I'm sure I could have found something at my mom's place that Esther used to wear."

"I'm okay."

"I know where to go so it won't take that long. And you could stay in the truck, if you want."

"Are you kidding? Cutting down a Christmas tree? In the woods?" Miriam held up her phone. "I'm documenting this. My friends back in Vancouver will be impressed."

"Can we decorate the trees when we get home?" Celia asked.

"We sure can," Miriam said.

"Do you know where the decorations are?" Duncan spun his truck around the next corner, part of his attention on the truckers chattering over the CB radio, the other half on his passengers.

"I found a box when I was cleaning up."

"I'm sorry that no one was around to help you with that job. I should have—"

"It's okay." Miriam waved her hand as if absolving him. "I didn't want to put any more burdens on your family. Your mom is busy, and your sister is in school."

"And I'm a workaholic, according to my partner."

"Are you really?"

Duncan shrugged, his mind shifting back to Les' comment. To the reason he started being so busy. Did it matter anymore? Did he still need to go full-tilt?

"I like to keep busy."

"I know the feeling," Miriam murmured.

"How much farther do we have to go?" Celia asked.

"Not much farther," Duncan said, unhooking the mic from the radio as he got close to the bridge. Truckers and loggers had been jabbering away on it ever since he got within receiving distance, but from what he could hear, things were going well. They hadn't met any logging trucks yet. They'd missed the morning run. He clicked the button on the side of the mic. "Pickup at Ten Bridge empty," he muttered into the handset, then hooked it back on the dashboard.

"What does that mean?" she asked.

Duncan shot her a puzzled glanced. "What does what mean?"

"What you just said. About Ten Bridge empty."

He laughed. "Sorry, it's so automatic, I didn't even realize I was doing it. I was just calling my kilometers."

"Still confused."

"See those markers on the side of the road? Each one marks a kilometer from the beginning of the haul road, the main road that trucks and equipment go down. So we're about ten kilometers down the haul road now. The markers let everyone know where everyone is. The road is narrow, and the logging trucks are big, and you don't want to run into one. So every vehicle that goes down this way calls out where they are. Empty means you're going in. Loaded means you're going out. So if I hear a truck call out on the radio that they're at fifteen and they're loaded, then that means it's either a log truck or another vehicle coming toward me, and I should watch out for them because we're at kilometer ten and he's at kilometer fifteen."

"So you actually do get to use that school-math equation."

Now it was his turn to be confused. "Which equation?"

"The classic, 'if vehicle A is driving sixty kilometers an hour and vehicle B is driving fifty and they are so many kilometers apart, how long before they meet each other.' I could never understand the practical application of that, but here it is. The whole reason for that equation's existence."

Duncan laughed. "Unfortunately, I'm not that smart. I just figure I should watch out for the next few minutes."

"Hey, you pirate," a familiar voice squawked over the radio. "You're supposed to be taking today off, too."

Les. Trust him to be sitting by the radio at just that time.

"I am," Duncan said into the mic. "Just taking Celia and Miriam out to cut down a Christmas tree before you mow them all down."

"There's a really nice patch just back of where Anton is working."

"I know. I pushed the road in there with the Cat the other day." Duncan glanced at the clock on the dash. "I'll be at the block in about ten minutes."

"Everything's going great. You don't need to check in."

Duncan hesitated. He knew if he stopped by the site he would see something going on that annoyed him. Or something that wasn't being done the way he liked. But he still felt he should.

"Let. It. Go." Les put heavy emphasis on each word.

"Are you sure?"

"All. Is. Well. Don't make me spell it out for you. Take the lovely Miriam and impress her with your manly lumberjack skills."

Duncan felt his neck warm and couldn't stop a glance Miriam's way. Though she was looking out the window he knew she had heard every word.

Did it matter? He wasn't sure, but for now he could look forward to some time with her, and for some reason it felt good.

"Then I'll see you Wednesday."

"That's soon enough."

Duncan hung the mic up, then turned down a spur road. This road was even narrower, and as Duncan called out where he was, he was glad to know they wouldn't meet a loaded log truck on this one. They rode past the block road that would lead to where his equipment was working, fighting down a feeling of the usual guilt. His men were working and he was gallivanting around getting Christmas trees.

No. He was spending time with his niece. As he promised Miriam he would.

For a moment he felt conflicted, but when he glanced over at Miriam and caught her looking at him with a curious smile, he felt better about the situation.

"We have to stop here," Duncan said, parking the truck in a pullout and turning it off. "We have to walk into the bush a ways."

"I'm getting a tree. I'm getting a tree," Celia sang, unbuckling her seat belt and standing by the door. Her excitement was infectious, and as Miriam took her out and brought her around the truck to join him, Duncan smiled down at her.

She reached out one mittened hand and grabbed his, swinging it.

His heart melted. Just a bit.

"I've got to lead the way," Duncan told her, releasing her hand, but patting her on her shoulder. "The trail is just up ahead." He looked at Miriam's boots. "Just step in my footsteps and hopefully your feet won't get too wet."

"I'll be okay," she said with a grin, her eyes bright, her cheeks pink.

He held her gaze a beat longer than necessary, attraction flickering through him. Then he grabbed the saw he had taken and plunged into the bush, taking small steps for Miriam and Celia, trying to shake as much of the snow off the trees as possible so that it wouldn't rain down on them as they came through.

At the clearing he waited for them to catch up.

"So, we can look around a bit," he said. "Let me know which one you want Celia and I'll see if it will be good."

Celia immediately ran up to the first one close to her. "I want this one."

"Let's get rid of the snow and we'll see if it's thick enough." He grabbed a branch and shook. Snow showered down on him, and Celia laughed. Aloud. The sound pierced his heart. This was the first time he'd heard her actually laugh. He shot a quick glance at Miriam, who was staring down at Celia, her lips pressed together. Then she looked up at him and smiled as she pulled her phone out of her pocket. She snapped a photo before he could protest.

"Documentation," she told him with an arch look.

Duncan just shook his head in response, then stood back, angling his head this way and that. "You know what, sweetie? I don't think this is the one," he said. "We can do better."

They tromped through the clearing, checking a few more trees out and dismissed them.

Then, finally, there it was. Duncan could tell in spite of the layer of snow on its branches that it would be a good one. And it was.

"That one looks perfect," Miriam said, full of admiration. She pulled out her phone and took another photo.

"What do you think, Celia?" Duncan asked.

She frowned, tilting her head to one side, perfectly mimicking his actions of a few moments ago, which made him laugh. "I think it's good."

"Then down it goes," Duncan said, saluting her with his wood saw. He pushed the snow away from the base with his boot, getting as close to the ground as possible. He hunkered down and, ignoring the remnants of snow raining down his neck, started sawing.

A few minutes and a neck full of snow later, the tree was down.

"You two will have to help me drag it out," Duncan said, looking over at Miriam who was now on the opposite side of the tree, taking pictures with her phone.

Celia ran over to join Duncan, then stopped and spun around, her eyes wide, frightened.

"What's the matter, honey?" he asked, concerned at the fear on her face.

"I left Jane in the truck," she said, looking horrified. "I have to go back. She'll be so scared."

Duncan caught her by the arm, just before she took off down the trail. "She'll be okay. She's just a doll."

Celia's eyes grew huge, and her mouth fell open in total shock. Then she flew at him, her arms flailing as she struck at him. "She's not just a doll. She's real. She's real."

Her voice was edged with angry panic, and Duncan dropped the tree trunk, catching her arms. Then, to stop her, he pulled her close, hugging her against him.

She squirmed against his restraint but he kept his arms tight as the fight slowly went out of her. Then she dropped her head against his shoulder. "She's not just a doll," she sobbed. Then she was clinging to him with a frightening level of desperation. "My mommy gave her to me. She said she was real. Mommy said she would be my own friend and that I could tell Jane anything. Jane is my friend. From my mo...mo...mommy." Her last words come out in a broken cry.

Duncan's heart ached for her as she wilted against him, sobbing. His own throat thickened, too easily remembering his own recent tears.

And it finally clicked for him why Celia had been acting the way she did with her doll. It was her connection to her mother.

His sister.

Duncan choked down his own pain, holding Celia close, and as he did, he looked up to see Miriam looking at him, her fingers pressed against her lips, her cheeks wet with tears.

We're all hurting, he thought, hooking his arm around Celia and lifting her up. Then he walked over to Miriam, opened his arm to her and she leaned in. He laid his cheek on her head, his own emotions veering from sorrow to a curious sense of connection. Of an emptiness in his life being filled.

They stood this way for a moment, joined by their sorrow. Finally Celia stopped crying and was the first to pull away, her hands planted on Duncan's chest.

"Can we go get Jane?" she asked, her voice catching on the words.

"Why don't you stay here," he said, his arm still around Miriam, holding Celia's concerned gaze. "It will be quicker for me to go get her. I'll be right back."

Celia nodded as she pulled in a shaky breath.

He gave her a reassuring smile then gave in to

an impulse and brushed a light kiss on her damp cheek.

"I love you, Dunkle," Celia murmured, laying her head on his shoulder.

Duncan closed his eyes, her words piercing his soul. His gaze sought and found Miriam's. Though he would have liked to kiss her as well, for now he was content with simply looking at her, his arm holding her, her one hand resting on Celia's back, the other on his shoulder. Awareness, as real as a touch, arced between them, connecting them.

This feels right, he thought, his lips curving in a smile.

Their gaze lengthened, and his heart did a slow flip as she seemed to come closer. Her face grew blurry, and his breath quickened. She was going to kiss him. And he wanted her to.

Then Celia pulled away, patting him on the chest, and reality intruded.

"Are you getting Jane?" she asked, frowning at him. "I don't want her to be scared."

"I'll do that right now." He pulled his shaken wits together, catching his wayward breath. "Then I'll come back and we can cut another tree."

Miriam pulled away as he set Celia down in

the snow. He touched her cold nose with his fore-finger, slipped his gloves back on, and trekked back to the truck. His heavy boots dragged through the snow as he left Celia and Miriam be-hind, but at the same time he felt a lightness in his being that he had never felt before.

He wasn't sure what to do about it, but he stopped himself from analyzing it.

For now, life was good.

"IS THIS THE GOOD SIDE?" Duncan looked over his shoulder at me from his position on the floor as he turned the heavy stand holding the largest tree.

I looked this way and that, then nodded, pulling in a deep breath of tangy, spruce-scented air. I couldn't remember the last time I had smelled a real Christmas tree.

"It looks amazing," was all I could say. The tree filled up the one corner of the living room, domi-nating the space.

"It's a big, big tree," Celia said, dancing from one side to the other, holding Jane up so the doll could see better. Her happiness surprised me. It was as if her breakdown in the forest had let out some of her own pain, and it helped me understand better why she acted the way she did with her doll.

Duncan pushed his way out from under the tree, sprinkling spruce needles on the carpet as he went.

"Sorry about the mess," he murmured getting to his feet and brushing the rest off his shoulder. "I'll clean it up."

"I'll take care of it," I said, standing back, still trying to take this all in.

A real tree. The wonder of it washed over me as I watched Celia skipping, her excitement making the coming festive season suddenly real. I glanced over at Duncan and thought of that moment we shared in the clearing. And the one before that. And before that.

I felt as if we had come full circle, and I couldn't deny the attraction building between us again.

I didn't want to spin plans and dreams around him. Plans always, always changed.

But yet…

"So, where are the ornaments and the lights for the tree?" Duncan was asking.

"I put them in the basement."

"Getting them now," he said, turning and walking away.

Part of me wanted to stop him. Decorating a tree with him would add another layer of intimacy to a relationship that was already getting too comfortable.

"What are we doing now?" Celia asked, setting Jane on one corner of the couch. "Are we making the tree pretty? Like my mommy and daddy did last year?"

I tried to mask my surprise at her addressing me directly. Though she had been doing it from time to time, ever since her little breakdown this afternoon, she stopped talking to me through Jane completely.

"We are," I said. "But first I have to give the tree some water so it stays nice and fresh."

Celia insisted on helping, and we managed to get most of the water from the watering can into the stand. By the time we were done blotting up the excess water and sweeping up the needles, Duncan was back, balancing three packing boxes one on top of the other. "Am I good or what?" he exclaimed setting the boxes marked 'lights' and 'ornaments' on the floor. "Plus, I found a fake tree down there, too, all packaged up."

"Well, if I had known that I could have saved myself cold, wet feet," I protested.

"I did offer to get you some other boots," Duncan grinned at me. "But you refused. Admit it. You enjoyed the adventure of getting our own tree."

His teasing tone made me smile. "I did. Truly."

The many pictures on my phone attested to that. I had given in to an impulse and sent Christine one of Duncan and Celia, dragging the tree through the snow. But as soon as it was sent, I shut off my phone. I knew she would call back with all kinds of questions. I wasn't ready to hear any other voice in my head. I was having a hard enough time sorting out my own emotions where Duncan was concerned.

"So, let's get this party started," he said with surprising enthusiasm.

"You sound almost as excited as Celia," I teased as he pulled open the flaps on a box.

He shot me a quick grin, which faded just a bit. "It's been a long time since Christmas has been fun for me."

Again, our eyes held. Again, other emotions were teased to the surface.

"Well let's see what we can do to make this one fun, too," I said, keeping my tone light.

While Duncan strung up the lights Celia and I went through the boxes of ornaments, trying to decide what we wanted to put on the tree. I couldn't believe the variety of colors and types. We could have decorated three trees with all the ornaments Francine had in the boxes.

Celia was sorting them according to how she wanted them hung on the tree. So far there was no rhyme or reason. Metal ornaments and wooden toys lay beside purple shiny balls and white snowflakes.

"I got this one last year," Celia said pulling out a small nativity set that hung from a gold ribbon, grinning as it swung back and forth, the glitter on the roof catching the lights already on the tree branches.

The sight dipped into my soul.

I had bought that ornament for her, and shipped it to Jer and Fran's place, struggling not to feel the sting of my brother's rejection when he suggested that I not come.

"It's a beautiful ornament," I said.

Celia gave me a shy smile. "My mommy told me you got it for me."

I bit back a gulp of surprise that she remembered. "I did buy it for you. Do you know why?"

She shook her head.

"That ornament is called a nativity scene. It shows Mary, Joseph, and Baby Jesus." I pointed each tiny figure out to her. "I wanted you to remember that Christmas is all about Jesus' birth. Christmas is Jesus' birthday."

I had wanted to send so much more but Francine and Jerrod said too many gifts from me would only confuse her. I had tried to tell them that I was her aunt as well, but in the end figured it wasn't worth the battle.

"Happy Birthday, Baby Jesus," she said, swinging the ornament back and forth, her smile growing.

"Happy Birthday indeed," I repeated, thinking that this Christmas I could buy her whatever I wanted. The thought tantalized me with visions of brightly wrapped parcels. Of gifts piled under a tree.

And if you quit your job? What will you buy all those presents with?

I shook the thought off. It hadn't come to that, though my practical self knew I couldn't leave Gillian dangling any longer.

But I also knew I couldn't leave Celia. Not yet. It had been difficult enough to think of leaving a few days ago.

And now? Could I walk away after everything

that has happened between my daughter and me?

Between Duncan and me?

"Let's sort out the rest of the ornaments," I said, pushing my thoughts aside. "And you can pick which ones go on this tree and which ones you want on the tree in your bedroom."

"Did you find the star for the top of the tree?" Duncan asked, joining us by the boxes. "I'll put it up right away."

"I think this is it," I said, holding up a glittery, five-point star and handing it to him. His smile was casual, but when his fingers brushed mine I felt anything but.

"We should have Christmas music playing while we do this," Duncan said, his smile deepening. Then he turned to the bookshelf that flanked the fireplace and turned on the stereo. He fiddled with the controls and suddenly rap music bounced out of the speakers. "Oops. Sorry." He squelched the heavy bass beat and chattering lyrics, then a few moments later, the soft strains of *Silent Night* floated out of the speakers. "That's more like it," he said.

"How did you do that?" I asked, quite impressed.

"I have the same system," he said, adjusting the volume. "Mom and Dad got them for us last year for Christmas, and Esther pre-programmed some internet stations on them. I took a guess and figured Francine and Jerrod hadn't changed theirs either." His expression held shadows of sorrow. "Like you said when we went riding, we'll be bumping up against these memories again and again. We may as well get used to it." He pulled in a slow breath, then picked up some of the ornaments. "Are these going on the tree?"

I nodded and he handed a couple to Celia. "Here, sweetie. Help me put them on."

As we worked, the music laid a festive counterpoint, filling the room with carols. Though no one talked while we worked, we shared a companionable silence. A gentle acknowledgement of our loss. I let my thoughts drift back to happy Christmases at the Carpenter household. How thoroughly I absorbed and took in every small tradition, storing them away in my memory box.

And now I was making another one.

When it was all done, we stood back from the tree, the spinning ornaments refracting the lights strung in the branches.

"It's beautiful," I breathed, filled with a sense of wonder.

"I love our tree," Celia said, hugging Jane, her eyes bright. "And I'm so excited for Christmas. I hope Mommy buys me a bike." Then she stopped and she shot us a panicked glance. Her lip quivered and tears glistened in her eyes as realization dawned.

Then, to my surprise, she ran directly to me, flinging her arms around me. "I miss my mommy and daddy," she cried. I knelt down and hugged her tight, rocking her, giving her unspoken encouragement to let her tears flow, just as we had in the forest. And, as before, Duncan knelt down beside me and placed his large arms around us both.

We stayed that way a moment longer, and in spite of my sorrow and Celia's pain, I felt a quickening of my breath as the memory of that moment amongst the trees drifted into my thoughts. When I almost kissed this man again.

Celia was the first to draw away, and she swiped at her tears with the palm of her hand. "Am I still getting presents?" she asked, her child's mind quickly shifting gears.

"Of course you are," Duncan said, his voice gruff as he smoothed his hand over her hair. "In fact, I think we should go shopping this week. For some presents. Would you like that?"

Celia nodded vigorously. "Can we go tomorrow?"

"Maybe not tomorrow. I should get some work done," Duncan said, getting to his feet. He held his hand out to help me up and I took it, his large callused palm easily engulfing mine. He gave my hand a light squeeze and added a smile. "But we can go at the end of the week if that's okay with you?"

The thought held more appeal than it should. Spending time with Duncan was getting to be a habit I could get dangerously used to.

He didn't let go of my hand and instead gave it a little tug. "What do you think, Miriam?"

I swallowed down a curious anticipation. "I think that's a good idea."

And what about Gillian? What about your job?

I felt a sense of resignation. I couldn't find any way around quitting. I couldn't expect Gillian to hold my job any longer. All I could do was hope for a good recommendation from her. I would need every ounce of goodwill on my quest for a new job when I got back to Vancouver.

Celia danced toward the tree to show Jane the lights and while her back was to us, Duncan shifted just a little closer to me, his arm brushing mine. "I'm glad you pushed me to spend time with Celia," he said. "Because it means I also get to spend more time with you."

I couldn't say anything. But I knew I felt exactly the same way.

"We should…should probably decorate Celia's tree," I managed past the thickness in my throat.

"Let's do that." Then, to my surprise and shock, he bent down and brushed a kiss over my forehead.

We made quick work of Celia's tree, with Jane 'helping'. When we were done, Duncan swept up the remaining ornaments and dropped them in a box while I struggled with his casual touch, trying to decide what to do.

Enjoy being with him. Maybe this time around things will end differently.

The voice teased me with the lost possibilities of our first meeting.

Was this really a chance to do that over? Had God really brought us together again?

And what would Duncan think when he finds out the truth?

I grabbed the other box and closed the flaps on it while my heart pounded with a mixture of anticipation and concern. I needed to tell him.

Just not yet. Not yet.

CHAPTER 14

"*A*re you sure you don't need any help?" I asked, as Esther took another sip of her coffee. She sat at the eating bar while I cleaned up the dishes from breakfast. Christmas music floated through the house. Combined with the pervasive scent of the spruce tree, the house held a festive air that chased away the gloom of the past couple of weeks.

Celia was up in her bedroom, trying to decide which clothes she wanted to keep and which to throw away. I had told her we would be cleaning her room today while Aunt Esther worked downstairs.

"It's better if I go through Jerrod's office myself before the lawyer does. I know what I'm looking for...I mean, what I'm doing," she said, clutching the coffee mug. It seemed to me that she wasn't looking forward to the job.

When she called this morning to say she was coming to clean the office I was grateful to leave that job to her. After spending the past week sorting and bagging Francine's and Jerrod's clothes and personal items, cleaning out the rest of the house, I was emotionally exhausted. With each picture and knick-knack I packed, each item of clothing I put away, the few memories I had returned. The sweater I sent Francine for Christmas one year that I agonized over for days then justified the cost by reminding myself she was the mother of my daughter. An old volleyball T-shirt I couldn't believe Jerrod had kept from his high school years. All brought back painful memories.

"Did you want to go through any of Francine and Jerrod's things that I've bagged?" I asked, leaning back against the island as I nursed my freshly brewed coffee. "See what you might want?"

Esther chewed her lip, as if thinking, one finger toying with her blonde hair. "Maybe another time," she said giving me a pained smile.

"Did you go through the pockets? Did you find anything important?"

"Nothing out of the ordinary," I said, wondering what she meant.

"Okay. But just don't give them away yet."

"Oh, no. Of course not. I've been moving everything downstairs." One corner of the basement was filled with bags and boxes, all labeled. I wasn't sure where things would go from there or who would do it.

Esther toyed with her mug as she shook her head. "This has been a rotten couple of weeks," she said, clenching the handle of her mug. "I'll be taking some time off school. So I can help Duncan with Celia," she said giving me a vague smile. "I'm glad he helped you get a Christmas tree."

"We had a great time and Celia really enjoyed herself. I'm sure she's redecorated her tree a dozen times."

"That's cute. I hope he can find the time to take her shopping."

"He is. In fact, on Friday he's taking Celia and me to the mall in Edmonton."

"Both of you?" She sounded surprised. "He didn't say anything to me."

"That's what he told me." I tried not to blush at

the thought. With each moment we spent together, my emotions grew more confused. It was like the years between Jerrod and Francine's wedding and now had faded away, and we were simply building on the attraction we felt then.

That was a more innocent time.

And yet, I felt as if Duncan and I were being given another chance.

You need to tell him everything.

"That's…surprising that's he's taking you along," Esther said, her tone puzzling.

"It's about a smooth transition," I said, playing things close, still unsure of my next move.

"I suppose, but I think it's important that Duncan spend some time with Celia on his own as well."

"He will."

"And when will you be leaving?"

"I'm not sure."

Last night, after Duncan was gone and Celia in bed, I made the fateful call to my boss. I couldn't leave her hanging any longer so I told her I was quitting. Gillian was more than gracious and promised me a glowing reference for my next employer.

I hated the uncertainty this brought into my life but right now my priority was Celia.

Christine was next. Thankfully she assured me she wouldn't sublet my room, though she had teased me that she was selling my paintings to pay my share of the rent while I was gone. I laughed and told her to go ahead.

"I want to make sure that Celia is settled, and that Duncan is ready to take on the responsibility," I continued.

"You don't have to worry about that now that I'm moving home."

"Will you go back to school? Once things settle down?"

"Not sure," Esther said. "Since Jerrod and Francine's death I haven't been able to concentrate. I haven't been doing well all term. "Too much on my mind, and now, with Jerrod gone. Francine gone—" Her voice broke, and she pressed the back of her hand against her mouth, jerking her arm away when I tried to touch her in sympathy. "Sorry. I'm sorry."

"No, it's okay. You've had a lot to deal with."

"Too much. I need a break and some time to reassess my life. Figure out what I want to do." She walked over to the box of tissues on the top of the refrigerator and tugged a few out, wiping her eyes and blowing her nose. She muttered an 'excuse me' as she pulled open the cupboard beside me and tossed them in the garbage. She sucked in a shaky breath, then gave me a trembling smile. "Now if you'll excuse me, I better get to work." She walked past me and closed the door behind herself. Then I heard the distinctive click of the lock. She really wanted to be on her own.

My cell phone rang right then, so I wasn't able to think any more on that.

"Hey Christine," I said, as I jogged up the stairs to Celia's room. "What can I do for you?"

"So after you lost your job I figured you could use a win. So ...I kinda stuck my neck out and sold one of your paintings."

"What? Where...who...how..." My brain was having trouble processing her words. "Already?"

"I sold it online. On Kijiji. To some guy who lives in Nanaimo."

"What? Kijiji? Are you kidding me?" I stopped in the middle of the hallway, trying to sort out what my friend was telling me.

"It was easier than listing it on eBay, and I wanted to avoid Craigslist. This way, I can sell to someone local and not worry about shipping."

"You seriously sold one of my paintings?"

"We talked about this." She sounded uncertain. "You said I should."

"We joked about it. You joked about it. It was a

joke."

"Oh." Christine went quiet. "I mentioned it when I said I wouldn't sublet your room. Then you laughed so I thought it was okay."

"You sold one of my paintings." I leaned against the hallway wall, still trying to wrap my head around what she had done.

"I don't know why you're so upset. You said you weren't attached."

"I'm not...it's just...you sold one of my paintings."

"I think we established that. Look, if it bugs you that much, I can tell the guy that I changed my mind. He's coming tonight. And he even asked if I had more paintings."

I scraped my hand through my hair, still surprised and somewhat stunned. I had done the paintings as therapy. Because Jerrod and Francine had discouraged visits, the paintings became a way of creating a fantasy life for Celia. They were sweet. Cute. An expression of my dreams and inner longings for my little girl.

"So how much did you ask?"

"A thousand bucks."

"What? A thousand?"

"Not enough?"

"A thousand." I couldn't wrap my head around

that amount.

"I Googled other paintings like yours and they were going into the mid four figures so I figured I could easy ask a grand."

"Wow. I didn't think anyone would be interested in them."

"If you want, I can put a couple more up tonight. See what happens."

"Sure. Okay." I was still trying to understand this. I hadn't painted or sketched seriously for the past couple of years.

"So can I try to sell all of them?"

"There's only about ten or fifteen more."

"So you should make more. This could totally be a thing for you. A way to make a few bucks. You could set up a website. Sell from there. Shopify here we come!"

I tried to ignore her chitchat but at the same time I couldn't dismiss it completely. "I'm pretty stoked about this," I said. "I'll need the bucks now that I'm out of a job."

"You'll get another one. I know Gillian was crazy about you." She was quiet a moment. "And I'm sure with the other thing…you'll find someone else willing to take you on."

We both knew what the 'other thing' was. I had been completely up front with her from the beginning about my time in prison. Once I told her how it happened, she understood completely. Turned out I wasn't the only one with a lousy boyfriend. We had that much in common.

I just had never told her about Celia. There was only so much 'heart-to-heart' that I could indulge in.

"And you'll have time to paint. Be all inspired by the great outdoors you're in," she enthused.

"I'm not staying, remember?"

She was quiet a moment. "Really? You won't even consider it?"

Thoughts of Duncan followed her questions.

"I saw the picture you sent me of the Christmas tree gathering. That Duncan is quite the hottie. And such a cozy little scenario. Going out to get a Christmas tree together. You could paint that." Christine's comment was heavy with innuendo.

I wanted to tell her it wasn't what she thought, but I would be lying.

"So, anything happening with you two, or am I being tacky again?"

"Celia was with us as well. And I have to be smart about all this."

"You're thinking about Celia, aren't you?" Christine asked.

"I'm always thinking about Celia." And didn't I sound sober and full of good judgment instead of the woman who lay awake last night thinking less about Celia and more about Duncan.

And what to do about the shift in our relationship.

"Honey, I know you want the best for her and I know you don't think you're that best, but don't discount what you can give to her. To other people. You have a really good heart and you're a loving person. I want you to be happy and I think you deserve it."

Each word Christine leveled at me underlined my own struggles, and at the same time, nourished my soul. "I have to keep my priorities straight. What I want and what Celia needs—"

"Celia needs a mother. The woman who adopted her is dead. I know she's only your niece but right now you're all she has," Christine said.

"My mom was all I had for awhile," I said trying not to get defensive at the 'only your niece' comment. Christine didn't know.

"You aren't your mom. Gracious girl. You're nothing like her. She was so selfish; bouncing you back and forth, wanting you then pushing you away. You're not like that." Christine sounded angry which gave my soul a much-needed lift.

"Besides, I'm not all Celia has. She has family and community. She's in a good place."

"But you seem like you're in a good place. I know you sound happier than you have in a while."

I felt a quieting in my chest that echoed her words. "You sound like you're trying to talk me out of coming back," I said with a light laugh.

"To what?"

The two words echoed down the phone line.

To what indeed?

"It's not like you love Vancouver. Or city living, period," she continued, as if pressing her point. "You never really liked your job—"

"I was thankful for my work," I protested.

"Of course you were, but you're not an office kind of person. Every time you talked about that farm you lived on with your foster parents and Jerrod your voice would get all soft and melancholy like you missed that place. And now you're back in that same type of community."

"I know." I spoke quietly.

"And it seems like you and Duncan are getting back together."

"We weren't together before," I said.

"Dancing most of a wedding night with him

and going out for a couple of dates? I'd call that being together."

I didn't reply to that.

"You're allowed to receive good gifts," Christine said, heaving out a sigh. "You always told me that God's grace and His love is a gift. Well, maybe this place is a gift, too. Maybe you're allowed to be a part of it, too. I know I'm only shooting myself in the foot here, because if you don't come back I'll need a new roommate, but I hear something in your voice I haven't heard since we first met. I hear joy. I hear enthusiasm. I think being with your niece, Celia, is doing that to you, and I think being with Duncan is doing it as well."

I felt like I was hovering on the edges of a wonderful world, hardly daring believe it might happen for me. Just like I did when I first came to the Carpenter home. But taking that step meant dragging with me all the things from my former life that were also a part of me. I couldn't see them fitting.

"I don't know. I just can't see how—"

"Maybe you have to stop looking at yourself through your eyes, and start seeing yourself through others' eyes."

The conviction in her words created a flicker

of hope.

"And now, after delivering my mini sermon I need to get back to work. And contact this guy about your paintings."

"Thanks. For everything. You're a good friend."

Christine was quiet a moment. "And you're a good person. Don't forget that."

We said goodbye and I stayed where I was, holding my phone in both hands as if capturing every word Christine gave to me. Wondering if I dared take them completely to heart.

Then I heard Celia calling for me. "I'm hungry," she announced, coming out of her room with a puzzle in one hand and Jane tucked under her arm.

"Let's go make some sandwiches. Maybe Aunt Esther wants some, too."

Esther was already in the kitchen when we came downstairs.

"I thought I would get started on lunch," Esther said, looking up from the bread she was buttering as we came in the room. "Celia, do you want soup with your grilled-cheese sandwich?"

Celia didn't reply. Instead she walked past Esther and dropped the box with the puzzle in it on the dining room table.

"Celia, sweetie," Esther prompted. "You didn't answer me."

"Jane doesn't like soup," Celia replied.

"She's still doing that?" Esther whispered as I opened the cupboard door right beside her. "Talking through that doll?"

"Sometimes," was all I said, surprised that she was doing so with Esther, when she seemed to have stopped doing it with me.

"I'm really concerned about that. Weren't you going to see a counselor about that?" Esther asked as she flipped the sandwiches.

"I talked to the principal, Mrs. Lansing yesterday. She can't get Celia in until the new year," I said in a lowered voice, hoping Esther got the hint.

"Celia, honey, do you and Jane want a sandwich?" I asked as I set the dishes out.

Celia just nodded, and I left it at that.

"How is the office cleanup coming?" I asked Esther as I returned for cutlery, hoping she would leave the topic of Celia alone for now.

"Slow," she said, flipping the sandwiches. She stopped, her spatula hovering over the frying pan as she drew in a shuddering breath. "It's much harder than I thought it would be."

I put my hand on her shoulder in commiseration. "I know what you mean."

She spun around, glaring at me. "Do you? Really? Jerrod was just your foster brother."

That her unexpected anger was directed at me was puzzling. And I tried not to take offense at the way she minimized my relationship with Jerrod.

"But he was still my brother," I said, making myself hold her gaze. "The only one I had."

Esther turned away again, her shoulders drooping. "Of course he was. I'm sorry. It's just too much. Too hard."

I wanted to offer to help again but I knew she would turn me down as she had each time I had suggested it.

So I just took the pot of soup and brought it to the table.

Lunch was eaten in awkward silence and I, for one, was glad when Celia slinked away from the table, giving me the excuse to leave as well.

CHRISTMAS SONGS FILLED the mall with their familiar, cheerful sounds. Stores lured people in with bright banners and posters proclaiming preseason sales. Bright-red balls and huge frosted snowflakes hung suspended over the open space connecting the first and second floor. In spite of the busyness of people scurrying about, all carrying shopping bags, a feeling of festivity and expectation filled Duncan's heart.

It had been years since he'd been to the mall, and though he forgot how busy it could be, he also forgot the energy created by being around so many people.

He glanced over at Miriam, who was clutching her purse, looking around with a sense of wonder, acknowledging that her presence was part of the reason for his mood. For the first time since Kimberly and Tasha died, he was looking forward to Christmas and daring to make a few plans.

"Never been to West Ed before?" he asked, when she slowed her steps to look around her.

"Never. It's huge." She was walking slowly as her head turned taking it all in.

"We'll have to check out the pirate ship and the water park," he said, grinning at her surprise.

"Water park? Pirate ship? Seriously?"

"And a roller coaster, amusement park, numerous food courts and movie theaters, mini-golf course, submarine rides, full-size skating rink, gun range, and, oh, yeah, stores. Lots and lots of stores, half of them selling shoes."

"Wow." She shook her head as if trying to assimilate all that information. "This isn't a mall, it's a resort. With shopping."

"And there's a hotel."

"Can we go to the toy store?" Celia asked, dancing along between him and Miriam, Jane tucked unceremoniously under one arm, her hair flopping with every step Celia took.

"Of course we can," Duncan said. "You'll have to show us what you want for Christmas."

He had counted on this happening. He had no clue at all what to get her.

"I want Shopkins, and a bike, and Jane wants a new dress and a kitchen," Celia said, skipping ahead of them to check out one of the many Christmas trees.

"Kitchen?" he asked Miriam with a puzzled lift of his hands.

"It's one of the accessories you can get for her doll."

"How much is this accessory?"

"About four hundred dollars," Miriam said, unsuccessfully hiding a smirk when his mouth fell open in shock. "Before tax."

"Four hundred," he sputtered. "Four hundred. Are you kidding me?"

"You can get a table and chair set for it, too, with dishes. That's only two hundred. And the pots and pans and fake food and appliances you can get would set you back, I think, another three hundred."

Duncan looked over at Celia, who held Jane at her side. "That's not a doll. That's an eighteen-inch tyrant."

"It's an investment in her future happiness and mental stability," Miriam said with a grin. "And you can't put a price on that, now can you?"

Duncan laughed and before he realized he had done it, he dropped his arm over Miriam's shoulders. Like they were old friends.

But she didn't pull away, and deep within something shifted into the right and proper place. Like a piece of him that had always been missing when he walked away from her the first time finally found its special niche.

This was right, he thought.

Celia came running back to them as they passed a bookstore. "Can we look at books?" she said, catching Miriam by the hand.

"Okay with you?" Miriam asked Duncan.

"Absolutely," he returned with a grin.

So inside they went. Celia quickly found the children's section and soon she and Miriam were on the floor, paging through books, pulling out some, rejecting others. Duncan was content to watch the two of them. Miriam with her shining copper hair, bent over Celia.

They could be mother and daughter, he thought, as he watched Miriam tracing out the words she was reading to Celia. The last few days he had witnessed the bond growing between them, and he wondered how Miriam felt. Did she really think she could leave this little girl behind?

His heart skipped a beat as an errant thought settled.

Would she consider staying?

And where did that put him?

He dropped down on one knee beside them, laying his hand on Miriam's shoulder, as if solidifying the thought. His feelings for her were growing. He couldn't dismiss out-of-hand their first meeting and that instant connection they shared. That had to mean something, too, didn't it?

Miriam looked up at him, her soft smile making his heart do a slow flip. He wanted to kiss her again, and when he saw her lips part ever so slightly, he wondered if she felt the same.

Then Celia grabbed a book and dropped it on

Miriam's lap. "Read this one to me," she said.

A strange look came over Miriam as she picked up the book and turned it over to look at the back. She touched the picture of the writer with trembling fingers.

"You okay?" Duncan asked.

Miriam nodded, a wistful look coming over her face. "This lady was the one who wrote the princess books I illustrated."

"Really?"

"I didn't think she was writing again. After we did the princess books together she was diagnosed with Hodgkins." Miriam released a light laugh. "She must have gotten through it."

"Good for her," Duncan said, feeling a bit puzzled at Miriam's reaction. "Is that why you quit illustrating? Because of her?"

Miriam released a harsh laugh. "No. My publisher wanted me to do more but, well, life got complicated."

"Boyfriend?" He threw out the word casually, realizing a woman as attractive as Miriam could not have spent the past few years on her own.

She released a harsh laugh. "Bad boyfriend." Then she gave him a warning look, putting her hand on Celia's shoulder. "Something I prefer not to talk about."

That only made him want to find out more, but he knew that this wasn't the time or place.

"I'm happy she's working again." Miriam gathered the books and stood. "Did you decide which one you wanted?" she asked Celia.

Celia pulled the last book they had looked at, the one by the author Miriam had worked with, out of Miriam's arms. "I want this one."

Duncan trailed behind Miriam and Celia as they walked to the cash register. They passed a table that held adult coloring books, as well as crayons and markers for coloring. Miriam slowed as she passed the table, her fingers trailing over the blank sketchbooks and packages of drawing pencils that took up one corner. A look of yearning came over her face, and a light winked on in his brain.

"Do you take any of your drawing things along when you came here?" he asked.

Miriam jerked her hand back and laughed. "I packed too quick. Just took the essentials."

"Aunty Miriam, I have to go to the bathroom," Celia announced, suddenly dancing beside them.

"Okay. I'll see if I can find one."

"There's one just down the mall a couple of stores," Duncan said. "Give me the book, and I'll wait here."

Miriam nodded and as soon as she left the store, Duncan waved a clerk over. The young man with a ring in his nose, purple hair and pants sagging halfway down his hips came sauntering over. "Do you know anything about these?" Duncan asked, gesturing to the art supplies.

"Yeah, man. I put that display together," he said, tossing his hair out of his face. "I do art."

He shouldn't have been surprised. "Perfect. You can help me figure out what I should get. It's a surprise for that young lady that just left with the little girl."

Mr. Purple Hair gave him a thumbs-up and a slow nod. "Impressive chick. Very."

Though Duncan wholeheartedly agreed, right now he had another focus. "She's a professional illustrator who's staying here temporarily. She doesn't have any supplies with her, and I want to get her some for Christmas, but I don't have a clue. So can you help me out here before she comes back?"

The young man became suddenly all business. "If she's a pro, you'll want to head to Peevey's downtown."

"No time. I need to get what I can now."

"Okay. What we got here isn't pro-level, but it's pretty good. You'll want a variety of pencils.

Some soft and some hard, and a blending tool." He pulled a few packages from the display and then handed him a pad of paper. "And this paper has a good weight and not too much tooth, but there's some paper in the back that really rocks."

"Can you get me the rocking paper?"

"Yeah, man. What about colored pencils?"

"Would she use those too?"

"If she does illustrating, possibly. Though she might use Copics or watercolors."

"We'll start with the pencils," Duncan returned, glancing at Purple Hair's name-tag. "Jeff. And thanks."

Jeff picked up a tin with a picture of an abstract looking tree in rainbow colors. "These are awesome. Smooth lead, blends great. Has wax in the lead so it lays down smooth as silk. Adult coloring is a huge deal and I recommend these to everyone."

Duncan tried not to look shocked at the price on the tin. "These certainly aren't the crayons I used in school."

"They're worth every penny," Jeff assured him so Duncan added them to the pile. "I'll get the paper and then I can ring you in."

Duncan brought everything to the counter, peering around the corner, hoping Miriam wasn't headed back. He grabbed a calendar as well so he could sandwich the supplies between it and Celia's book.

"Can you double bag the stuff?" he asked as the clerk rang his purchases through.

"Course." Thankfully, Jeff was efficient and quickly had the items wrapped up. He handed him the bag and added a wink. "That's an awesome gift for an awesome woman."

Duncan just grinned, pleased with himself that he had found such a perfect gift for Miriam.

He exited the store and walked to a kiosk in the hallway that held maps to the mall. While he was paging through a map, he glanced up in time to see Miriam and Celia walking toward him. Miriam was holding Celia's hand, looking down at her and Duncan caught the same smile she often had when looking at their niece.

How could Miriam think she couldn't take care of Celia? She was clearly connected to her.

Then Celia saw him, released Miriam's hand and ran up to him, looking at his bag, her eyes wide. "Did you buy my book? Did you buy me a present?"

He touched her nose with his fingertip. "You're not allowed to ask questions this close to Christmas."

Miriam joined them, her smile encompassing both of them and she too shot a meaningful look at the bag hanging from his other hand. "You all done?"

"I am. Unless you wanted to get something else?"

Miriam glanced past him, and he wondered if she was thinking about the art supplies. She shook her head then reached into her purse for her wallet. "How much was the book?"

"We can settle back at the house," he said, putting his hand on hers to stop her. She gave him a secretive smile. "Okay, but make sure you do. Otherwise I'll have to come up with something else for her majesty."

Duncan chuckled. "Of course. And now, I have a suggestion for our next store."

"Lead the way." Miriam fell into step beside him while avoiding oncoming shoppers. "I have no idea where to go."

As they walked he looked at the map, then at the stores around them to get his bearings. "We need to get to the other side, over there," he said, pointing to a shoe store across the large opening.

They threaded themselves through the crowd and found a way to cross over to the other side. Duncan walked into the store, glancing around.

When he saw what he was looking for, he grabbed a couple of pairs of boots, turned, and showed them to her. "Which color do you prefer? These light-blue ones with the gray bottoms and yellow laces, or the beige ones with brown laces?"

"Why?"

"What did I just tell Celia?"

Miriam laughed. "That rule is for kids."

"That rule is for Christmas," he returned, giving the boots a shake. "Which ones?"

A wry smile curled over her mouth. "I can buy my own boots."

"I'm sure you can." He cocked her a questioning eyebrow. "Don't fight me on this. I'm bigger, and I'm tired of you getting cold feet when we go out." He could see her hesitation. "Fine. I'll pick then." He set the beige ones aside and started walking to the counter.

"Okay. Okay. I like that color in a size seven."

"Whoa, you have tiny feet." Then he turned back to the saleslady that had zeroed in on him, showed her the boots and gave her the size. Miriam sat down on the backless bench, Celia beside her, giving him a quick smile.

"You don't want to look around?" he asked as he dropped down beside her. An assault of Christmas music declared peace and joy coming to earth in the midst of the thronging shoppers and noise, a contradiction if ever there was one.

He looked over at Celia who was now sitting beside Miriam, swinging her legs and it hit him again. How alike they looked.

"What are you thinking," Miriam asked, giving him a poke. "You're looking pensive."

He shifted his gaze to her. "Just thinking how alike you and Celia look. You seriously could be mother and daughter."

She stared at him, her eyes wide, then she waved off his comment with a laugh. "I think it's just the time we've been spending together. I heard that can happen."

Before he could say anything more, the saleslady returned with a large box, and as she pulled the boots out of the rustling paper Duncan felt a sense of déjà vu. He and Tasha had spent more time than he cared to remember in shoe stores as the clerks opened box after box and Kimberly tried on shoe after shoe. Thankfully Tasha was a patient toddler.

He bit his lip as an unexpected sorrow raked through him. Yet another memory to acknowledge and move on from.

He glanced over at Miriam, who had started him down this path to healing. She was smiling as she laced up the boots. "Wow. My feet are warmer already."

"That's the point," Duncan said, forcing a cheerful note into his voice.

She shot him a puzzled glance, as if she sensed something was off.

"I like those boots," Celia said, jumping off the bench to get a closer look. "Can I have a pair?"

"I believe we have matching boots for your daughter," the clerk said, a hopeful tone in her voice.

Duncan didn't bother to correct her though. And of course, Celia looked directly at him, the one who was financing these proceedings.

She tilted her head just so, gave him exactly the right smile, blinked her eyes, and he was undone.

Two pairs of boots and many dollars later, they walked out of the store.

Miriam stopped, clutching the carrier bag holding her boots and laid her arm on Duncan's arm. "Thank you. That was so generous of you. You didn't have to."

"Merry Christmas," he said, touching her cheek with his finger.

"You have to touch her nose," Celia said,

swinging her own bag back and forth. "Like you do with me."

Duncan chuckled and obliged, and then Celia caught his hand in hers, handing him her bag. "Can you carry this for me?"

It joined the other bag he was carrying, and then Celia frowned. "Dunkle, can you put Jane in the bag?"

"Do you think she'll like being in there?" Duncan asked as he obliged, surprised at this turn of events.

"I want to hold your hand and Aunty Miriam's hand, and I can't if I'm carrying Jane," Celia said matter-of-factly, as she grabbed Miriam's free hand.

As the three of them walked down the mall Duncan shot Miriam a curious glance and wasn't surprised to see her watching him. She gave him a cautious smile and then, together they looked down at Celia.

We're like a little family.

And somehow, the thought didn't bother him like it once would have had.

And somehow, he knew that Christmas, a holiday he normally dreaded, might not be so bad this year.

If Miriam was staying that long.

CHAPTER 15

"*H*ave you had a chance to try out your new boots yet?" Duncan's deep voice resonated in my ear, making me smile.

"They're on my feet as we speak." I tucked my cell phone between my ear and shoulder as I knelt down and helped Celia untie her boots "Celia and I just came back from a walk." It was Saturday now and Esther had come over again. I wanted to give her some privacy, so I thought this would be an excellent opportunity to try out my new boots.

"Did Celia wear hers, too?"

"Oh yes." I pulled her boots off, then helped her with her jacket. She was humming a song, clearly in a good mood. Her cheeks were a bright red that made me smile. "We have a play date this afternoon at a park to go sledding, so she'll get to use them then as well."

"And so will you."

"With much gratitude. How is work going?" I asked, as I rose and hung her coat up and put her boots away.

"Can I have a snack?" Celia whispered and I nodded.

"It's going." I could hear equipment running in the background that slowly faded away, then the slam of a door. "Somehow the crew managed not to break anything while I was gone, so that's a plus."

Duncan had apologized for not coming by today or doing anything with us. I tried to tell him that it didn't matter. I knew he had to work.

Besides, in spite of me wanting him to be more involved, things had shifted so much between us, I needed a bit of mental space to process my own changing emotions. The new place I had found myself in. I didn't need to hurry back to Vancouver but I knew I couldn't stay forever.

Can't you?

I pushed the thought aside. Too soon.

"Thanks again for the boots." I placed said

boots on a rack inside the porch entrance, smiling at their cheerful color. "I feel like I should have protested more, but they kept my feet warm so I'm happy you thought of them."

"If you're happy, I'm happy," he said as I walked into the kitchen. Celia was already sitting down at the eating bar, patiently waiting for her snack.

"I got a call from Phil early this morning," I told him. "He says he'll need access to Jerrod's office in the next week before he finalizes the estate." I poured her some milk and pulled a cookie out of a container that I had taken out of the freezer this morning.

"I'd say finally, but that would be redundant."

"Someone pulled out their thesaurus this morning."

"Someone is smarter than someone else thinks," he returned. "I'm not just a dumb logger-slash-rancher."

"I never thought you were."

I felt a tiny shiver at the delightful inanity of our conversation. The kind between...well...girlfriend and boyfriend. Which was crazy, because we hadn't even gone on anything resembling a date.

"Did he say what time he wanted to come?" he asked.

I leaned my elbows on the counter, allowing myself this domestic moment. Watching my daughter eating a cookie, drinking milk, humming her pleasure while I talked to Duncan.

"First thing Tuesday morning. I'll have to let Esther know."

"She still cleaning up the office?"

"I guess." Though it didn't seem like she was making a lot of headway.

"So what are you doing tonight?"

The words, so ordinary, seemed rife with meaning.

"Putting Celia to bed early. Watching a movie."

"You want some company?"

Another shiver fingered down my spine.

"I think I'd like that a lot."

While we made plans, Celia jumped off the chair and hopped over to the living room, where Jane sat on a chair. To my surprise, she had left Jane behind when we went for our walk, stating that Jane didn't have the same boots that we did, so it was better she didn't come on the walk or the play date.

I was surprised how much I looked forward to the play date. After my morning with the women in the café, I found I missed the company of other women.

"I can bring some pizza and maybe we could all eat together," he suggested.

"And that would be nice, too."

The door of the office opened, and as Esther stepped into the kitchen I felt guilty that I was talking to her brother and that I didn't want her to know. Everything between Duncan and I was so fragile. New. I wasn't sure myself what to do, only that I felt as if I hung suspended between past and future, not sure which direction my life would take.

Esther was looking down at the envelope in her hand, then jumped when she saw me.

"I thought you and Celia...I didn't hear you..." She held the envelope close, as if it held some treasure she had discovered. "I didn't know you were back."

I held up my phone instead of replying and she nodded, walking quickly toward the porch.

"I should go," I said, turning my head and lowering my voice. "Esther is here."

"See you tonight?"

"You bet." And that's all I was going to say with Esther just around the corner.

I ended the call, then walked over to Esther.

"Sorry. I didn't know you were talking on the phone," she said, zipping up her coat.

"That's okay. How is it going cleaning up the office? You sure you don't need any help?"

Esther shook her head as she grabbed the envelope off the deacon's bench, frowning as she looked at me. "So, how are things with you?"

Her question puzzled me. "Fine, since last we spoke."

She took a step and looked around the corner, probably to see where Celia was, then stepped back, lowering her voice. "I thought you were moving back to Vancouver after Celia's birthday."

I held her narrowed gaze, wondering why this mattered to her.

"I'm not sure anymore..." I let the sentence trail off. I didn't think I wanted to tell her that I had quit, or been pushed to quitting.

"Not sure about what?"

I almost stepped back at the harsh tone in her voice.

"A week ago, you and I both agreed that Celia needed to be with Duncan," Esther continued, her frown deepening with each word she spoke. "You told me that this was your plan all along and that you were leaving. What aren't you sure of?"

How I feel about your brother. The hope creeping into my life.

But I couldn't say any of these things aloud.

"You still agree that Celia should stay here, don't you?" she pressed.

"I believe that firmly," I said, thankful I could say this with conviction. I just wasn't sure where I fit in the scenario.

"Good. You also need to know that I'm willing to help Duncan out when you leave."

When I leave.

"Because I think it best if you still do," she continued.

I didn't want her to see how much her comment bothered me, so I kept my features impassive and said nothing.

"We can't have Celia feeling confused," she added, then glanced at her watch. "I better go. I promised Mom I'd help her do some baking for tomorrow. She said Duncan is bringing Celia home tomorrow after church. So that's good that he's showing some initiative."

I just smiled, forcing myself not to feel edged out. Then I reminded myself that Duncan had invited me, as well.

"Will you be finishing up in Jerrod's office soon?" I asked.

She gave me an odd look, her eyes narrowing. "You haven't been in there at all?"

"No. No need to."

"Okay. I'll finish up on Monday. Will you still be here?"

I just nodded, wondering why she thought I was leaving that quickly when I hadn't said anything one way or the other. It was as if she was hinting to me to leave sooner.

"I see," Esther said. "I'll see you then."

She closed the door behind her and I stayed where I was a moment, gathering my tumbled emotions.

Trouble was, I wasn't sure where to put them. The more time I spent with Celia, the harder I knew it would be to go. The thought of leaving her was like cutting off my arm, yet I knew I couldn't take her with me.

And the more time I spent with Duncan, the more I felt I had a reason to stay.

I felt as if I were balancing precariously on a rope, not sure how quickly to move to get across this uncertain place.

Or what would be on the other side when I got there.

* * *

As he waited for Miriam, Duncan eased himself back on the couch staring at the Christmas tree. The twinkling lights and the music flowing from the stereo created a festive air. And now he was drinking a cup of coffee and waiting for Miriam to come downstairs. He had offered to help her put Celia to bed, but was secretly thankful when Miriam said she could do it herself. He was exhausted.

It had been a busy and tiring day. Skyline's rep had come out and given them yet another list of new quality control standards they had to follow. Plus, told them that they might be cut back on their quota next year. He was getting more tired of all the crap he had to deal with. He should get out while he could.

He took another sip and put his feet up on the leather ottoman, easing out a sigh as he rubbed his temple. The lights of the Christmas tree twinkled from one corner of the room, and he had put on the Christmas music station again. He pulled in a sigh, just taking in the ambience.

The best part of the day was coming here. Stepping into this house, seeing Miriam in the kitchen smiling at him, having Celia come running up to him with her usual enthusiasm and throwing her arms around him.

It wasn't his house, but it sure felt like home.

Eating supper together around the kitchen table eased away the hundreds of times he ate alone, in front of the television, half of the time not even aware of what he shoved into his mouth. Or the many times he ate in the café because he didn't want to sit at home alone.

As they shared the meal and listened to Celia's chatter about all the sledding she did on her play date and how much fun it was, he felt a sense of well-being rise up.

And the thought that he could really get used to this.

A creak on the stairs made him look up, and he smiled again as Miriam came down. She was looking at him as well.

"She settle down okay?" Duncan asked, sitting up.

"She was tired. That walk this morning and the play date this afternoon wore her right out."

"You wouldn't have guessed from the way she was yakking at supper time," Duncan said getting up as Miriam walked into the living room, hesitating, as if not sure where she should sit. He thought he would help her out. "Come here. I've got something for you."

"What?"

Duncan reached beside him and pulled out the bag holding the gifts he had taken with him, and laid them out on the coffee table.

He had found some old wrapping paper in the closet in Tasha's room and had taken the time to wrap up the pad of paper, the pencils and the pencil crayons, spurred on by a comment she had made all those years ago. The first time they had been together. He remembered her saying how exciting it was the first time she got a gift that was wrapped up in pretty paper. So he had taken the time to wrap each item up individually.

"What's this all about?" she asked, slowly walking closer, as if drawn on by the shiny packages reflecting the lights of the Christmas tree and the fire in the fireplace.

"It was supposed to be a Christmas present, but I couldn't wait. I know you are probably running out of things to do, so I figured you could use something to keep you occupied." He threw out the words casually, assuming that she would need to fill her days here in Holmes Crossing. Not in Vancouver.

She released a light laugh, shaking her head as if trying to figure this all out. "But I didn't—"

"Get me anything?" He finished for her. Then

laughed. "It's okay. Sometimes you are allowed to just receive."

"I meant to say, I didn't expect to get anything," she said as she sat down beside him.

"Oh. So I might be getting something after all?"

"No questions at Christmas, remember?"

He laughed again, watching her as she reached out to touch the packages almost reverently, making him glad he took the time to wrap them up. "It seems a shame to open them," she said, fingering the ribbon that took him about fifteen minutes to tie just right.

"You could just look at them."

"That's what I feel like doing." She laughed again. "When I lived with Jerrod's family, I used to sneak down early Christmas morning, sit on the floor and just look at all the gifts. I never even wanted to unwrap them."

Duncan felt a twinge of sympathy for a young girl whose life was so devoid of joy and happiness that all it took was the sight of a wrapped gift to make her happy.

"How many Christmases did you have with them?"

"Enough to know how it was supposed to work," Miriam said giving him a grin. "Don't worry, I won't sit and stare at these all night, though I can't believe you wrapped them so nicely."

"A job worth doing is worth doing well," he said, taking one of the packages of pencils and handing it to her. "Start with this."

She unwrapped it slowly, carefully peeling the paper back. She stopped and stared at the pencils then looked over at him. "You bought these at the bookstore."

"I did, and although I was told that Peevey's had better supplies, I thought you could start with these."

"They're perfect." She opened the package and took one out, testing the point with her fingertip. Then she picked up the other presents and just as methodically unwrapped them as well, saving the tin of colored pencils for last.

"Oh wow. These are amazing," she said, her voice filled with awe, holding up the tin as if to examine them better. "I had a set like this..." She stopped, then set it down, turning to him, her smile tremulous. "I can't believe you did this for me." She hooked her arm around his neck and kissed him. She drew back, her eyes still shining. "That's the nicest thing anyone has done for me in years."

He slipped his arms around her and held her closer. He wasn't sure what to say, so instead, he kissed her again. She melted into his embrace, her fingers tangling in his hair as their lips moved over each other, arms tightening, breaths mingling.

Slowly, she drew away, her hands trailing down his neck, coming to rest on his chest. He saw her swallow again and his own breath came quicker than before.

He traced the line of her cheek, her soft lips, exploring her features, then he cupped her face in his hand, his other arm still holding her close.

"You make me feel alive," he whispered, afraid that speaking too loudly would ruin the moment.

Her eyes met his, and in their depths he read an answering emotion.

He toyed with her hair, trying not to think too far ahead. Instead, he chose to go back. To the first time they were together.

"Do you ever think about that summer?" he asked.

She said nothing for a moment, her fingers toying with the button on his shirt. "I do, actually."

"So I know I might sound like a total loser, but why didn't you ever call me? After Jerrod and

Francine's wedding. Why didn't you return my calls or texts?"

* * *

DUNCAN'S WORDS dug up old memories. Old insecurities that returned to haunt me. I wanted to push away and give myself some distance.

"Why do you want to know?" I asked. "That's old history."

"Maybe, but I want to get it out of the way. And I want it out of the way because I feel like that will help us move forward."

Did I dare think this could happen? With this man who had always occupied a corner of my heart and life? With the past I would drag into his present?

I rested my head against his shoulder, carefully picking through my memories. "I enjoyed our dates and our time together. You need to know that. I started to think that maybe things could work between us," I said, deciding which words to pry out from my past. "But when I got back to the States and my lousy job and my crappy apartment, I really saw the differences between us. I wasn't…wasn't living a good life. I had made some wrong choices, and seeing you and your family only underlined how different my life was from yours. I didn't feel like I was worthy of you. It didn't help that I got a text from Jerrod a few days after I got back. He told me that you were a great guy and I should be careful. I knew what he was saying." I took a breath, my heart pushing hard against my chest as I debated what to tell him next.

"He told you that?" Duncan's voice held a harsh edge. "And you believed him?"

"Well, for one thing, he was right."

"No. He wasn't. And neither was my mother," he said, derailing my train of thought.

"What do you mean by that?"

"Kimberly and I had been dating off and on, and my mother always thought she was so perfect for me. She was heartbroken when we broke up. Then, when I met you at the wedding, she told me the same thing. To be careful. That maybe things would be different for me when you got back home. Then, when I didn't hear from you, I figured that's what happened."

"I...I wanted to call you back," I said. "To return your texts. But the longer I waited, the more pointless it seemed. And then I found out you got married."

Duncan's chest lifted in a sigh. "I don't know

why you thought you weren't worthy. I was no better. Kimberly and I got back together, and a few months after that she got pregnant. With Tasha. We got married. Which was a mistake."

I released a harsh laugh. If I were to tell him everything, my confession would have so neatly dovetailed with his. Only, I didn't get married after I got pregnant by my drug-dealing boyfriend.

"Anyway, that's my sad history," he continued. "And now that I know you didn't ignore me because you didn't like me I feel like we can move on. We can talk about good things. I want to talk about you and me."

You and me. The promise in those words thrilled me even as shadows from the past hovered in the background.

"What about us?" I asked, still prevaricating and testing.

"Are you still thinking of going back to Vancouver?" he asked.

I held that thought, weighing, measuring. Did I dare take this step across that space between us? That one step farther along the tightrope?

He was smiling at me, and I thought of the gift he had given me. Wondered if what we had would survive what I needed to tell him.

"Do you want me to stay?" Another tiny step.

He grinned down at me and I felt a weight slip off my chest. "You're going to make me say it, aren't you?"

I wanted to ask what, but felt that would only underscore what he was teasing me about.

"I'm just playing my cards close to my chest," I said, returning his smile. "I have to confess that my life has given me mixed messages about allowing myself to accept gifts and think that things will turn out well for me."

"Of course. I get that. I've got my own hang ups, but I'll stick my neck out. I want you to stay. I want you to take a chance on me and see, this time, where this goes. I feel like God has given us a second chance and though we both seem to have stuff to deal with, I like to believe that we can trust He'll help us through."

His little speech twined around my heart, anchoring me in a safe and secure place.

"Then I'll stay."

He pulled me close and as his lips met mine I sank into his kiss, his embrace, feeling that, for the first time since I came to the Carpenter home, that happiness was a possibility in my life.

You have to tell him.

Just not yet, I told that pernicious voice. Just a

few more days to explore and establish this new relationship.

And then, once I knew I stood on a solid foundation I would tell him everything.

I slowly drew away, giving myself some space for now. Some time to think and absorb what had just happened.

So I focused on the gift he had given me, picking up the sketchpad. I flipped it open, feeling a long-buried sense of anticipation at the sight of the clean paper.

"You want to give it a test run," he teased, leaning back against the couch, holding his head in his interlaced hands.

"I do," I said, suddenly itching to try a sketch. To put pencil to paper and discover and create.

"Go for it," he said with a grin.

I didn't need any more encouragement. I grabbed the pencils and set the paper on my raised knees. Soon the pencil was dancing over the page as I quickly sketched out lines delineating Duncan's face, his hair, and the lines of his chest, his arms.

I smiled as I worked, a curious happiness bubbling up inside me.

"What are you drawing?"

"You."

"Hey. Let me see."

"Artists never let people see their work before their time," I protested, holding my paper pad against my chest, pushing him away with my other hand.

"But I'm the subject," he said with an aggrieved tone as he picked at the corner of my sketchpad with a forefinger.

I shook my head, enjoying the teasing in his tone.

He slumped back on the couch and shot me a warning glance. "Make sure you work hard at making me look handsome," he said.

"I don't have to work that hard," I said, giving him a smile.

"Flattery. I like it."

I returned to my sketching, shading and filling in, catching the angles of his features, the flow of his hair.

Then I heard Celia cry out, and my heart stuttered as I stopped, waiting. Listening.

Then she cried out again, and I set the pad aside, hurrying across the room and up the stairs. Duncan was right behind me.

Celia was still deep in slumber, but twitching in her sleep, muttering, her arms thrashing. I knelt down, taking her hand, talking to her.

"It's okay, honey," I said, stroking her head, trying to calm her down.

She suddenly sat up, her eyes wide as she stared at me. "Mommy?"

The word slivered my soul. I wanted to say yes, lay claim to that title. Instead, I wordlessly pulled her close, cupping her head as she fell against me, crying. "It's okay. I'm here," I said, my hand making rhythmic, soothing circles over her back.

Duncan sat down beside her, his hand resting on her shoulder. I looked at him over her head and then, when his other hand cupped my neck I felt as if the circle was complete.

Celia's sobs slowed, and with one last shuddering breath she pulled back. To my surprise, she leaned forward and kissed my cheek. Joy melted into my soul, filling parched and empty spaces. I wanted to grab her again and stake my claim to her. Instead, I grazed her cheek with a kiss.

"Love you, sweetie," I said.

She sniffed then settled back in her bed. "I just had a bad dream. About Mommy. I thought she was back, and then she ran away." She sniffed once, remnants of the sorrow that had woven around her sleep. "But I still miss Mommy and Daddy."

"Of course you do," I assured her. "You loved them."

She nodded her acknowledgement of this. "I wish they didn't go."

"I wish they didn't go either," Duncan put in, planting his one hand beside her head, touching her nose gently. "But we're here for you."

She gave us both a wavering smile, then drew in a long breath. "I'm glad you're here. Will you stay with me?"

"We'll be here until you fall asleep," Duncan said, taking my one hand, as my other rested on Celia's warm, damp forehead.

Celia snuggled down and slowly her eyes slid shut as her breathing slowed and deepened.

We both stayed a while longer, until we were sure she was asleep. I was the first to get up, slowly easing my hand from her head. Duncan came to stand beside me, and we watched.

"Poor little kid," he whispered. Then he slipped his arm around my shoulder, anchoring me against him. "But, she's got us now."

He sounded so sure, and as I watched my daughter sleeping, I felt again the gift of a second chance.

We could do this, I thought. We could take care of this little girl.

We could be a family.

I just had to pray that when the time came to explain everything to Duncan that he would understand.

Soon I would tell him, I thought as he brushed a kiss over my forehead.

Soon, but not yet.

CHAPTER 16

$\mathcal{A}$ sudden blanket of warmth enveloped me as Celia and I stepped into the Tiemstra house Sunday afternoon. The porch was achingly neat, and I felt guilty as my boots dripped melting snow onto the floor. But beyond the door, Christmas music wafted through the house and the smell of soup cooking made my mouth water.

Celia kicked her boots off and shrugged out of her coat, which I tidied up, trying not to rush myself. Though I would have preferred to see Duncan on my own, the thought of being with his family had an added appeal.

"Hey, Celia. How's my little girl?" I heard Esther ask. "You're finally here."

But Celia simply ignored her and marched into the house.

I felt a tremble of concern as I heard Esther's voice and caught her angry glare. As if I was the reason Celia wasn't talking to her. Being around Esther made me feel like I was overstepping my bounds. Like I shouldn't still be here.

Just as I was hanging up my coat I heard footsteps, then Duncan's arms circled around me from the back, and he was pulling me against him in a tight hug. "Glad you're here," he whispered in my ear, gently turning me around to face him. "I wanted to give you this before you came inside."

And then his lips were on mine as he shared a long, lingering kiss. He rested his forehead against mine. "I missed you. Sorry I didn't come to church."

I had wondered about his absence but didn't want to say anything about it.

"Les got some of the guys working today, even though we don't work Sundays, and of course something went wrong and of course Les needed help." He sighed heavily as he pulled away. "Don't know why I'm telling you all of this."

"I'm a good listener," I teased, cupping his chin and enjoying the bristly and rough feel of it.

He pressed a kiss into my hand, then wrapped

his fingers around mine, giving them a light squeeze. "We should go inside. Esther's been antsy ever since I came home, wondering when you were coming."

This puzzled me. Why should she care?

I thought of her curious behavior yesterday at the house. Did she find something in Jerrod's office she needed to talk to us about?

Duncan's parents were already at the table when I came in, and I hurried to find an empty spot, feeling guilty that I had made them wait.

"Come and sit by me," Celia demanded, slapping the empty chair beside her. "And Dunkle you have to sit beside Aunty Miriam."

"Really?" Duncan asked, pulling out the chair for me to sit down. "Why do you get to decide who sits where?"

"Because I know you like Aunty Miriam." She put her hand over her mouth and giggled, looking down at Jane. "We saw them kissing, didn't we, Jane?"

My breath stuck in my chest, my heart suddenly taking off as I heard Esther's shocked cry.

Her mother looked from Esther who was trying to compose herself to me, then to Duncan as if trying to connect the dots.

"Kissing?" she asked.

I shot Duncan a concerned look but he was just grinning. As if he didn't care. And then, to underscore what Celia had just said, he brushed a kiss over the top of my head, his lips teasing at my hair.

"Yeah, Mom. Kissing."

I couldn't speak. Didn't know what to say or where to look, so instead I focused on getting the cutlery beside my plate and bowl sitting exactly right.

"I'm rather confused," Mrs. Tiemstra was saying. "What is going on?"

"I can't believe this," Esther said. "Francine and Jerrod are...it's only been three weeks...how—"

"I think we should eat first," Duncan said, settling in his chair and giving me a smile of encouragement.

I swallowed, trying to slow the emotions rushing over me. Too soon. Everything between Duncan and I was still changing and growing. To be put under his family's scrutiny already scared me.

"I agree," his father said. "So let's pray."

Everyone bowed their heads and I felt Duncan's hand reach for mine under the table. He gave me a squeeze of encouragement, which I returned, my heart rate slowing.

"Our Father in heaven and on earth," his father prayed. "Thanks for food and for life. For healing and strength. Help us through this time and give us Your comfort and hope. Help us to cling to the promise of peace You give us. Amen."

His simple prayer wound its way around my soul. Church this morning had been comforting again. The minister had preached on peace. How God never promised us a life without difficulties, but that the peace He offered transcended this world and its chaos. I clung to that hope now, as my own brain scurried around, chasing down concerns and worries.

"So, did you get your problems solved in the bush?" Duncan's mother asked, as she stood to serve everyone up some soup.

"Yeah. I did. Don't know what Les was thinking, sending the guys out. He knows we don't work Sundays."

"He's a go-getter, that Les," his father said. "He may come across as a bit of an idiot, but he's not so dumb when it comes to the business."

Duncan and his father chatted back and forth about the business while we ate, but all the while I caught Esther and her mother sending me surreptitious glances, as if trying to understand what was going on between Duncan and myself.

The conversation slipped to the community and I was content to listen, wondering if I would be able to remember the names I heard Esther and her mother discuss.

I felt a momentary panic as I thought of me staying here. If Esther and Cora reacted the way they had to the news of me and Duncan kissing, how would they to me staying?

And where would I work?

I dismissed the fearful thoughts, reminding myself of what Duncan's father had just prayed. That I knew I could receive God's peace no matter what.

"I think Jane is full," Celia said to her grandmother, looking down at her half-empty bowl. While I was glad she ate most of her soup, it bothered me that she still spoke by way of her doll. At least to her grandmother.

"And what about you, honey?" Esther asked, leaning closer to Celia. "Are you full?"

"Jane doesn't want to talk to you," Celia said.

I was taken aback at her blunt comment. "Celia, watch your manners. That wasn't polite."

"My mommy didn't like Aunt Esther," Celia said in a matter of fact tone. "And Jane doesn't either."

"Celia. You shouldn't say that," Mrs. Tiemstra reprimanded her as Esther's face grew pale.

"That's not true," Esther said.

I frowned glancing over at Celia who didn't seem bothered by the reactions of the Tiemstra women.

Celia just shrugged, then stepped away from the table.

"We're not finished with lunch," I said to her, but I could see that Celia had slipped into a stubborn mood and seemed to sense I wouldn't do anything about it around Duncan's parents and Esther.

"I want to watch television," she said.

"It's okay, honey," Mrs. Tiemstra said with a quick nod, getting up from her chair. "Go into the playroom, and you can watch there."

"What have you been saying to her?" Esther asked me, her tone accusing as her mother left the table, holding Celia's hand. "Why is she talking like that to me?"

"I have no idea," I protested, surprised at the edge of panic in her voice.

"You must have done something. Told her something."

"What could I possibly have told her?" I was puzzled at Esther's growing antagonism.

"Esther, relax. It was just Celia being Celia," Duncan said.

Esther dragged her gaze away from me then looked over at her brother, her features softening. "Of course. I'm sorry."

By that time, Mrs. Tiemstra returned. I could hear the television quietly playing from the play-room, and though I couldn't see Celia, I could hear her singing along. She sounded happy.

"So do you have any plans for the coming year?" Duncan's father was asking him, clearly returning to the conversation they had before.

Duncan sat back from the table, slowly pulling in a deep breath, as if getting ready to say something important.

"I did, but lately I've been thinking more about the farm and less about the logging."

"What do you mean?" his father asked.

"I'm thinking that I might find a way to ease out of the business," Duncan said.

"Why would you do that?" his mother asked.

Duncan's hand was resting on my knee so I took it. Squeezed it to give him encouragement.

"I'm tired, Mom," he said. "Tired of juggling work and trying to keep things going. I want to focus on the ranch and the horses, and stop running around trying to keep everyone happy. And, well, I have other dreams. Other plans." His eyes slid sideways toward me for a fraction of a second, then back to his mother, who was looking at him like he had grown an extra head.

"But the business...it used to be Dad's," Esther was saying looking from him to me, her look almost accusing.

Not something I had anything to do with, I wanted to say.

"I know, and I'm sorry, but I don't want...I can't..."

"End up like me," his father put in with a heavy voice. "I don't blame you, son. The longer you're out there the higher your chance of getting hurt."

Duncan gave his father a smile and my hand an extra squeeze.

"And what other plans do you have?" Esther insisted. "What are you doing that will keep you so busy?"

"See, that's just it," Duncan said. "I don't want to be that busy. I want to have a life."

Esther's gaze slid to me and I saw her slowly shake her head. "With her?"

"You mean Miriam?" Duncan asked.

Too fast. Things were moving too fast. I wanted people to stop talking about me, about us. It was all so new and fresh. To have it now under such close scrutiny gave me the willies. And I certainly didn't understand Esther's sudden antagonism.

"Esther, keep your voice down," their mother said, but she was looking at me as well. "We're not discussing this."

"Of course not. We don't talk about things that are right in front of us," Esther snapped.

"Have you heard anything more from Phil?" his father asked, breaking into Esther's comment.

"He wants to come on Tuesday to the house." Duncan sounded relieved at the switch in topic.

Then Esther pushed away from the table, tossing her napkin down. "Duncan, we need to talk. Privately."

She looked directly at me, her eyes narrowing.

She knows something. She found something in Jerrod's papers. Ice slipped through my chest, blooming outward.

"What on earth do you need to say to Duncan that you can't say here in front of us?" his mother asked.

"Please, Duncan. It's important." Esther was quiet now, sadness pulling her features down.

When Duncan's hand slipped out of mine, I felt as if my blood was filling my chest, surging into my throat. I wanted to call him back, as a sense of urgency pervaded the atmosphere. I didn't want him to go. So strong was the compulsion I almost got to my feet, but Esther showed me her palm. "Please, Miriam. I need to talk to Duncan, just the two of us."

It was about me. Had to be.

But I couldn't say anything, so I just nodded.

And then I started praying.

* * *

"First off, I don't appreciate what you said to Miriam," Duncan said, closing the door behind him. "Nor the way you were talking to her."

Esther shook her head as she leaned back against their father's roll-top desk, her hands resting on either side of her hips. The desk was as cluttered with papers as it was when his father ran the business. "I'm sorry. I don't know what got into me. I'm still dealing with Jerrod's death. And Fran's."

"We all are," Duncan said. "So what is so important that you couldn't talk in front of everyone else? And please don't tell me it's about me getting out of the business."

"Why can't I talk to you about the business?"

"Because it's none of yours. I've worked my

butt off for too many years trying to keep people happy, and I'm not doing it anymore." Duncan walked over to the window of the office and looked out over the yard. His parents' home was on one corner of the ranch, looking out over the river valley. He pulled in a deep sigh, the ticking of the grandfather clock in one corner of his father's office measuring out the time in heavy, solid increments.

"You tired of it?"

"I am. It's exhausting."

"And Mom and Dad?"

"They're fine. The money I paid Dad to buy him out is invested in solid stock. Plus, they have the insurance money from the accident."

"Speaking of insurance money, is that why Phil needs to come? Because of the insurance company?"

"He needs to go over a few things. Sounds like the mortgage insurance will pay off the house, but Jer and Fran's life insurance company are balking about paying out. Said because they were involved in a risky sport they aren't covered. He also wants to check on Jerrod's business dealings. Go through some of his old tax files because of this guy who is putting a claim against the estate.

He figures he can get it dismissed but just wanted to cover all his bases."

"So if the insurance company doesn't pay out there might not be any money for Celia?"

Duncan wasn't interested in dealing with all of this. "The house can be sold. That money can be put in trust."

"Sold? But it was Jerrod's home—" she stopped there, pressing her fist against her mouth.

Her reaction was curious. "Fran's, too," he added.

Esther nodded, swiping at her eyes. "Yes. Of course." Then she released a harsh laugh as she pulled a tissue out of her pocket and dabbed at her eyes. "Not that she ever took care of it. It took Miriam the whole time she was here to clean it up. She did a good job."

"She is a tidy and organized person." While he was happy to hear praise for Miriam it bothered him that Esther would talk that way about their sister.

"You like her?" Esther asked, sniffing again. "Miriam?"

"I do. I like her a lot."

"You liked her already when you met at Fran's wedding, didn't you?"

"I did." He wasn't ready to talk about Miriam.

Not when things were so new between them, so he shifted his attention back to his sister. "So, now that we're in private, away from everyone else, tell me what you couldn't tell me back there."

Esther bit her lip, looking down at the tissue she had been worrying while she talked. "I wanted to talk to you about Phil going through Jerrod's papers."

"You pulled me away in private just to tell me that?"

"I didn't want Mom and Dad asking a bunch of questions."

Duncan felt puzzled, but Esther wouldn't catch his eye. He grew suspicious. "What's the deal, Esther? Miriam said you didn't want her going through the office, either."

"I didn't think she had any right to."

"Miriam was his sister, and probably had more right to do it than you did."

"Not really. She's just—"

"She's just his foster sister, right?" he said, annoyed with the insinuation that Miriam's relationship was less important than Esther's tenuous one.

"No. I didn't think that."

"At any rate, she is Celia's guardian," he pressed. He had made the mistake of not fighting for Miriam the last time. He wasn't making that mistake again. "You should have left all that to her."

"I couldn't," Esther said, an edge of panic in her voice, folding and unfolding the tissue she couldn't keep her eyes off of. "I couldn't leave it to her. I couldn't leave it to anyone else."

"Why not?" he asked, anger edging his voice.

"Because." She stopped there, her hands still torturing the tissue.

"That's no answer."

Esther took a quick breath, tears suddenly spilling down her face. "I couldn't let her get into Jerrod's office for the same reason I can't let Phil in the office. I'm not done yet. I haven't found—" Again, she stopped.

"Found what? What are you looking for that's so important?"

Esther shook her head, her breathing shallow.

"Esther, look at me. What is going on? Why did you feel only you should clean out Jerrod's office?"

She spun around, away from him, still saying nothing.

"Tell me why," he pushed.

"I didn't want anyone to find all the letters or the e-mails," she said finally, her voice quiet.

"What letters and e-mails?"

"The ones Jerrod and I wrote each other. The ones when we were..." She stopped, her voice breaking.

"Were what? When you and Jerrod were what?"

Esther took another breath. "When we were having an affair," she said, her voice a hoarse whisper.

"What?" Had he heard right? "An affair?"

She turned to face him now, holding her hand up, her eyes wide with fear. "Be quiet. I don't want Mom and Dad to hear."

He moved closer, lowering his voice. "You and Jerrod?" He couldn't wrap his head around the idea. Tried to put the information in some place that made sense. "How long?"

"For the past three years. He was going to leave Francine, but said he couldn't because of Celia."

"Nor should he have," Duncan said, his own heart heaving at the thought.

"But they were fighting all the time—"

"So that's what was going on."

Esther shot him a frown. "What do you mean?"

"Miriam said something about Celia complaining about the loud voices. She'd asked me if Fran and Jerrod ever fought. And they did." He turned on Esther. "Over you, I imagine." Then another thing clicked in his mind. "And that's why Celia talks to you the way she does. She must have overheard them fighting about you."

She straightened. "Don't look at me like that. It wasn't something I chose."

"But it's something you could have stopped. He was married. He had a daughter."

"He was hoping to take Celia with him. So we could be a family."

"That's not a family," Duncan said, anger slowly rising. "That's a disaster."

Then, as he said the words, he felt things finally clicking into place. "Is that why Fran named Miriam as Celia's guardian? Was it because you were cheating with her husband?"

"Don't talk like that. It wasn't like that," Esther countered, holding up her hand. "I loved him."

"That's a lame excuse and incredibly unoriginal. If you really loved him, you would have left him alone. You would have put his interests before yours."

"Like Miriam did with Celia?" Esther shot back, her eyes blazing with anger. "Like those kind of interests?"

"What do you mean?" A sense of dread trickled down his neck. "What do you mean like Miriam did with Celia?"

Esther just stared at him, then swallowed, her eyes bright, her breathing shallow. She shook her head, waved him off. "Nothing. Never mind."

"You're hiding something else. I know it. What else are you hiding?"

"It's not my secret to tell."

"You said something about Miriam. You said, like Miriam did with Celia. What did you mean?"

Esther's face contorted, and he could see she was struggling. The niggling sense of dread wound more tightly around his gut.

"What did you mean?" he pressed, fear making him more angry than he liked. He grabbed her by the shoulders, feeling as if he had to shake it out of her. "Tell me what you meant?"

"It's Miriam," Esther spat out. "Miriam is Celia's natural mother. Jerrod and Fran adopted her from Miriam."

Her words floated past him in a fog as he tried to absorb what she was saying. He stepped away from her, clenching his fists.

"They never told us who the mother was, but it's true," she said, the words flowing out of her now. "I found the adoption papers in Jerrod's office. Miriam Bristol is named as the mother."

"Miriam Bristol? Miriam is Celia's mother?"

"Yes. And that's why, I'm sure, Francine named her guardian."

Duncan felt like his legs couldn't hold him up. Like he would fall over, so he caught the edge of his father's desk, steadying himself. "Miriam gave Celia up? For adoption?"

"Yes. I didn't want to tell you, but you pushed me."

Duncan shook his head, trying to sort things out. Too many emotions had been dredged up the past few weeks, piling on top of what he and his family had already lost. He felt as if he'd been balanced on a knife's edge for so long. Only during the past few days had he felt like he'd found his footing again.

And now? This?

Miriam and Celia. Why hadn't he seen it himself? The joke he made in the mall about how Miriam could be Celia's mother, and she just laughed. Like it was nothing. She could have said something then. Or a dozen other times.

He thought they were close. That they had something. But she felt she had to hide this important piece of information from him.

Did she think he would never find out? Did she think this didn't matter?

A deep chill seeped into his soul, encasing his heart, rising up his throat to his face.

Miriam gave up Celia. She didn't want her own daughter.

Just like Kimberly hadn't wanted Tasha.

CHAPTER 17

I helped Mrs. Tiemstra clear the table, while Mr. Tiemstra wheeled his chair to the playroom, Celia right behind him. Then he closed the door. It was as if he sensed that the muted voices in the office, rising and falling, would soon spill over into the rest of the house.

What did Esther think she needed to tell Duncan in private? And they sounded like they were arguing.

I couldn't still my anxious thoughts. With trembling emotions I struggled to cling to what the pastor had preached about this morning as I rinsed dishes and put food away, listening to Mrs. Tiemstra's inconsequential chit-chat about people in the community and plans for Christmas.

Peace. God's perfect peace casts out fear. So why did anxiety wrap its chilly fingers around my gut? Why did I have this unyielding sense of impending doom?

Because anytime anything good comes into my life, it's yanked away.

I snapped the lid on the container holding the leftover soup, disappointed to see how my fingers trembled.

The door of the office burst open, and Duncan's heavy footfalls thundered down the hall. He came into the kitchen, stopped, and looked directly at me, his eyes cold. Hard. Unfeeling.

And there it was. My fears come to fruition.

"Why did you do it? Why didn't you tell me about Celia? Were you ever going to tell me you were her mother?"

My panicked gaze shot backward but, thankfully, the door to the playroom was closed.

My legs grew weak, undependable, and I grabbed the counter to steady myself. My breath came quick. Duncan knew. I didn't have a chance to tell him myself.

"I couldn't," was all I could say, as I tried to

find my footing in the face of his battering anger. "I couldn't tell you."

"Why not?"

I looked at him, his blazing eyes and behind the anger saw confusion and a hurt betrayal.

And what would he say if I told him the truth? If this was how he reacted to my first secret, how would he to the second?

"I had to. I had no choice."

"Choice." He shook his head, emitting a disgusted sigh. "There's always a choice."

"No. There isn't." I struggled to keep my own growing anger in check. "I did what I thought was best for Celia. I'm not sorry I did it and I would do it again."

"So you were willing to give up your child."

I tried to separate his anger from his words and find my footing in the storm that was washing over me. "I had to," was all I could say.

"Did you ever really want her?"

For a moment my mind sifted back to that moment when I found out I was pregnant. When I realized that Gregg was the father. After all he had put me through. After I took the fall because of him. After I ended up in prison because of him. How he avoided me. The confusion I felt, and the fear.

And those emotions must have shown on my face, because as I hesitated, Duncan stepped back. Away from me.

"You couldn't trust me with the truth? You couldn't tell me that you gave up your own child?"

I had no defense.

"Then you had a chance to take her back. But you couldn't do it then either? You told me over and over again that you couldn't take care of her."

His growing anger battered at me as my mind floundered for reasons. Excuses.

"You're no different than Kimberly," was all he said, before I could formulate my thoughts, his words piercing like darts. "You're just like her."

Then he strode out of the kitchen, slamming the door of the porch behind him, the sound echoing like a shot.

I could only stare at the closed door, my heart banging against my ribs.

"My goodness, girl. Is it true?" Mrs. Tiemstra asked, turning to me as if I knew. "What he said about you and Celia? About you being her mother?"

But I was spared replying by the sound of Esther's crying. She stood in the doorway to the kitchen, one arm hugging her midsection, the other resting on the doorframe, as if to hold herself up.

"Honey, what's wrong?" Mrs. Tiemstra turned away from me, tossed the towel she'd been drying the dishes with aside, and slipped an arm around her daughter's shoulders, pulling her close.

But Esther held herself stiff in her mother's arms. "Where's Celia?"

"She's with Dad in the playroom," Mrs. Tiemstra said. "They're watching cartoons. Honey, what is going on?"

Esther turned to me, tears now streaming down her cheeks in earnest. "I'm so sorry, Miriam. I tried to keep quiet. I didn't want to tell him, but I made a mistake and he kept pushing me. I told him. About you and Celia."

"What do you mean you told him about Miriam and Celia?" Mrs. Tiemstra looked from me to Esther, genuinely confused. "Duncan said something about Miriam being Celia's mother."

I could hear Celia giggling beyond the closed door, Mr. Tiemstra's deep chuckles joining in. This was what I had wanted for my daughter, I thought. This family. These roots.

I yanked myself back to the moment and the time at hand. "It's true," I said, my voice barely above a whisper. "I'm sorry I didn't say anything sooner."

"We need to talk, Miriam," Mrs. Tiemstra said in a surprisingly matter-of-fact tone. "Esther, you go make sure Celia is taken care of." She laid her hand on her daughter's shoulder before she left and gave her a faint smile.

Esther just nodded, and though I was curious as to what that was about, I had larger things weighing on my shoulders.

A few moments later, we were all bundled up, walking down the sidewalk, our boots squeaking on the cold snow, the air cooling my heated cheeks.

Mrs. Tiemstra tucked her hands in the pockets of her down jacket, looking up at the trees covered with layers of snow like frosting on a cake. "I usually love this time of the year," she said, her breath making puffs of fog in the chilly air. "That sense of expectation. But this year..." her voice broke, then she gave me an uncertain smile. "This season will be hard for you as well, I'm sure."

I just nodded, not trusting myself to articulate the many reasons why it would be. Right now, Duncan's anger with me was the most pressing reason. That moment of joy and peace I thought

I could hold on to had been torn out of my hands.

And yet, at the same time, another measure of relief flowed in behind the pain. I didn't have to keep it a secret anymore. I could tell people the truth about Celia. I could lay my claim to her.

"I have a secret of my own to tell," Mrs. Tiemstra said, looking ahead as she spoke. "I know you and Duncan cared for each other when you met at Francine and Jerrod's wedding."

I didn't reply. I was still processing my own emotions.

"I need to tell you that I still feel bad about what I had said to Duncan. After the wedding. How I told him not to waste his time with you. To get back together with Kimberly." She released a light laugh but it held no humor. "I loved Kimberly. I watched her grow from a little girl into a beautiful woman. Her parents were our good friends, and remained so even after they moved away a year after the accident." Her voice grew wistful. "Too many losses in the past while."

Again, I kept quiet, not sure where this conversation was going, but thankful for her apology.

"I was being an interfering mother, thinking I knew what was best for my boy and that Kimberly would be the perfect wife for him. I was so sad when he broke up with her. Then when I found out that he was going on a date with a girl he'd been dancing with all night..." She sighed. "A girl I only knew as Jerrod's foster sister, I got a little nervous. I spoke with Jerrod to find out more about you. When he said that he didn't think the relationship was a good idea and that he had his own reservations about you, I overreacted. I am afraid that what I did wasn't very Christian. I judged based on what someone else had told me."

Funny that it could still hurt, my brother's estimation of me. And yet, how far off was he?

"He was partly right," I said, keeping pace with Mrs. Tiemstra, staring at the opening in the trees at the end of the driveway.

"What do you mean?"

I stopped, needing to see her face to face, to deal with this head-on, so to speak. "I made bad choices in my life," I said, forcing myself to hold her gaze. "I could blame my absent mother, my turbulent childhood, but I had a good example in Sally Carpenter." I shoved my fisted hands deeper in my coat pocket, hunching my shoulders against a chill that came from within and without.

"And you lost her, too."

The sympathy in Mrs. Tiemstra's voice was almost my undoing.

"After I met Duncan I thought I had a chance at normal. I thought I could find a happy-ever-after, but—" And once again my voice trembled.

"We stopped that."

I shook my head. "It wasn't just you. It was me. Duncan tried to text me, but I ignored the texts. I wasn't in a good place in my life and I dove right back into it after Jerrod told me to leave Duncan alone. I believed his view of me. I started hanging out with the wrong people. I went back to a man I knew I shouldn't be with, but one that I thought I deserved, and I got pregnant."

A stillness fell between us, and I felt as if every word I spoke was dragged out of me. But I finally found the words and drew them out. "I got pregnant, and I couldn't take care of the baby. Not in…in my circumstances at the time, not where I was at the time, so Jer and Fran adopted her."

"So Celia really is your daughter," Mrs. Tiemstra breathed, her gloved fingers resting beside her mouth.

I swallowed, unable to speak past the boulder now lodged in my throat. I couldn't tell her anything else. This was hard enough.

Then, to my surprise, Mrs. Tiemstra placed her hand on my shoulder, squeezing lightly. "My dear girl. I'm sure you had your reasons, and I'm so sorry for you. But you need to know that Celia has been a blessing in so many ways to this family."

I felt sorrow clawing up my throat. I didn't want to cry in front of this elegant and contained woman. But her unexpected caring was my undoing and my eyes welled up with tears. Then to my surprise, she pulled me close. Like a mother would.

I laid my head on her shoulder, and the tears came. Tears for losing Celia, Jerrod, Francine and all the other losses in my life. Tears for the anger I saw in Duncan's eyes. For what I thought we had, and the uncertainty that seemed to be my lot in life.

I felt like a boat tossed in a storm, but Mrs. Tiemstra's arms were a surprising and unexpected anchor.

Finally I drew away, swiping my mittened hands over my face, sniffing loudly, the moisture on my cheeks growing suddenly cold in the winter air.

Mrs. Tiemstra's expression was all sympathy and understanding. She pulled a tissue out of her pocket and handed it to me, then pulled another one out and wiped her own red eyes.

"It's been kind of a lousy month, hasn't it?" Her comment surprised me, coming from someone who always carried herself so elegantly.

I thought of Duncan and the moments we shared. My time with Celia. "There have been some good moments," I murmured.

"So, now what?" she asked me as we both turned, moving back toward the house.

"I don't know." I was exhausted mentally, emotionally.

"You know, we can take care of Celia for the rest of the afternoon. Why don't you go home, have a nap. Give yourself some space. We'll bring Celia back after supper."

Though I didn't like the idea of being away from Celia, the thought of a few moments alone held a strong appeal.

"I think I'll take you up on that."

"It's just for an afternoon. Give yourself some time alone." Then she gave me a nervous smile. "As for Duncan, I know he was badly hurt by Kimberly, and losing Tasha gutted him. But in the past few days I've seen a lightness and a purpose return to his life. I think it's because of you."

I clung to her words, even though I sensed

that she didn't know the entire story about Kimberly and Tasha. And I wasn't about to enlighten her to explain how deeply betrayed Duncan was by his wife's actions. To be compared to her was an indictment I doubted I could recover from.

"He's angry that you didn't tell him and I can understand why, to a point. Duncan can't abide it when people hold secrets. But I think you're good for him. I think you can give him what he needs." Then she gave me a sideways hug, our hips bumping against each other. "He'll come around. I'm sure. Just stay optimistic."

I wished I could believe her. Optimism was like a plant that needed nourishment. Mine was wilted and lifeless.

By the time we got back to the house, the kitchen was all tidied up. Celia was asleep on the couch, so this was my chance to leave. Esther was nowhere to be seen, so I said a whispered goodbye to Mr. Tiemstra, received a final, quick hug from Duncan's mother, and a few minutes later I was driving down the road, back to the house. The empty, lonely house.

When I got home I took a bath, wishing my anxious, twisting thoughts would pop as easily as the bubbles I was soaking in.

I should have told Duncan sooner about Celia.

I knew that. But when would have been the right time?

I got out of the tub, dressed and wandered around the house, looking for something to do, my footsteps echoing in the heavy emptiness. I re-plumped pillows and rearranged the pictures on the mantle, then turned to the coffee table.

The sketchpad, crayons, and pencils Duncan had given me still lay in a neat pile. The sight of them created a wave of sorrow.

I grabbed both kinds of pencils and the pad, curled up in a corner of the couch, and tried to channel my chattering thoughts onto paper. When I opened the sketchpad, the sketch I made of Duncan jumped out at me, and what I had just lost loomed large, unattainable.

Another sob thickened my throat, but I stifled it. I was alone, as I usually was. I simply had to endure it. Like I had before.

With a quick flip of the page he was gone, and I wished I could as easily remove him from my life. But I knew I couldn't. It had been hard enough the first time. This time? Impossible.

And Celia? What would become of her?

I had to release the thoughts that doubled back on themselves. Instead, I let them flow through my pencil, capturing the curve of Celia's cheek, the wispy curls of her hair, so like mine when I was young. I drew pictures of her walking through fields, flying a kite, living the life I had dreamed for her. She wasn't supposed to be alone, without her parents. I made the sacrifice so she could have what I didn't. A home and a family from when she was a baby. I had loved her and wanted the best for her.

But what would happen now?

Another sketch to drown out the questions, but this time it was Duncan who appeared on the paper. Tall, broad-shouldered, hair hanging to his collar, holding his hand out to a little girl. Celia, who was reaching out to him.

There was room on the other side of Celia for another person. Another adult. A mother.

My pencil hovered over the space as tears slid down my cheeks. Did I deserve to be in this picture?

You're just like Kimberly.

Duncan's words rang in my ears.

I could make all the excuses I wanted for how my life turned out. How I thought I had found something wonderful in Duncan after my brother's wedding. How I thought he was a second chance. An opportunity for a new life.

And then, how rejected I felt when Jerrod warned me away from Duncan.

How alone I felt, how afraid. Gregg found me in a bar, made me feel good. I thought he was my salvation, when he turned out to be my condemnation.

I had paid a high price for my stupidity, but it was paid. I set my sketchpad aside, got up, and went upstairs to my room. I found my Bible and brought it back down, settling back in the couch as I opened it. My movements were random as I turned pages, idly seeking. Here and there a passage struck me, and then, there it was in Psalm 32.

Blessed is the one whose transgression is forgiven, whose sins are covered...I said I will confess my sins to you and you forgave the guilt of my sin....you are my hiding place, you will protect me from trouble.

The words flowed over me, reminding me of the journey I had taken. The time when I had confessed. When I had let go of the guilt that clung so tenaciously to me.

I shook my head as I re-read the words. What would have happened if I had told Jerrod that he was wrong at that time? That yes, I had made mistakes, but in Christ my sins were forgiven?

What if I had truly believed that, instead of believing what Jerrod said?

What if I had fought, instead of rolling over and believing those lies? What if I had fought for Duncan then, fought for myself? What could have happened? Would I have so quickly believed Gregg and his promises? Would I have thought he was all I deserved?

An unexpected anger with Jerrod surged through me, which was immediately followed by guilt. How could I think ill of the dead?

Actually, it wasn't that hard. What Jerrod had done was wrong. And because of that, he had pushed me back into a space I didn't belong. I didn't belong there then, and I didn't belong there now.

I wasn't like Kimberly. I wanted my daughter, and I wanted what was best for her. I needed to tell Duncan that. I needed to fight for myself. To show him that I was worthy of caring for.

And will you tell him everything?

Would he be able to stand the truth?

He had to. And if he didn't, well then he wasn't worth fighting for, was he?

CHAPTER 18

*D*uncan parked his truck by the coffee shack, shivering as he stepped into the cold winter weather.

I won't miss this, he thought as he zipped up his jacket and slipped on his gloves. In the distance, snow shivered off a spruce tree as the buncher buzzed its blade through the base. Then another. And another.

He could hear the roar of skidders dragging the cut trees to the block, where the processor was working. Beyond that, a loader was dropping logs onto a truck. Each piece of equipment required maximum production, which created higher maintenance, which put a dent in the bottom line. Every day, it was about that all-important bottom line.

And he was tired of doing the math required to make the numbers on that bottom line black and not red.

A dusty blue pickup, crusted with snow, bounced across the block road, then stopped a few feet from him. Les jumped out, still wearing his safety vest and ever-present hardhat.

He was on his phone, frowning and gesturing wildly with his free hand.

"It's not necessary," he was saying as he strode toward Duncan. "You guys are going way overboard on this." He gave Duncan a quick nod of his head in acknowledgement. "Okay. We'll meet for coffee to see how we can make this work for both of us." He stabbed the screen of his phone and dropped it into the holder on his belt. "Did Allistair talk to you about this new deal?" he asked with a note of disgust.

"He tried to call yesterday, but I don't take calls on Sunday."

"Right. Forgot." Les shook his head. "They want us to hold safety meetings every morning now, instead of once a week. Like that won't cut into the production they keep pushing us to maximize."

"Do the guys know?"

"Just found out. We're meeting to figure out another plan. All part of the business." He shrugged as if shaking it off then gave Duncan a grin. "So, you back to work? Or are you getting used to being away?"

Duncan paused a moment, second thoughts chasing each other around his brain.

Then he pushed them aside. If anything, yesterday had shown him that he needed to take care of himself. To do what worked for him.

"Come with me." And before he could catch Les' reaction, he walked into the coffee shack. He poured himself a cup of coffee from the coffee maker, dumping in his usual two packets of sugar.

Les closed the door behind him and got a coffee as well. "So. What's up?"

"We need to talk about the business."

"Sure." Les sat down, but then his phone rang and he glanced down at the screen. "Sorry. It's Small Power. I got to take this."

Duncan nodded, sipping at his coffee, thinking of the many conversations that had taken place in this coffee shack. All the gossip, the chitchat, the griping and comparing. The friendly competition and ribbing. The complaining and the jokes. It had become ingrained in the routine of his life. The plans he made. Could he really let go of this?

He thought of the phone conversation he'd had with Phil on the way into the bush this morning. Good news on all fronts. The mortgage insurance would be paid out. And though Jerrod's life insurance wouldn't, Francine's would. Jerrod's ex-partner had dropped his claim against the estate—which meant Phil wouldn't need to go through Jerrod's personal papers at all.

Esther had panicked for nothing.

And if she hadn't panicked, he might not have found out the truth about Celia. The truth about Miriam.

"You okay, man? You look kind of sick."

Duncan pulled his thoughts back to the present, and slanted Les a lame smile. "Yeah. I'm fine." He was anything but. He hadn't slept more than an hour at a time last night. He kept going over what Esther had blurted out.

Miriam was Celia's mother. Miriam had told him from the start that she couldn't take care of her own daughter. She was no different than Kimberly, and that thought cut deeper than he thought it could.

"So what do you want to talk about?"

Duncan set his coffee mug aside, and crossed his arms over his chest. "This business. I want out. Are you interested in buying me out?"

Les' eyes grew to twice their normal size, his mouth actually falling open. He blinked a few times, then pulled himself back together. "You serious, man? You really want to sell out?"

"Dead serious. I'm tired of all the stress and the work." This morning, he had made his final decision. Had told his father, and was surprised at the support he got. All the way here, going down roads he'd often driven too fast on, one hand on the steering wheel, the other often holding a phone or the mic of the two-way radio, head in two places at once as he dealt with trouble and disaster, he'd gone over and over what he wanted to do.

At one time, he wanted out because he'd harbored a vague notion of him and Miriam. And Celia. A little family.

And now? Now he just wanted to move on. Start a new life and leave this behind.

"Not gonna lie, I'm kind of shocked," Les was saying. "So why are you doing this now?"

Why now, indeed?

"I just found out this morning that Jerrod and Francine's estate is settled. I don't need to worry about Celia. And I'm tired of living a complicated and stressful life."

And some of that stress came from what he'd found out about a woman he cared for. He knew he felt angry and betrayed, and assumed the final push to do this came from hearing about Miriam.

"I took on this business to pay for a lifestyle that...that Kimberly wanted. Then, when she and Tasha died, I stayed in as a way of keeping myself busy. To try to forget how much it hurt to lose them." He stopped there, but was surprised that the thought didn't hurt as much as it would have at one time. He was getting over it.

Just in time to be cut down again.

"Anyway, it's time I make decisions for myself. Time to live life on my terms."

"Those are good reasons," Les said, nodding his agreement. "And you're sure about this?"

Duncan thought back to the conversation he'd had with Cor DeWindt just a week ago. How Cor had told him he'd been trying to fill the empty spots in his life with the wrong things.

But how would he fill them now?

He thought of Miriam, and his stomach clenched. He'd thought she was different. He thought, when they met again, that they'd been given another chance.

"I'm sure. I've been tired of this for a long time. It's not what I love doing. I've just about got the ranch paid for. I've got a chance at expanding. Cattle prices are decent. It's a good time. I love being on the ranch, working with horses and cattle. It'll be good for me."

"That's good. 'Cause it's no secret I've been wanting a bigger slice of the pie."

"And now you've got it all," Duncan said.

Les nodded, still looking surprised. "So we need to talk price and all that other fun stuff."

"I'll come up with a figure, you come up with a figure, and we can get an assessor to come up with a figure. Between the three we should be able to come to a fair price," Duncan said.

"Sounds good to me." He got up and walked over to Duncan, holding out his hand. "Shake on it?"

Duncan stood and took his friend's hand, grasping it between both of his. "Welcome to the business," he said with a wry grin.

* * *

"How was Celia last night?" I asked, tucking my cell phone under my ear as I sat down on the bench in the porch to pull my boots on. The boots Duncan had bought for me.

"She slept just fine," Mrs. Tiemstra was saying. "And right now, she and her grandfather are playing a game. What about you? How did you sleep?"

I switched my phone to the other ear as I tugged on my winter jacket, stifling a yawn at her question. "I didn't sleep that great, but that's okay."

"Oh, my dear girl. I hope you know I was praying for you."

"I appreciate the prayers more than you can know," I said. "But now I have another favor to ask of you. I have...I have another job to do. Would you be willing to watch Celia this afternoon yet?"

"Of course."

"And one more thing, could you tell me where I can find Duncan today?" I zipped up my coat one-handed, grabbed my mittens and toque and shoved them in my purse as I walked out the door of the house.

"He's not home. We called him today because Phil, the lawyer, contacted us, but we had to get hold of him on his cell phone. I suspect he's in the bush. At the logging block."

"Phil called?" I asked as I unlocked the SUV and climbed in. I had started it before I got dressed so it was warm and ready to go. "What did he want?"

"He said he tried to contact you as well, but he didn't get an answer."

"I turned my phone off."

"Anyhow, it's good news. The estate is finally being settled and the insurance company will pay out for Francine. Not Jerrod, though. And the mortgage on the house will be paid off as well. Apparently the man who filed a claim against the estate dropped it. So things are finally settled."

"And Celia will be well taken care of," I said relief flooding through me.

"Francine's policy was enough to help her through her formative years." Mrs. Tiemstra was quiet. "So, does this change any of your plans?"

"I'm not sure." I had a few things to get out of the way before I made any decisions.

"Because in spite of what Duncan told you, I want you to know that we would like to help and support you taking care of Celia. If that's your choice. I know you said that you wanted Duncan to do so, but I firmly believe that you should reconsider. I know you love her, and I believe God has given you a second chance with her. I hope you will take it for your sake as much as hers."

Though her words encouraged me I also knew my life was so untethered. I had no idea where I was headed, or what I wanted to do. Once again, I felt like I was at a fork in my life's road.

I had fallen in love again with my daughter, as well as with the man who was also supposed to take care of her. And I wasn't sure what step to take next.

Just deal with what's in front of you.

"Thank you for that. I do love her," I said, staring out the window at the front of Francine and Jerrod's house. Trying to imagine it as a home for Celia and me.

And Duncan? Could you stay so close to him?

My throat thickened at the memory of the anger in his face. His denunciation of me.

Just deal with what's in front of you.

"Again, we'll be praying for you," Mrs. Tiem-stra said. "And as for Duncan, I believe he spoke out of a hurt and broken heart. I'm sure he didn't mean what he said."

I was certain she didn't know the entire truth about Kimberly, so I just murmured a vague re-ply. Then I said goodbye, and dropped my phone in my purse. I buckled up, reversed the SUV out of the driveway, and headed out.

My mind was a whirl of thoughts and worry as I drove. What would Duncan say? Would he understand?

I shook off the questions. I was forgiven. My sins were covered. I paid for my mistakes. Dearly.

Songs from Sunday's service floated through my head, and I let the words soothe me. Remind me that God wanted me to put my burdens at His feet. That my life was His.

I slowed down as I came to the road that I was sure Duncan had gone down when we had gotten the Christmas tree. It had snowed last night again, a wet, sticky snow that clung to the signs and the branches, and though the road hadn't been plowed, it was fairly well packed from the traffic. I recognized an old log cabin Duncan had pointed out to me, and I felt more confident as I turned down the road just past it.

I just hoped and prayed that Duncan was at the logging block when I got there.

And if he wasn't?

Well, I would find him. This time I wasn't letting him go without a fight. Without letting him see me for whom I was.

I slowed down as I came around a tight corner. The snow had started up again, and I couldn't see far through the falling flakes. The road grew narrower and tighter.

I drove a ways farther and then with a flicker of panic realized what I had done. I remembered Duncan talking on the radio. Calling his kilometers, he'd said, so that anyone coming down the road toward him would know where he was. I didn't have a radio, and now I was driving down roads that logging trucks ten times my size were also traveling on. In my determination to set the record straight, I had put myself in danger.

The snow was falling more heavily, and I rolled down the window just a bit to hear more clearly. But the only sound was the faint rustle of the wind through the snow-covered tree branches.

I knew I had to turn around and get out of here, but the road was too narrow.

And then I heard it, the muffled sound of a vehicle approaching. Fast.

Now what? I slowed down even more, and as I came around a corner my heart thudded as I saw the road go downhill to a narrow bridge spanning a snow-covered creek. The bridge was only wide enough for a single vehicle, and right now a pickup truck was approaching it from the other side. There was no room for both of us.

I tried to brake, but I was going downhill already, and my tires slid on the icy road. I had no traction, and the truck was now directly below me on the bridge. I had no choice—I took a deep breath and swerved right, tires spinning, and with a thud and a sickening crunch, I plowed the SUV into the creek.

The hood of my vehicle was buried in the ice I had broken through, water now flowing past, but my back tires were still on the bank. I had to get out. I pushed on the door, but it was stuck against the snow. I pushed again, trying not to panic as the vehicle slid slowly, inexorably, farther into the water, the ice crunching against the engine.

My fingers shaking, I opened the window all the way. Finally, I was able to clamber out, struggling to find purchase in the deep snow, my feet slipping and sliding. I made it to the road, and my trembling knees gave way as I crumpled to the ground.

I started to shake violently, adrenaline working its way through my system, ice spreading from my heart outward.

"Miriam?"

I slowly got to my feet, my limbs quickly chilling, to see Duncan running toward me, his truck tilted off to one side on the top of the hill.

"Are you okay?" He grabbed me by the arms, hauling me to my feet, his wide eyes ticking over me, checking me out.

"I'm fine. Just scared. But fine."

He gave me a light shake as if to reprimand me. "What were you thinking? Driving down this road?"

"I'm sorry. I made a mistake. I realized too late that I shouldn't be here. I'm sorry." I was babbling and I blamed my loose tongue on the close call I'd just had. "I forgot that you used a radio and that you called your kilometers." I shot a panicked look behind me, the deep tracks I plowed in the snow leading to the SUV that now sat half-buried in the creek. "I'm sorry about the car."

He heaved out a sigh and then, to my surprise, he pulled me close, enveloping me with his arms.

"It's okay. We can pull it out. I'm glad you're okay." He held my head, rocking me slightly.

I leaned into his embrace, my own legs still wobbly, and I clung to him, needing this momentary anchor. We stayed together for a moment, the silence surrounding us, snow kissing my heated cheeks, tangling in my hair.

Finally I pulled away, knowing I couldn't read

more into his embrace than simple reaction to the situation.

"Come into my truck. You're like ice," he said, taking me by the arm and gently leading me up the hill. My feet slipped on the snow, and he wrapped his arm around my shoulder, holding me up, his other hand holding my arm.

Finally, we made it to the top, and he walked me around his truck, through the deep snow to the side. He had to fight the door open, but finally got me inside. He hurried around and climbed in, turning the engine on again. Blessed heat poured out of the vents and I tugged my mittens off, holding my hands to the warmth.

"You sure you're okay?" he asked again, his hand resting with comforting weight on my shoulder.

I nodded, still shaky from the encounter.

He pulled his mic off the holder and clicked it. "Duncan at Fifteen bridge. Got an SUV in the creek. If there's a picker truck empty we could use your help."

Almost immediately, the radio squawked back. "Karl here. Just at checkerboard corner. I'm probably the closest. Be there in twenty."

"Thanks Karl. Any trucks coming on Y road loaded, watch for vehicles at Fifteen bridge."

I heard a faint, "Copy," from the radio. "Truck loaded at kilometer forty. Hope you get that idiot out before I get there." This was followed by a chuckle.

"Don't worry about that," Duncan said, turning to me, one arm resting on the steering wheel, the other on the back of his seat. "That's just guy talk."

"He was right. I was an idiot." I pulled in a deep breath, trying to still my pounding heart. Only now it wasn't just because of the accident. Duncan's nearness, the intensity of his gaze, was as much responsible as my near miss.

"So what were you doing out here?" Duncan asked.

"Looking for you."

He said nothing to that, but kept looking at me.

I sorted through my thoughts seeking the right way to start. The right words to use. But there was no way to ease into this conversation. So I dove straight in.

"You need to know why I gave up Celia for adoption," I said, looking away from him, focusing on the snow gently falling down and accumulating on the hood of his truck.

I heard the sudden intake of his breath, but

kept my eyes resolutely ahead, praying as I found the words.

"Jerrod was right to warn me away from you. Before I came to Jerrod and Francine's wedding, I wasn't living a good life. I was hanging around with the wrong group of people. Partying way too much, and wasting my time. Then I met you. And I saw an alternative to the life I was living. I saw a family that cared about each other. Something I'd always wanted for myself. After the wedding, after our dates, I thought my life had come to a good place. I really liked you and I thought you liked me. But then I got that text from Jerrod and though it made me angry, part of me knew he was right."

I took a breath but Duncan stayed silent so I kept going.

"I went back to the guy I had broken up with. Except he wasn't a good Christian guy, though I thought he was decent enough. I found out too late that he was dealing in drugs. I confronted him, and he beat me up. I got scared and I took off. I was living in Minnesota at the time, and I wanted to get back into Canada. Only I didn't re-alize, that he had been using my car to store his drugs. I got caught with four kilos of cocaine as I tried to cross the border."

I heard an intake of breath, and in spite of his reaction I glanced over. But he was looking ahead as well, as if trying to absorb my story. "I didn't know. I had no idea. You have to believe me." A pleading tone had entered my voice and I hated it, but I needed him to believe me.

He frowned, and for a moment I thought he was going to condemn me.

"What happened after that?" he asked, instead.

"I got hit with five years. I served three of them. And then was extradited to Canada. Jerrod and Francine took care of that. I think it was a way of paying me back."

"For what?"

I wove my fingers together, hoping, praying, that he would understand. And if not, at least hear me out.

"I was pregnant when I got sent to jail. With Celia." I stopped there, my throat suddenly thickening. I pressed my trembling lips together trying to regain my composure. I had thought I could tell him without breaking down. And in spite of everything I had felt last night, in spite of knowing I was forgiven, knowing that being sent to jail was just a combination of bad luck and bad choices, the shame of it all still thundered down on me. "Celia was born when I was in prison."

"And Jerrod and Francine adopted her then?" Duncan asked.

"I wrote Jerrod from prison, telling him what happened. And about my situation. He came to visit, and he talked me into letting them adopt Celia. They had just found out they couldn't have children. I wanted what was best for my little girl. I didn't want her ending up in foster homes, waiting for me to be released. I wanted her to have a home. It was so hard to give her up but I had to do what was best for her. So when I found out that Francine named me as guardian, after she died, I was scared. I couldn't take care of my daughter when she was a baby, I didn't think I could do it now." I stopped there, turning to him, silently pleading for his understanding. "I wanted her more than anything. Then and now. But I saw your family, the community, and the home that you guys could give her. I couldn't begin to give her half of that. I had a hard enough time finding the job I did. I live in a small, crappy apartment that I share with a good friend. I have no way of supporting Celia. I wasn't rejecting her. I was rejecting me."

Utter silence fell between us, thick and heavy.

Well, this was it. I had told him everything. I had entrusted him with my deepest, darkest secrets. Other than Jerrod and Francine, he was the only other person that now knew the complete story of my sordid past.

His head was bowed, his hair hiding his face. I swallowed down the tears that threatened, and yet felt relieved. I had released my final secret.

"Why didn't you leave this man sooner?" Duncan asked finally, a note of condemnation in his voice.

"Because I had nowhere else to go." I lifted my chin, a defiance entering my voice. "You have had the privilege of choices in your life. You have parents who have taken care of you, who have backed you. Your home, your farm, and your business—that was all a legacy given to you via a secure family and parents who could afford it. You have had a good example of relationships. I know there came a time in my life when I was responsible for my own choices, and I accept that. But I only spent seven years with Jerrod's family. When Sally died, I lost my only anchor to normality. Jerrod was out of the house and finding his own way through life. I drifted through my life. And when I met you, I thought something good had happened. Then Jerrod warned me off you and I let myself believe that he was right." I stopped, releasing a harsh laugh. "So I went back to Gregg. I know I should have left him. It's easy to say that looking back, but at the moment he was all I had."

I stopped there. I didn't want to defend my decisions anymore. Duncan would have to take what I said at face value. If he didn't...

Then, to my surprise, I felt Duncan's hand rest on the back of my neck, his fingers gently caressing.

"I'm sorry," he whispered. "I'm sorry for all the things you've had to deal with. You're right. I'm condemning you from a place of privilege. I've only ever known a family. Community. Security."

He turned me to face him. "I'm not trying to justify my actions last night. I'm just hoping you can see how it looked to me. I thought you were just like Kimberly. I thought you didn't want Celia. You talked that way when we first met right after the funeral."

I held his gaze, my own hand coming up to grasp at his arm. "I have grieved every day that little girl has been out of my arms. I have shed more tears over losing her than anything else. I only wanted what was best for her. I didn't think I could be a good mother to her then, I didn't think I could now. I was scared I was like my mom."

Duncan's gaze softened, and his eyes wandered over my face as if trying to see me in a different light. "You did what was best for her," he said. "You made a sacrifice for her sake. That's what a mother does. A real mother. You were willing to make yet another one for her, as hard as it was for me to see that. I'm sorry you've had to go through all you have. I can't imagine the life you've lived. But you came through. The fact that you were willing to put your needs behind Celia's shows that you are a good mother."

He took a deep breath, his fingers making soothing circles on my neck, easing out the pain that had gathered in my soul. Then, to my surprise and joy, he leaned closer, brushing his lips over mine. Warm. Soft. Tender. Then they moved with a deeper urgency as his hand held my head close.

I caught his shoulder, pulling him near, returning his kiss with abandon and joy.

Could this be? Could this man still care for me after all I'd told him?

After a moment we both drew back, our eyes locked on each other.

"You have no idea what I would give to turn back time. To make better choices," I whispered, needing him to understand. "I'm not that person anymore."

"I believe that," he said. "I don't know if you were ever that person. The girl I met at Jerrod's wedding had an innocence about her that I still see in you. A gentleness and a desire for love." He laughed briefly. "I'm no knight in shining armor, like the princes in the books you illustrated. I've made my own mistakes. Kimberly didn't get pregnant on her own." He stopped there, his thumb gently caressing the side of my mouth, as if to discover the kiss we had just shared. "But we're here together. And I don't think that was chance."

"Actually it was Jerrod and Francine's doing. In their own strange way."

"I found out why they were split on the guardian issue. Why Francine named you and Jerrod named me."

I frowned at him. "How did you find out?"

He sighed, pulling me close, resting his head on mine. "You talk about our family like it is some amazing group of people, but we have our own secrets and problems. Apparently, Jerrod and Esther were having an affair. That's why Francine and Jerrod were fighting. That's why Esther wanted to clean out Jerrod's study on her own.

She didn't want anyone to know about the two of them. She was hoping to get rid of any evidence."

I sat utterly still, trying to absorb this, even while pieces of what I'd been dealing with the past few weeks hinted at this very situation.

"I think that's partly why Francine named you guardian," Duncan continued. "Because of the affair."

"I thought it was a way of giving Celia back to me," I said.

"I'm sure that was the main reason." Duncan pressed a kiss to my head, his chest lifting in a sigh. "So you see, my family isn't perfect by any stretch, either. We all have our dark secrets and silent sorrows."

I sat quietly in his arms a moment, my mind reeling with these unbelievable new details.

"But it's still a family," I said finally, resting my hand on his chest, feeling his steady heartbeat under my hand. "And it's still part of a community. It's still a good place."

"It is," he agreed. Then he drew back again, brushing another kiss over my forehead. "And I think you should stay here. Experience it for yourself. Christmas is ten days away. Stay until then. And then, stay after that. Be Celia's mother. Be...well, be a part of my family."

I looked at him, hardly daring to guess what he hinted at and what he offered.

Then he smiled, as if he understood my hesitancy. "This is a good thing," he said, tucking a strand of hair behind my ear, his callused fingers rough against my face. "I want you to stay. I want us to try again. Like I said before, I think we've been given a second chance. I don't want to throw it away. I know you don't have a job or anything lined up here, but I'm sure you could find a way to support yourself."

"My friend Christine just sold one of my paintings. On Kijiji, of all places. I might find a market for more of my work."

"And now you've got some amazing sketching supplies, bought for you on the cheap."

"They're great," I said, giving him a smile. "One of the best gifts I've ever received."

"Now you're just trying to make me feel all generous and manly."

"Takes a real man to buy pencil crayons," I teased, surprised at the lightness that had entered our conversation. Thankful for the removal of the heaviness, curious as to where it would go now.

"Seriously, I want you to stay. I want you and me to become an us. Holmes Crossing is a good place to get a second chance. The people here are good."

"Would they hire an ex-convict?"

"You could talk to Terra DeWindt. She did some time in jail."

"Really?" I could hardly believe that. "She's married to a Mountie."

"How do you think they met?"

I couldn't help but laugh at that.

"Seriously? She was in jail?"

"I think it was only about four hours, but still…"

"Hardly the same."

He grew serious. "I know. But I mean it. The people here are good people, like you said. I know you could find something to do. Meaningful work that would make you fulfilled. So, what do you say to my suggestion?"

Beneath his steady gaze, a sensation started inside of me, of my life opening up, like a flower moving from bud to bloom. I thought of the women in the Bible study group who said they would pray for me. I thought of Duncan's family. Flawed, but still intact.

He kissed me again. "I want you to have time to think about this. I want to give you space to find where you fit here. I want you to make this place your home."

"I think I could do that," I said, as new possibilities opened up to me. And for the first time in a long time, I felt the promise of a future.

And when Duncan kissed me again that promise became solid and real.

* * *

"I THINK she's wiped right out." Duncan knelt down, laying Celia in her bed.

"I'm not surprised." Miriam tucked the blankets around her. "It's almost eleven and she's been going steady since six this morning."

They had just come back from his parents' place, where they had unwrapped their Christmas gifts. Duncan had been surprised to find a couple of gifts for him under the tree from Miriam and Celia; a pocketknife and a flashlight. Celia had been as excited about that as she was about the doll bed that his father had made for Jane.

He watched as Miriam gently ran her fingers down her daughter's face.

This was so right, he thought, resting his hand

on her shoulder. This was as it should be. Where Miriam should be.

The past few days had been a time of adjusting. Of getting used to each other.

Miriam had, to her surprise, found a job working for Terra in the café, and discovered that she loved it. She had also found time to do some more sketching. He was awed every time he saw a new piece.

He also hoped to take her to the city after Christmas to buy some real art supplies. At Peeveys.

Encouraged by Christine's sale of three more of her paintings, she'd taken it up again as well. He helped her convert Jerrod and Francine's room to a studio and she had been working there the past week.

Miriam bent over and brushed a kiss over Celia's cheek, then stood aside. Duncan did the same, feeling an unexpected ache blended with joy. Bittersweet, he thought.

They stood by her bed a moment.

"She's been sleeping much better the past while," Miriam whispered.

"Maybe the ghosts of Francine and Jerrod are finally at rest," he said.

Miriam swatted him gently. "Don't talk like

that. I won't be able to sleep."

He kissed her, just because he could. Then he took her hand and led her downstairs.

The lights of the Christmas tree glowed softly, the only light in the room.

"Why don't you go sit down on the couch and I'll get us a glass of wine," Duncan said, giving her a nudge toward the living room.

"I have wine?"

"No. You don't. I brought wine," he said, nudging her again.

She frowned her surprise but he just ignored her, pulling a couple of glasses out of the cupboard above the stove. He uncorked the bottle and poured the wine. Miriam was curled up on the couch, her shoes on the floor when he came back with the glasses.

He sat down beside her and gave one to her.

Then he lifted his glass. "A toast. To Christmas. And blessings of the season."

"Blessings of the season," she echoed, her glass tinging lightly against his.

They both took a sip from their glasses, and then Miriam gave a quiet chuckle.

"This feels a little odd, in a way," she said. "Celebrating Christmas at my brother's house."

"Does it bother you?" he asked, hoping she

wasn't dwelling on what they had lost. Not now. Not when he had other things he wanted to discuss.

"A little. Jerrod and I weren't that close, but I still miss him." She turned to him. "I'm sure you miss Francine, too."

"I do. I know Christmas was hard for Mom and Dad but they're happy that Celia is staying here." He gave her a tender smile. "And I think they're glad we're together."

"And Esther?"

"She'll come around, I'm sure."

He was quiet a moment, thinking of his sister. She had made a brief showing this evening and then left after the presents were unwrapped. She had claimed to have a previous engagement in the city. In spite of Celia's previous outbursts, she hadn't said anything more to her Aunt Esther. In fact, she seemed to ignore her.

"Don't condemn her too hard," Miriam said quietly. "She's your only sister."

"It's hard to know what to do with what happened between her and Jerrod. I've tried not to think too much about it. If they hadn't been fooling around I wonder if Francine and Jerrod would have taken that trip."

"I don't think it's fair to put that much on her shoulders. Jerrod made choices too," Miriam said.

Duncan gave her a gentle smile, then touched her nose with his forefinger. "You are an amazing person."

"Hardly. I just know I'm not in any position to condemn anybody."

He couldn't help a flash of anger. "You did nothing wrong," he said. "You were truly a victim."

Miriam's lips trembled and she looked down.

"That you can defend me-"

"How can I not?"

She gave him a shy smile, which dove into his soul. Then he thought of the other plans he'd made for tonight and an unwelcome tension gripped him.

He'd had this all planned out, but now that the time had come, he didn't feel as confident.

Too soon? Too much? Should he wait?

But when she leaned closer and brushed a kiss over his cheek, his uneasiness subsided. He set his wine glass aside and pulled open a drawer of the coffee table.

She was watching him, and as he drew out the small velvet box her eyes widened, and her soft lips parted.

He swallowed down another attack of nerves. Should he go down on one knee? Stay where he was?

Then he figured he might as well just go for it and opened the box, tilting it her way.

"I know things have felt rushed the past month and we've had to deal with a lot. I don't think you and I are the type to dilly dally and I really feel this is right," he said as she gasped her surprise. "Miriam, will you marry me?"

She just stared at the ring, which sparkled in the light of the Christmas tree. Then a shimmer of tears glistened on her cheek.

"Oh, no, don't cry," he said. "It's okay. We can do this another time."

Her only reply was to grab him by the neck and kiss him. Hard. Then she drew back, touching the box lightly with trembling hands. "No. This is a good time. This is the best time."

He yanked the ring out of the box and then, taking her hand, gently slipped it on her finger. It was a bit loose, but it was on. Then he raised her hand to his lips, kissing her fingers slowly. Gently.

"I love you, Miriam Bristol. And I want to spend the rest of my life making sure you know that."

"I love you, too," she whispered, her hand tightening on his. "And I promise to make a home for you. And for Celia. Here. In this place."

And their kiss sealed their promises and claimed the future.

* * *

I hope you enjoyed reading about Miriam and Duncan and their journey to love.

I often buy books based on other people's reviews so I'm hoping you're willing to leave one on this book to give future readers some idea of what to expect. You can leave a review by clicking on the link below

REVIEW ALL IN ONE PLACE

* * *

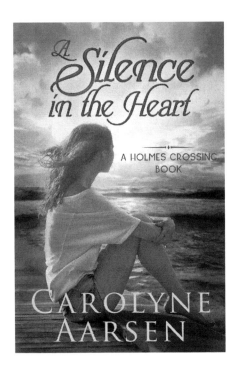

The next book in the series is A Silence in the Heart. Read an excerpt here:

A SILENCE IN THE HEART

She thought she heard the cry of a child.

The haunting sound slid through the early-morning quiet just as Tracy stepped out of her car. Still holding the door, she canted her head to one side, listening.

There it was again. Softer this time.

Tracy strode around the concrete-block building trying to pinpoint the origin. But when she came around the side, the street in front of the clinic was empty as well.

The tension in her shoulders loosened and she shivered, pulling her thin sweater closer around herself. Ever the optimist, she had left her warmer jacket hanging in the hallway closet of her apartment this morning, counting on the early-September sun to melt away the coolness of the fall morning.

Then a movement caught her eye.

She stopped and turned to face whatever might come.

Then a small boy shuffled cautiously around the corner of the clinic, his head angled down, his thin arms cradling something. He looked to be about six or seven.

Tracy relaxed as she recognized him. For the past two weeks she had seen him walking past the clinic in the early morning on his way to school. The last few days he had stopped to look in the window. It had taken a few encouraging waves and smiles from her to finally tease one from his wary face.

She always felt bad for him, going to school on his own, remembering too well her own early morning treks as a young child.

Tracy might have been inadequately dressed

for the weather, but this little boy was even more so. He wore a short- sleeved T-shirt, faded blue jeans and in spite of the gathering chill, sandals on bare feet. As she watched, he shivered lightly.

"Hey, there," Tracy said quietly, sensing he might startle easily.

"I want to see the doctor," he said, sniffing lightly as Tracy came nearer. "This kitten got hurt." He angled her a suspicious glance through the tangle of dark hair hanging in his brown eyes.

"The veterinarian isn't in yet." Tracy crouched down to see what he was holding. The tiny ball of mangled fur tucked in his arms looked in rough shape. One eye was completely closed, the fur around it matted with blood. A leg hung at an awkward angle. Probably broken.

"What happened to it?" she asked quietly.

"I dunno. I just found him laying here." The little boy stood stiffly, his body language defensive. "Can you fix him?"

Tracy's heart sank. She knew the little boy couldn't pay the vet fees, and from the looks of his clothes, doubted his parents could.

"Where's your mommy?" she asked, touching the kitten lightly.

"I dunno."

Those two words dove into her soul. Too familiar.

"Is she at your home?"

He kept his eyes down, looking at his kitten. Tracy looked over his worn clothes and the dried smear of tomato sauce on his face and stained shirt and filled in the blanks. She guessed he had gone to bed looking like this and that there was no one at his home right now.

"I wanna keep him," the little boy wiped his nose on the shoulder of his T-shirt, a hitch in his voice. "He can be my friend when I'm by myself."

Tracy's thoughts jumped back in time. She saw herself a young girl of eight, standing in the kitchen of her apartment she and her mother shared, saying the same words, also holding a kitten, hope lingering.

"Not enough money," her mother had said, though Velma managed to use those same limited funds for lottery tickets and liquor. How Tracy had longed for that kitten. A friend. Someone to hold when there was no one around.

Tracy pushed herself to her feet. "Let's go inside."

The boy slanted her a narrow-eyed, wary look, holding back as she unlocked the door and opened it.

"It's okay," Tracy said quietly. "We have to go inside to look at your kitten."

He nodded and slowly stepped inside, his head swiveling around, checking out the reception area of the clinic.

"What's your name?" she asked as the door fell shut behind them.

"Are you a stranger?" he asked, suspicion edging his voice. "My mom says I'm not s'posed to talk to strangers."

"I'm a vet technician," she answered, sidestepping the guarded question. "And my name is Tracy Harris."

He stood in the center of the room, a tightly wound bundle of vigilance, clinging to the kitten like a lifeline. His eyes darted around—assessing, watchful. They met Tracy's as he straightened, as if making a decision. "My name is Kent," he said with a quick lift of his chin. "Kent Cordell."

She had been given a small gift of trust and in spite of the kitten that might be dying in his arms, she gave Kent a smile. She skimmed his shoulder with her fingers. "Good to meet you, Kent."

The back door slammed and a loud singing broke the quiet. Crystal, the other vet technician burst into the room with her usual dramatic flair, bright orange sweater swirling behind her. "And a good morning to you, my dear," she called out snatching a knitted hat off her deep red hair, then stopped when she saw Kent.

Kent tucked his head over the kitten, his shoulders hunched in defense. Like a turtle he had withdrawn again.

Crystal angled her chin at Kent as she tossed her hat on the desk. "Who's the kid?"

"This is Kent, and I'm bringing him and his kitten to an examining room. As soon as Dr. Harvey comes in, can you send him my way?"

"Not Dr. Braun?" Crystal asked, her voice holding a teasing tone.

Tracy was disappointed at the faint blush warming her neck. From the first day that David Braun had started at the clinic four months ago, Crystal had been avidly watching the two of them, as if it was only a matter of time before they started dating. Because, you know, two single people were always on the lookout for a mate.

Negatory.

There was no way Tracy was putting herself there again. Her old relationship with Art was the textbook version of 'bad relationship'. And she wasn't putting herself there again.

But that didn't stop her from feeling extra self-conscious around David—which in turn annoyed her.

"Just send Dr. Harvey in when he comes," she said.

Crystal pouted. "Okay, okay. I'll just be in the supply room." She swung around, her lab coat flaring out behind her as she strode down the hall. But from the glance she tossed over her shoulder and the wink she gave, Tracy guessed Crystal hadn't gotten the hint.

At all.

Purchase A Silence in the Heart by clicking on the book cover or the title below:

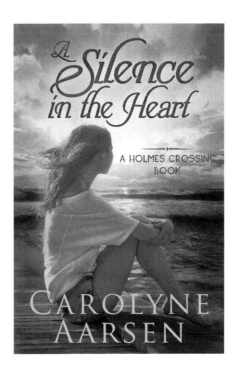

A SILENCE IN THE HEART

WANT to find out instantly about any new releases? Follow me on Book Bub to stay updated.
https://www.bookbub.com/authors/ carolyne-aarsen
Or my Amazon Author Page here:
https://www.amazon.com/ author/carolyneaarsen

OTHER SERIES

FAMILY BONDS

#1 SEEKING HOME

A rancher who suffered a tragic loss. A single mother on the edge. Can these two find the courage to face a romantic new beginning?

#2 CHOOSING HOME

If you like emergency room drama, second chances, and quaint small-town settings, then you'll adore this romance.

#3 COMING HOME

He thought she chose a hotel over him. She thought he loved money more than her. Years later, can they fill the emptiness in their hearts?

#4 FINDING HOME

She's hiding a terrible truth. He's trying to overcome his scandalous history. Together, forgiveness might give them a second chance.

FAMILY TIES

Four siblings trying to finding their way back to family and faith

A COWBOY'S REUNION

He's still reeling from the breakup. She's ashamed of what she did. Can a chance reunion mend the fence, or are some hearts forever broken? If you like second chance stories, buried passions, and big country settings, then you'll love this emotional novel.

"I enjoyed this book and had trouble putting it down and had to finish it. If the rest of this series is this great, I look forward to reading more books by Carolyne Aarsen." **Karen Semones - Amazon Review**

THE COWBOY'S FAMILY

She's desperate. He's loyal. Will a dark lie hold them back from finding love on the ranch? If you like determined heroines, charming cowboys, and family dramas, then you'll love this heartfelt novel.

"What a wonderful series! The first book is Cowboy's Reunion. Tricia's story begins in that book. Emotional stories with wonderful characters. Looking forward to the rest of the books in this series." Jutzie - Amazon reviewer

TAMING THE COWBOY

A saddle bronc trying to prove himself worthy to a father who never loved him. A wedding planner whose ex-fiancee was too busy chasing his own dreams to think of hers. Two people, completely wrong for each other who yet need each other in ways they never realized. Can they let go of their own plans to find a way to heal together?

"This is the third book in the series and I have loved them all. . . . can't wait to see what happens with the last sibling." - Amazon reviewer

THE COWBOY'S RETURN

The final book in the Family Ties Series:

He enlisted in the military, leaving his one true love behind.

She gave herself to a lesser man and paid a terrible price.

In their hometown of Rockyview, they can choose to come together or say a final goodbye...

'This author did an amazing job of turning heartache into happiness with realism and inspirational feeling." Marlene - Amazon Reviewer

* * *

SWEETHEARTS OF SWEET CREEK

Come back to faith and love

#1 HOMECOMING

Be swept away by this sweet romance of a woman's

search for belonging and second chances and the rugged rancher who helps her heal.

#2 - HER HEARTS PROMISE

When the man she once loved reveals a hidden truth about the past, Nadine has to choose between justice and love.

#3 - CLOSE TO HIS HEART

Can love triumph over tragedy?

#4 - DIVIDED HEARTS

To embrace a second chance at love, they'll need to discover the truths of the past and the possibilities of the future...

#5 - A HERO AT HEART

If you like rekindled chemistry, family drama, and small, beautiful towns, then you'll love this story of heart and heroism.

#6 - A MOTHER'S HEART

If you like matchmaking daughters, heartfelt stories of mending broken homes, and fixer-upper romance, then this story of second chances is just right for you.

* * *

HOLMES CROSSING SERIES

The Only Best Place is the first book in the Holmes

ABOUT THE AUTHOR

Carolyne Aarsen, originally a city girl, was transplanted to the country when she married her dear husband Richard. While raising four children, foster children, and various animals Carolyne's résumé gained some unique entries. Growing a garden, sewing blue jeans, baking, pickling and preserving. She learned how to handle cows, drive tractors, snow machines, ride a horse, and train a colt. Somewhere in all this she learned to write. Her first book sold in 1997 and since then has sold almost forty books to three different publishers. Her stories show a love of open spaces, the fellowship of her Christian community and the gift God has given us in Christ.

To find out more about me go to.....
www.carolyneaarsen.com

Made in the USA
Middletown, DE
06 February 2022